The DRAGON and the Mask

The Dragon and the Mask
Copyright © 2017-20 by Deanna Cooner, PhD, All rights reserved

Stones in Clay Publishing
P.O. Box 1302
Newcastle, Ok 73065

> *Living stones, being built up as a spiritual house for a holy priesthood, to offer up spiritual sacrifices acceptable to God through Jesus Christ. . . .*
>
> *1 Peter 2:5,*
>
> *But we have this treasure in jars of clay, to show that the surpassing power belongs to God and not to us.*
>
> *2 Corinthians 4:7*

Cover Design and Graphics by Mindi Stucks
Book Design by Gary Cooner
Edited by Jeanne Marie Leach
Published in United States of America
ISBN: 978-0-9989522-0-8
Young Adult Fiction / Religious / Christian / General
2020.2.3

Stones in Clay
PUBLISHING

> *Suffer hardship with me, as a good soldier of Christ Jesus. No soldier in active service entangles himself in the affairs of everyday life, so that he may please the one who enlisted him as a soldier.*
>
> 2 Timothy 2:3-4 (NASB)

ACKNOWLEDGEMENTS

The creation of a story may come from one individual but it does not remain with one individual. We all love stories: the ones we've heard, ones we've read and the ones we create are valuable each in their own right. It is the work of various talents that bring the conception of a story to a complete memorable story. I have had many people help make this first book in a series a work that hopefully will endure through each of the up-coming novels.

My husband, partner best friend and Administrator of Stones in Clay Publishing makes this happen with his expertise in technology. He is my rock on the days I say, "I can't," and my encourager on the days I say, "I did."

My most talented and adorable graphic artist, Mindi Stucks, who does so much that is a mystery to me. She designs covers, and creates wonderful promotional materials.

A great Christian author and editor who isn't afraid to hurt my feelings both makes a better end product and me a better story creator. I appreciate Jeanne Marie Leach for her input.

My first reader of this book, Benjamin Mykytiuk, who overlooked all the grammar mistakes and became involved in the story enough to stay up until two a.m. to finish it. My second reader who found the mistakes and offered criticism, Levi Mykytiuk.

I thank you all for your contributions and encouragement to make *The Dragon and the Mask* a reality of a parable of the Book of Jeremiah. For more in depth Bible Study there is a Leader's Guide to accompany the novel with an application of the book of Jeremiah based on the novel character's and their story. This book is available from Stones in Clay Publishing, P.O. Box 1302, Newcastle, OK 73065. It will be available for on-line purchase at AlongSideYou.Org, the parent ministry of Stones in Clay Publishing.

Along Side You is a counseling and teaching ministry dedicated to the spiritual needs of teens and young adults, their parents and leadership. All profits from the sale of novels and materials help support this ministry.

Tragedy upsets the boundaries of all that is normal, but none more strangely than the spiritual boundaries by which a person governs themselves.

Author

Contents

1

Nature?

I remember concerning you the devotion of your youth, the love of your betrothals your following after Me in the wilderness, through a land not sown.
---Jeremiah 2:2 NASB

BUSTER SLOWLY CLIMBED down from his old tractor, letting his foot touch the ground with a light touch, hoping it wouldn't swallow him. Otherwise, he'd simply disappear, never to be found. Just like his grandfather.

Buster trembled as he watched the soil quiver. A loud roar like a lion slapped his ears. The earth fell from beneath his feet, he ran for his life to higher ground. He turned around. To his surprise the flat field remained solid, and his tractor remained in the same spot, mocking him for his fear.

Again Buster felt the ground tremble and shudder; he staggered a bit. Still, it didn't fall away. Instead, a shadow darkened the soil. He looked up unprepared for what he saw.

A scaly reptilian creature with giant yellow-green eyes stared down at him. A red liquid flowed from its maw which resembled a giant cavern. It writhed its long neck in front of Buster and dropped the blood-soaked body of a Limousin bull at Buster's feet, in the same manner as a cat offers a dead mouse.

The sheer shock of seeing such an abomination kept Buster glued to the ground where he stood. Was this real? The logic of a monstrous dragon staring at him escaped his thinking.

Even though Buster hadn't seen hand-to-hand combat in his four years of military service, he did learn to stand firm in the face of the enemy. Problem was, he never faced an enemy such as this before. He wanted to run. He stood still for it would make no difference. The neck of the beast would simply reach out and spear him.

He shuddered with loathing at the disemboweled animal at his feet. The cattleman's brand on the bovine's rear was the brand of Garrett Boseley, Buster's neighbor. He'd paid Garrett a sizable stud fee to inseminate his cattle with this bull. This dead animal was no apparition.

The ugly thing winked at him with a mocking smile. He could do nothing but stand there and hope the creature would go away and leave him alive. He had no weapon or defense against this monster.

The creature stepped closer creating the sound and feel of an earthquake. The wind from his nostrils nearly burned Buster's fair skin. Even with a farmer's tan, his face often suffered painful sunburn.

The copper smell of a busy slaughterhouse on a hot summer day overcame Buster. He gagged and tasted the bile rising from his stomach. He swallowed it and stood straight, staring directly into the creature's eye. He may not have a defense, but he would not give this hideous creature the satisfaction of seeing him become sick and weakened by the encounter, even though he was both.

A large stream of saliva dripped from the creature's mouth, quickly pooling around Buster's feet. Even though Buster was fairly tall, the rising drool puddle engulfed his ankles. With the dexterity of a stealth athlete, he backed up to higher ground. The creature either didn't notice Buster's movement or didn't care.

Shaking with fear, Buster determined to remain steadfast and firm in the face of absolute destruction. With the creature watching his every move, he did the only thing he could do: he prayed.

Buster remembered the disappearance of his grandfather and the long-lasting effect it had on his father. The townspeople spread rumors about his disappearance until the vile lies were accepted as truth. Buster knew he too was about to disappear without a trace, and he prayed his children would not endure the same treatment.

When Buster opened his eyes, the creature was gone, but the disturbed soil revealed where the creature had been. The evidence of the encounter was verified by the dead bull and saliva puddle left by the animal.

He stood in the middle of his field alone and shouted to relieve the tension in his body, "What was that?"

2

The View on the Road

Lift up your eyes to the bare heights and see; where have you not been violated? By the roads you have sat for them like an Arab in the desert, and you have polluted a land with your harlotry and with your wickedness.

- Jeremiah 3:2

BARBARA TROYE GASPED. Her brothers stopped arguing.

"What's wrong, sis?" Rance asked.

"It's okay, boys. Just look." She pointed out the front window toward the sky.

"Wow!" both boys said as they climbed out. They sat upon the hood and stared at the sky. The three snuggled close to each other for warmth and they watched the beauty of the plains play out on the clear sky in the form of a reverse mirage.

Too soon, the vision began to fade. The three didn't move for a few seconds. Finally, Rance spoke up and said, "Great show."

"What causes that?" Zay asked.

Zay, the likable, silent twin, would usually only speak up after pondering things in his head. Even as a thirteen-year-old boy, he expected a full answer.

"I'm not sure," Barbara said. "But it has something to do with the flat land and the warm and cool air." They continued to stare at the fading phenomenon as long as possible.

"We gotta go," Barbara finally said. "I'm going to be late by the time I deliver you."

"Sis, look!" Zay exclaimed as he pointed south toward their farm home. "What's that?"

Barbara glanced over toward the other side of the road and saw a huge dirt devil in one of the fields.

"You think that's at our place?"

"Can't be," piped Rance, "We can't see our farm, it's five miles away. It has to be on Overstreet's place."

The three stared into the distance at the second strange sight of the morning.

"It almost looks like it has wings," Rance said.

"Yeah," Barbara and Zay agreed.

Again Barbara had to bring them back to reality. "Come on guys, I really need to get on the road." She hurried them back into the car. Zay and Rance turned and watched the swirl of dirt.

"Strange, it's not moving," Rance said.

"It's just a big dirt devil——another strange thing that happens out here on the plains."

"That sounds good for the explanation of the dirt. But I want to know how you can explain the big snake in the middle of it," Zay said.

Barbara shuddered at the word snake, and if Rance had said it, she would have laughed, thinking he was making a joke. Zay didn't waste words; he wouldn't say it unless there was something to it. She had to turn and look.

Suddenly, the car jerked and made a kerthump noise. Barbara quickly hit the brakes and pulled over.

"What was that?" Rance asked.

Once the car stopped the three of them searched the highway. There in a curled up clump of scales lay the dying body of the largest rattlesnake any of them had ever seen. Barbara shrank back and shuddered in revulsion but at the same time she couldn't take her eyes off the creature. He was so big and…he started twisting and wiggling on the highway on this cool September morning. It didn't make sense. Snakes don't like cool weather.

"Don't get close," she warned her younger brothers. "He's not dead. He can still strike. In fact, let's get moving."

They all took one last look at the snake. To their horror and surprise, it raised its head, flicked its tongue, and coiled up. It shook a thick tail and made a loud noise with ample rattlers.

"Get out of here!" Zay screamed.

The three of them were silent for the remainder of the trip.

When Barbara reached the junior high building, she turned to the boys. "You guys okay?" she asked.

They both nodded but hesitated to get out of the car.

"Sorry, guys, you gotta go. I only have a few minutes to get to the high school. I'm probably going to be late now."

They reluctantly got out of the car and half-waved at her, "Bye, sis."

Barbara parked in the far west parking lot on the opposite side of the school office; now ten minutes late to first hour. She hated being late. Her thoughts about the evil-looking snake wouldn't leave her alone. She desperately wanted to talk to someone—anyone—about her morning experiences.

As she entered the building, the click of her shoes echoed with each step. She made the trip to the school office to get a tardy slip. At least someone in the office would hear her explanation. It didn't work out that way. The office was empty except for Mrs. Paul, the school secretary, who sat behind her desk with a tissue in her hand and her head bowed.

"Mrs. Paul," Barbara said softly.

Mrs. Paul wiped her eyes and turned toward Barbara. "Yes."

"I need a tardy slip."

"It's okay, go on to class," the secretary answered.

This was a disappointing turn of events. Barbara wanted to explain why she was late, but instead she was given a free pass with the wave of Mrs. Paul's hand.

"Is something wrong?" she ventured to ask.

"Yes, we received word that a carrier ship suffered a huge fire."

This news should have some significance, instead it was merely another piece of war news that flooded the television airwaves every day. An active part of her life since the first U.S. troops joined the Vietnam skirmish in 1965. To Barbara, Vietnam was nothing more than a news clip. She prayed it would end before her brothers were drafted into the horrible battles the family witnessed on the television screen.

Mrs. Paul looked at her blank stare and continued, "It was the USS Forrestal."

Barbara wished she had been keeping up with the events in Vietnam better. "I'm sorry, Mrs. Paul, but I still don't know what you're talking about."

"It's the ship on which Barry Lawson was assigned."

Now the news made more sense. Barry Lawson was a favorite son of Church Creek Falls. He joined the air force soon after graduation. That was all Barbara knew, other than the tidbits of gossip about Barry and his girlfriend. Today's news didn't fall in the category of whispered gossip. This very real loss of life affected the Lawson family and would send repercussions of grief throughout the whole community.

Barbara ducked her head and held her books tighter to her body. She let out a deep mournful sigh. This was the first casualty of the war from her hometown. She prayed it would be the last. She didn't say anything more but left the office and headed for her first-hour math class on the other side of the building.

3

Exploring the Roots

> Then I said, how I would set you among My sons and give you a pleasant land, the most beautiful inheritance of the nations! And I said, how shall call Me, My Father, and not turn away from following Me... A voice is heard on the bare heights, the weeping and the supplications of the sons of Israel; Because they have perverted their way, they have forgotten the LORD their God.
>
> —Jeremiah 3:19, 21

BUSTER WOULDN'T BREATHE easy until he reached the other end of the field. But the end meant turning the tractor around and heading back to his starting point. Normally, the mundane work of plowing a field suited him. He enjoyed the time to think and pray. Even this old tractor was so much better than the horse and plow he had to work as a young boy.

As he neared the spot where he first saw the creature, his heart pounded hard in his chest. He thought he could see a transparent outline of the creature. He had to be hallucinating, which made him question his sanity. The plowing continued until lunch. Never had Buster been so happy to head home. Except this time, he needed to decide how much of his morning adventure he could share with his wife, Merilee.

Returning to the field in the afternoon was not an option today. Buster needed to know more. He pondered about where one would go to find information about a dragon in the field. Buster was a farmer, not a student. Only one person he could trust with this—Barbara, his seventeen-year-old daughter. School would dismiss in a few more hours. He would ask her about it when she arrived home.

When he opened the back door, Merilee looked up from preparing lunch, "Hello, handsome."

He gave her a weak smile and hoped she didn't detect his inner terror still lingering from the morning's event. She must not have noticed; she continued to hum as she prepared lunch plates for the two of them.

Buster loved lunchtime. It allowed him to come in from the hot sun, but mostly, he enjoyed spending time alone with Merilee. Then an idea hit him. Merilee always wanted them to do something together. After washing the dirt from his hands and face and removing his straw hat, he walked over to her and gave her a squeeze from behind and a peck on the cheek.

She let out a little giggle and leaned her head back against his shoulder.

"How about a little adventure today?" he asked.

She stopped and turned to look him in the face. "Buster Troye, do you really want to go out in the middle of the day?" she said. Then she furrowed her brow, "What's going on?"

Buster sat down at the dinner table and took a big gulp of iced tea. He loved the feel of the ice-cold liquid trickling down his dirt-parched throat and cooling him from the inside out. He set the glass down. "I'm not sure, but I had a strange experience this morning. I thought I was over a sinkhole. It started me thinking and I was wondering if there had been any sinkholes in our area before." The sinkhole had been Buster's original thought until the…creature appeared. Maybe that would be a good place to start. Whatever that thing was, it was occupying a large hole in the ground.

Merilee set his plate of food in front of him and sat at the table with her own plate. She took a couple bites. "Where do you go for that kind of information?" she asked.

"Not sure," Buster responded.

"Maybe the library," Merilee said.

Silence engulfed the table for a few minutes, then Merilee dropped her fork as if the realization just hit her. "What do you mean you think you saw a sinkhole? Were you in danger of falling into one?"

"I thought I was, but it turned out to be a huge dirt devil instead. It made me wonder what's under our ground. I really want to know more about this land we're farming."

"Why? It's been good to us," Merilee responded.

"We inherited the land and started farming. We don't know anything about the history of this place or the geologic makeup," Buster responded.

"Humm, I guess we took it for granted, having lived here all our lives," Merilee said, and then her eyes lit up. "There's a new museum in town. Barbara's history teacher is the curator. She's retiring at the end of the year to work it full-time, but until then she opens at 1:00 p.m. when she finishes her school schedule."

"Sounds like the perfect place to find some history of our home territory."

The museum parking lot was empty. Merilee and Buster wondered if the museum was open. Merilee turned the knob and the door opened. A disembodied voice responded to the tinkling of the overhead bell.

"Be there in a minute," the voice said.

"Merilee, look at this," Buster said, pointing to a glass case.

"What is it?" Merilee looked at the map.

"It's a map of the Ogallala."

"What's that?"

"It's the water reservoir below us; it's where we get our irrigation water."

"Oh."

Buster thought that might mean Merilee did not understand the significance of the maps, "If what I experienced was a sinkhole, this would be the reason why," Buster started to explain. He looked at the blank expression on Merilee's face.

"I don't understand. Are you saying that you would have fallen into that water?" Merilee was interested.

"Sort of. A sinkhole is created when part of the underground is hollowed out, usually by water. We don't hear about them often because there's plenty of water in them, and so the ground is stable."

"So if the ground is stable, why are you afraid of falling into one?' Merilee asked him. Buster wasn't sure what he was going to say next. Fortunately, a woman came around the corner giving him some time to think about his answer.

"Hello," the woman behind the voice entered the room, sweeping dust from the front of her apron. "Sorry, I was up on a ladder and it takes me a little longer to get down than it used to." Mrs. Wallace's face lit up when she saw Merilee.

"Merilee Troye, it's so good to see you. What brings you here today?" Mrs. Wallace put her arm around Merilee and gave her a big hug. "How can I help you?"

Merilee introduced Buster. After the niceties were finished, Mrs. Wallace said, "You look as though you have questions?"

"You are indeed a teacher," Buster said with a good-natured smile. He already liked this woman.

"I had a bit of a scare this morning," Buster said. Thought I was about to fall into a sinkhole."

"A good scare and he decides to take me out. I like it when he gets scared." Merilee chuckled as she grabbed his arm and gave it a body hug.

"Thanks, but she's right," Buster continued. "Obviously I didn't have a sinkhole and I didn't fall in, but it scared me, made me curious about our land."

"So you come to the museum?" Mrs. Wallace asked with a bit of skepticism.

Buster nodded with a downward glance, as it sounded rather silly now. Why would one come to a museum if they were scared of sinkholes? He couldn't tell anyone the truth' that he'd been scared out of his wits by a huge dragon with a dead bull. How could anything in a museum give insight to a mythical creature in his field?

"I see you found the Ogallala map," Mrs. Wallace said, interrupting Buster's thought. "That's a good start to understand the theory behind a sinkhole, but truthfully, I don't know that we have ever experienced one in the entire county. Did you actually see one?" Mrs. Wallace asked.

"No, I heard a loud roar."

"Oh." Mrs. Wallace ducked her head.

"But since we are here, can you show us around? It's the first time I have been in the museum, and maybe it will help take my mind off my near-death experience this morning," Buster said with a forced laugh.

"I would love to show you around. I actually don't get many visitors. I have become more of a collection center for people cleaning out their closets and finding things they can't throw away but no longer want to keep."

Merilee looked around. The museum was quite orderly and interesting, even if the objects were fairly new.

"We are not a very old community. The original founder, Phillip Donnigan, came here in the late 1800s after the Civil War and settled the area. So there isn't any history before that era."

Buster picked up a book and thumbed through it. It had a lot of pictures. "Is this Donnigan?"

Mrs. Wallace took the book and looked at the picture. "Yes, it is."

"He was a good-looking man," Buster said as he thumbed through the pictures.

"Well, on the outside."

"What do you mean?"

"History proved him to have a black heart and evil spirit. Probably came from his time in Andersonville POW camp during the Civil War."

"Just because he was a POW doesn't make a bad man."

"No, he started life as a street urchin after his family came to America during the Irish potato famine. Apparently, he raised himself on the streets, became quite a con-artist and manipulator. He didn't have any allegiances to either side of the Civil War. He was one of many street urchins that joined the army for free food." Mrs. Wallace smiled at Buster.

"So, how did he end up out here in Texas?"

"He came to fight the Indians with General Mackenzie. He was recruited from Andersonville to participate in the Texas Indian wars," Mrs. Wallace said. "Like I said, he was an opportunist, and this little community of ours became his greatest opportunity. He entered history as our greatest sorrow."

Buster wondered at her statement but didn't ask anything because Mrs. Wallace and Merilee soon became involved in a conversation about bridge club. Buster wandered around the museum by himself. The bit of history he obtained from Mrs. Wallace calmed him from his morning scare. He didn't want to leave; there was safety in the building, a security of knowledge.

Buster found a small section with more pictures and information about Donnigan. He was surprised he hadn't heard the name especially since the man founded the town.

"Mrs. Wallace, why is our town called Church Creek Falls if the founder's name is Donnigan?"

"Good question," Mrs. Wallace said. "No one really knows. The only details I have been able to dig up is that there was once a church where the courthouse now sits. Not sure about the Creek or Falls since we have neither."

"Seems we live in a most interesting place, even if there is no scenery," Merilee interjected. They all chuckled at her little joke.

The information about Donnigan from Mrs. Wallace left Buster with more questions than answers. The only information he gained from the visit was the lack of sinkholes in the county. Probably no history of dragons either, since it wasn't mentioned.

Donnigan was an opportunist and this place had been his final opportunity.

"Did Donnigan have a pet dragon?" Buster asked with a smirk on his face.

"Hum, possible, people said He did have a fiery temper and mean disposition," Mrs. Wallace answered with a similar smirk.

I can't believe I said that out loud. Buster was certain he was blushing from his mistake.

Merilee picked up a little trinket, a turquoise blue broach or amulet. "What's this?"

"It's just a piece of junk jewelry someone brought in here, probably homemade," Mrs. Wallace answered as she looked away. She quickly changed the subject back to Donnigan, and Merilee put the piece down on the counter.

"There's not much about Donnigan around town, but the old-timers know a little about him. If you're interested, you can talk to them," Mrs. Wallace instructed.

"Thank you," Buster replied, knowing the old-timers were the last people who would talk to him.

The real question he really wanted to ask was if there were sinkholes below the earth that would be large enough to contain a …large dragon. He moaned to himself as he thought the word, but no other description would be adequate. Buster needed this information in order to restore some sanity to his "vision." But those weren't questions he could ask of Mrs. Wallace. What had started as a search for information regarding sinkholes in the county quickly became a history lesson of the county. Although the history and the geology were not in the same realm of research, this history felt important to his vision. He wondered if Donnigan the opportunist did more than settle the land. What had he brought to the land?

"Mrs. Wallace, do you know exactly how Donnigan started the community?" Buster asked, hoping there might be a morsel of information to lead him to discover why he had seen a dragon that morning

"The town was started by Donnigan as a settlement, but the town gained its standing with a gunfight over the location of the county square. It is said that everyone in Church Creek Falls is related to Donnigan," Mrs. Wallace said.

"Oh, how is that?" Buster asked.

"He never married, you know."

"Yeah." Buster didn't know that, but he didn't want to delay the details. The urgency still resided in his mind and he needed peace over his encounter more than ever. He was no closer to an answer. Instead he was getting further away from an explanation but still felt an urgency to pursue this line of thought. The memory of the creature's eyes prodded Buster to learn more about Donnigan. Why? Because he had seen those same eyes in the picture of Donnigan. Donnigan didn't bring the dragon…he was the dragon.

4

Undeclared Rebellion Is Still Battle

> Let us lie down in our shame, and let
> our humiliation cover us; for we have
> sinned against the LORD our God, we
> and our fathers, from our youth even to
> this day. We have not obeyed the voice
> of the LORD our God.
>
> ---Jeremiah 3:25

BEFORE BUSTER AND Merilee left the museum, Buster turned and asked Mrs. Wallace one more question. "Do you think ill treatment in a POW camp would turn a good man bad?"

"No, at least not in Donnigan's case, I don't. I think Phillip Donnigan went into Andersonville a bad man and came out a worse man."

"I see."

Mrs. Wallace and Merilee started talking when Buster didn't ask any more questions. He looked over some of the farm displays while waiting. Then he noticed a picture of an old house leaning at a strange angle. It was the one in which he lived when he was a young boy. But Buster had no memory of his house sitting at that strange angle.

When Barbara and her brothers arrived home after an unusually quiet ride, she noticed that their father's tractor was beside the house along with his pickup, which meant he would be home.

"Yippee, Daddy's home," Rance yelled as he clamored out of the car before Barbara brought it to a full stop.

Zay followed close behind, and although her feet wanted to race to her daddy too, she knew Rance and Zay would have his full attention first. She would wait. Daddy would seek her out as soon as Rance and Zay went on their way to their next adventure.

Barbara went in the back door straight to her bedroom and put her books on her desk. She changed her clothes and then came out to the kitchen where her mother was preparing the evening meal.

"Can I help?" Barbara had learned that by offering to help, it made her mother happy and gave them a little girl time alone. Barbara set the table before getting an answer from her mother.

"Did you hear about Barry Lawson?" Barbara asked her mother.

"Yes, I hurt so badly for Mrs. Lawson."

Merilee looked over at her two boys who were laughing and talking with their dad.

Barbara was certain she could guess the thoughts floating through her mother's mind. The same impressions in her mind all day. What if this war lasts long enough for them to go? She almost said out loud. Even though the family thought it, no one expressed the thought since the boys' tenth birthday, three short years ago.

While watching the news and seeing the battle scenes, Zay had started crying hysterically saying he didn't want to go fight in the war. Buster had assured him that no one under the age of eighteen would have to go fight a war. But now at age thirteen, the war was escalating, not slowing, and the family wondered if Zay may have to face a war that frightened them all. It didn't matter that the official term was a police action, it was still war. The possibility of the Troye boys being called up to the "police action" took on new horrors at the death of Barry Lawson.

"We will bake a cake tonight for you to take to them tomorrow," Merilee said. Then she stopped her task of preparing the vegetables. "No, I'll take it. Since I have my car back now, I can go into town. I think I'll go play bridge."

Typical Merilee thinking: first she wanted to offer comfort to a grieving mother, and second remembering they had become a two-car family and finally turning the entire sympathy to a joyful thought about herself playing bridge again.

"What made you decide to start playing bridge again?" Barbara asked.

"Your dad."

She looked at her mother, a bit shocked. "Why would Dad encourage you to play bridge?"

"Oh, he didn't encourage me, he took me to the museum today, and we talked to Mrs. Wallace and she let me know I have been missed and invited me back into the club."

"You and Daddy went to the museum and talked to Mrs. Wallace?" Barbara questioned.

"Yes. We had the most delightful time listening to the history of our town. I like Mrs. Wallace as a friend, but now I understand why you like her as a teacher. She really makes history alive."

"Barbara, tell Dad about the snake," Zay said.

"You go ahead." She smiled as she listened to Zay and Rance tell their tale about a ten- foot snake that rose up its thick, long body until the head was almost eye to eye with them. "And that was after we ran over him," Zay expounded and stood up on the edge of the couch.

"Well, it seemed like that at the time," Barbara said. "But when we were returning home, I saw the thing on the highway about two and a half feet long and very dead and flat. However, at the time, I could have sworn he recoiled and shook his little rattle thing at us," Barbara divulged in a distant voice. Then she shuddered. "The size doesn't matter. It was ugly and mean."

"Remember the noise it made when we hit it?" Rance said, making a face.

"Yeah, it sounded like we ran over a bicycle or something big and metal," Zay said.

Buster sat listening to his children tell this story of their morning. "Did you see anything else?" he questioned.

Zay shouted, "Yeah, we saw this big dirt devil and it had wings!"

Barbara laughed at him. "It appeared to have wings the way it was blowing out."

Buster tried to laugh with his children. "How could you see wings on a dirt devil?" "When did you see this?" he asked.

"About the same time we hit the snake," Rance added.

Buster's heartbeat accelerated as he gripped the arm of his chair. Had his children really seen a ten-foot snake? Could they have seen an image of the snake in the "dust devil"? Were the children at risk?

A small bead of perspiration trickled down Buster's temple, what's going on?

"Umm," Buster finally said in response to Rance. He didn't want to talk about this; he wanted to forget it all, if possible. He decided to change the subject, hoping his voice did not sound as shaky as he felt inside. "Barbara, have you ever studied the Great Potato Famine in Ireland?"

"Yeah, we talked about it in Mrs. Wallace's class."

"She's a good teacher, isn't she?" Buster inquired.

"The best. She makes history important to me."

Barbara paused for a moment then added, "Why did you ask about the potato famine?"

"Mrs. Wallace mentioned it when your mom and I were at the museum today."

"How come you went there?" Barbara and the boys turned to look at him.

He realized his children didn't consider him an intellectual. "Don't look so surprised. I enjoy information too."

"I just didn't think you did anything except work on this farm," Barbara said.

"I know. That's mostly what I do, but after the big dust devil today, I got a little scared."

"Scared of what?" Rance asked.

"A sinkhole," Buster answered in a matter-of-fact tone of voice.

"What's that?" Barbara asked.

"Oh, I know." Rance proceeded to give a geological lesson to his sister and explained how a sinkhole could happen here because of the Ogallala water reservoir under them.

"Is that true, Buster?" Merilee asked.

"Afraid so."

"What made you fearful of that?" Merilee stopped cooking and came over and sat on the couch next to Buster.

"The dust devil the kids saw…I saw it too, and it was so big it looked like it had wings. Made me afraid the ground was going to cave in. It really shook me up."

"Dad, why would a sinkhole happen now?" Zay asked.

"For us, this drought we've been experiencing could have something to do with it. The water reservoir beneath us is not filling up at the same rate in which our irrigation is draining it."

"How come we are having such a long drought?" Barbara pondered.

"Silly, it hasn't rained more than a few inches in the last three years," Rance informed his sister.

"I know that, but why hasn't it rained? Could it be weather patterns or what?" Barbara restated.

Buster smiled at his children as he pulled a cigarette from his pocket and lit it, but when the heat of the match came close to his face, he felt a sting and he put the cigarette down, deciding it was time to quit.

"Barbara, I sense there's something you're trying to say," he said as he blew out the match and tossed the cigarettes into the trash.

Zay watched as he tossed the whole pack, he didn't say anything.

"I guess I am, Daddy," she said. "I don't think the rain just stops without a reason, I'm not sure what that reason can be, but after studying earth science and the formation of clouds, it seems the system is pretty much on a steady basis, so what interferes and makes it stop?"

Zay spoke up adding to Barbara's thought, "We do live in a land-locked area. That's a good question, because the rains usually come. What's different now?"

"Maybe I need to go to the library and check out books on weather patterns." Buster grinned. "I might even become a weatherman." The family laughed.

Rance stood up, pretending to hold a microphone like a weather man, "This is Buster Troye bringing you your weather today."

The other kids laughed.

"Daddy, you'd make a good weatherman," Zay grinned.

"Better not, Daddy, right now everyone thinks you're an honest man. That would ruin your reputation," Barbara expressed with a silly grin.

Buster's expression turned serious. "In the Bible we see that when God began to discipline His children, He started by withholding the rain."

"Wow! Listening to this conversation, that dust devil caused quite a stir," Merilee declared. The family snickered at her pun.

"What are you all laughing at?" she asked with a smile she caught from their laughter.

"You, Mom, you're funny and don't even know it," Rance said.

Buster rose from his chair and walked into the kitchen. He poured himself a glass of milk and turned to face the family. Merilee joined him. She put her hand on Buster's arm to rub it. "Can you take me to see where it happened?"

What a strange request, but it would be good to return with someone.

"Sure, there's still enough daylight. We can go now," Buster answered.

"Could it swallow our house?"

"Yep," Rance answered.

Merilce looked to Buster who raised an eyebrow.

Everything looked somewhat normal as the family peered out the car windows, Buster and Merilee from the front seat and the three kids from the pickup bed. They stopped and looked over the field for a few minutes.

"See that little swirl of dirt there where the tractor tire prints are disturbed?" Buster pointed to the spot. "That's where it happened."

"Did it rain too?" Merilee asked.

"No, why?"

"There's a huge pool of water."

Buster got out of the pickup and walked over to the familiar puddle of drool. He'd hoped it would be gone so that he could attribute the entire event to a wild imagination. Fortunately, Garrett had pulled the bull carcass back to his place.

"What is it?" Barbara asked as she started to reach down and dip her finger in it.

"Stop!" Buster yelled at her. "It may not be water. It may be poisonous or caustic." Barbara withdrew her hand quickly and didn't argue.

"Here, let's collect it safely."

Buster pulled his empty gallon glass water jar from the back of the pickup, along with a shovel. He scooped some of the drool and dropped it into the wide mouth jar. Barbara put a lid on and held up the jar to gaze at the stuff.

"This is sure strange-looking, the swirls of color make it look as though it could be oil or antifreeze."

Buster took the jar and stared at the stuff.

He knew where it had come from, but he didn't know much about it either.

"I think I'll take this into the agriculture lab in the city tomorrow and have it analyzed," Buster said.

"Good idea," the scientific-minded Zay added.

Mrs. Paul entered Principal McCoy's office.

"Some of the teachers think we should dismiss school the day of Barry Lawson's memorial service," Mrs. Paul said.

"I know," Principal McCoy answered. "I'm not sure what to do. Mr. Lawson is on the school board, but Barry graduated three years ago."

"When will the remains arrive?"

"There won't be any. None were found," Principal McCoy said.

He shook his head and continued, "Such a shame. I remember Jim saying his boy would make it home because he was on an aircraft carrier and wouldn't see battle."

"So what happened?" Mrs. Paul asked.

"Fire on board the ship."

"You mean he was killed by our own military?"

"In a sense, yes, the Forrestal carried armed ammunitions for the planes. A spark from one of the planes caused an on-board fire, which ignited the bombs."

"Oh, I think I'm going to be sick." Mrs. Paul sat down.

Principal McCoy arose from his chair and approached Mrs. Paul. He extended his hand over her shoulder to comfort her but just couldn't make his hand touch her. Not that she was repulsive but rather that she was so desirable. McCoy walked back toward his desk and stood in front of it.

"I think you're right, Mrs. Paul," McCoy said. "We should allow those students and teachers who desire to attend the memorial service to go without a tardy or absence. Those students who stay can be incorporated into the classrooms of the teachers who stay."

"You know that means you and I will probably be taking on classroom duties along with much of the other administrative staff."

"Oh." He hadn't realized the largest portion of his teaching staff would leave under those circumstances since many of them had taught Barry.

"You're right. We'll dismiss school early. The service is at 2:00 p.m., so dismiss class at the lunch hour." He knew this was a better decision. It left him free to attend the service. In fact, most all of the people living in Church Creek Falls would be found at the memorial.

As Mrs. Paul gained her stamina and rose from the chair, McCoy went back to his desk and stared out the window, his thoughts jumbled with many things. He remembered the first time he had met Barry Lawson, a shy young man with slight build but handsome face. He was smart and could easily have risen to the ranks of CEO in any major company. McCoy knew his entrance into the Air Force was most likely a forced decision. A decision based on McCoy's accidental encounter with Barry. It was a few days later when McCoy mentioned the encounter to Barry's parents. McCoy sighed as he thought, If I had not said anything to them, he would probably be alive and living right here in Church Creek Falls.

McCoy shook off the regrets, knowing they would not change anything. As he stared out the window pondering the situation, he noticed a large dust devil south of town. At first he thought it might be a tornado and his heart quickened, but it stayed in one place. He stood and walked to the window to watch the cloud of dust rising in the air. After it disappeared, he went back to his desk to work.

<hr/>

Mrs. Paul wiped the tears from her face as she entered her office across the foyer from McCoy's. What a cruel joke of fate. He went to fight a nonexistent enemy in a nonexistent place by a nonexistent war, and he dies with the bombs destined to explode on a land far away. How could this be reality?

The sadness Mrs. Paul felt brought to mind her own anguish. Her husband had left her for a younger woman. He left her with two small children and no money. Mrs. Paul didn't become bitter, instead she became frivolous with her life, her body, and her reputation.

Barbara Troye entered the office in the middle of Mrs. Paul's thoughts. She turned her pensive demeanor into a welcoming smile. She didn't know Barbara very well, but she knew her dad, Buster, and his reputation for integrity. It wasn't that Mr. Troye did anything, it was that his very presence made her feel so guilty. Nonetheless, his daughter stood in front of her at this moment.

"Hello, Barbara, what do you need?"

"I need a class change," Barbara said.

"Sure, what do you want to change?" Mrs. Paul asked as she pulled out a class change form.

"I'm not sure, but I have four office hours and…I would really like to have more class time."

Mrs. Paul took Barbara's schedule and wondered what had happened. She truly did have four office aide classes. This was an unusual event for any student, but a bright student like Barbara usually spent their senior year taking chemistry, calculus, a foreign language, or something beneficial for college.

"Are you planning to attend college?" Mrs. Paul asked, now getting into her business frame of mind.

"Yes."

"You're right, this schedule is not suitable. Let's see what we can find for you."

After several minutes they came to the conclusion there was nothing offered that she could take during the hours she needed something else.

"I don't know what to do about this, Barbara. Would you like to talk to Principal McCoy?" Mrs. Paul wanted to make this situation right, but she didn't have the ability or authority to help the girl.

"Yes, I think that would be a good idea," Barbara smiled and gathered her papers preparing to go to Principal McCoy's office.

"Oh, you can't meet with him now. Let me set up an appointment for you. In the meantime, I think Mrs. Johnson might need some help. Would you like for me to ask her?"

"That would be nice," Barbara said. "Where do I go now?" She looked a bit bewildered.

"Stay here and I'll go talk to Mrs. Johnson now," Mrs. Paul said as she left the office, leaving Barbara sitting alone across from her desk.

The quiet was almost eerie. It was a strange time. With Barry Lawson's death, a quiet pallor had overtaken the school.

Barbara looked around Mrs. Paul's office where she sat alone. It had the same flowery smell of perfume that always surrounded Mrs. Paul. Pictures of Mrs. Paul's children and a few group pictures of different classes hung on the walls, and some sat on her desk.

Mrs. Paul had often helped sponsor senior trips. Barry Lawson's class enjoyed the last of that benefit. Barbara looked at the picture of that class. She scanned it for Barry's face. Even though she didn't know him, she felt a sadness knowing he was gone. She placed the photo back on the credenza. At the new angle she noticed something odd. Barbara realized one of the men on the back row did not look into the camera as all the other people. She didn't know who the man was, but there was no denying the look of love—or lust—on his face as he stared directly at Mrs. Paul.

"Good news, Barbara. Mrs. Johnson is delighted to have you. If you'll go to her room, she has a stack of things for you to do."

Barbara still held the photo in her hand. "It's a good picture of Barry, isn't it?" Barbara said as she sat it down.

"Yes, I guess it was probably one of his last. He joined the air force shortly after that trip." Mrs. Paul's gaze lingered on the scene, and Barbara was almost certain it wasn't Barry's face upon which she focused.

"Thank you, Mrs. Paul, I'll see Principal McCoy in the morning."

"Hum, yeah," Mrs. Paul responded as she turned away from the picture with a slight crooked smile on her face as she remembered the day that picture was taken. It had been one of the best days of her life. She traced the outline of one face recalling the events that followed that day. It had all begun with that smile captured forever in that photo. Completely unaware of his interest until after the group broke up, Mrs. Paul turned and looked at the most handsome Mr. Jase Hamlin smiling directly at her. When they made eye contact, he had winked. She could still remember the feel of the blush rising to her checks as she had "DTs" about him or dirty thoughts. Even now the dirty thoughts returned. Five years ago and she still had not forgotten that most memorable day and night. A repeat of that night would be most welcome now.

5

Scientific Explanation?

He has swallowed me like a monster,
He has filled his stomach with my
delicacies: He has washed me away.
                    ---Jeremiah 51:34

THE RINGING PHONE insisted upon an answer with each loud ring. It had been over a week since the "stuff" had been delivered to the agriculture lab in Burlington Heights. Buster knew he would hear from them soon. But as the phone rang, he wasn't sure he was ready for the results.

"Hello," Buster answered.

"Hello, I am calling for Buster Troye," the deep male voice on the other end announced.

"This is he."

"Mr. Troye, I have just finished doing my analysis of the stuff you brought in about a week ago."

"Yes."

"I wonder if I could come out to your farm and look at the location where you found this."

Buster paused for a minute. His first instinct was to say yes, but he hesitated because he wasn't going to tell anyone how the stuff came to be in that location.

"Mr. Troye? I need directions," the voice came over the phone a little louder.

Buster decided his need to know what the voice on the phone knew was greater than his fear of admitting to his vision. He decided he didn't have to tell the man what he saw.

"Oh, sorry, yes, I will give you directions."

Buster drove out to the site to meet the man from the lab. When he arrived, he saw Rance, his son, digging in the dirt at the site. He wondered what Rance could be doing. Nonetheless, he was glad Rance would be there with him when the man from the lab arrived.

"Hi, son. What are you doing?"

"Looking for our fortune," Rance replied.

"What do you mean?"

"Well, that stuff looks like it could have some oil. I got to thinking maybe we had oil on our land and we could find it and get rich."

Buster smiled at the enthusiasm of a thirteen-year-old looking for riches.

"Son, we are rich. We have the best family in the world, this farm, and the Lord. We don't need anything else. Besides, we don't own this land."

"But you said it was the family farm." Rance seemed puzzled.

Buster chuckled at the interpretation of his statement. "Yes, we call it the family farm because no one but our family has ever farmed this land. Mr. Kearney promised my father that if he decided to sell the land, we would have first chance."

"Why doesn't he sell it to us?"

"Because he makes money off the land with the rent we pay him."

"So he gets rich off our work," Rance said in disgust.

Buster shook his head, wondering how to explain to his son without instilling his own bitterness toward Mr. Kearney in him. "He makes a living off his land by leasing it out."

Buster continued without giving Rance an opportunity to speak. "If there is any oil on it, Mr. Kearney would be the one to reap the financial rewards."

"So he would be the one that would be rich?" Rance asked. Buster pressed his lips firmly together and nodded in the affirmative.

"But he's already rich… I want you to have a nice tractor with a cab and a nice pickup…" Rance's voice drifted off into bitter disappointment as he stopped shoveling and started walking toward Buster's 1958 short bed Chevrolet pickup.

"Whoa boy, we would all like to have nice things, but you know the Bible says to be content with what you have."

"I know…but…"

"No buts about it, when God says it in His book, we have to accept it and obey it."

It was times like this that Rance wished his dad wasn't such an honest man and didn't trust in the Bible so much. According to the boy's thinking, a little greed could be a good thing if an opportunity presented itself.

Rance saw the white pickup with the official-looking seal on the door drive up onto their property. A distinguished fiftyish looking man stepped out of the pickup and walked up to Rance and Buster. He extended his hand.

At the same time Zay rode up on his bicycle.

"Where'd you come from?" Rance hollered out to Zay.

"I saw that pickup pass the house with the official government farm lab logo on the side, so here I am."

"Okay let's go see what is going on," Rance said.

"Hello, I'm Dr. Winegren," he said.

"Buster Troye," he said as he shook the man's hand. "And these are my sons, Rance and Zay."

"What kind of doctor are you?" Zay asked.

Buster was a bit embarrassed by his son's forwardness. Since he wanted an answer too, he felt a bit of pride in Zay's inquisitiveness.

"I'm a herpetologist," the older man said.

"I was expecting a young tech."

"Normally, that would be the case, but this substance seems to contain signs that you may have some African cobras on your farm."

Zay gasped, "Cobras, here?"

"I didn't say they were here, I said the fluid seems to have signs of African cobras in it."

"So, if we do have cobras, how did they get here?" Zay asked.

"That's why I'm here, to further define the substance and rule out cobras and fire-breathing dragons."

Buster raised his head and looked Dr. Winegren in the face. Was he serious or making a joke?

"What is a herpetologist?" Zay queried.

Dr. Winegren squatted down beside the largest pool of liquid and pulled on thick rubber gloves while he continued talking. "A herpetologist is a person who studies reptiles and amphibians, like snakes and frogs. I'm mostly here to gather more information, that is, if you don't mind."

After the dragon remark, Buster wished he had not sent the sample.

"Wow!" Zay said as he asked questions nonstop to Dr. Winegren, barely leaving him time to answer before the next question popped out of his mouth.

Dr. Winegren smiled and said, "I'm enjoying the interest in my work because I usually don't get that from young teens, but right now, I need to ask you and your dad some questions."

"Shoot," Zay said with a puffed up chest and a broad smile on his face.

"I would like to do a little experiment, if I may," Dr. Winegren looked to Buster for permission.

"I…I guess so." Buster couldn't think of a reason to say no. He wanted to know all this man could tell him.

"Young man, I have a shovel in the back of my pickup. Would you bring it to me?"

"I've got a shovel right here, Dr. Winegren," Rance said.

"Thank you, son, but I need my shovel. It has been sterilized so no other matter will be mixed in my tests."

Buster caught a glimpse into the big box Dr. Winegren carried. He saw test tubes and bottles of different colored liquids, along with a set of fierce-looking tools—most likely used to handle venomous snakes without getting bitten. Dr. Winegren removed a blowtorch from the case.

"Stand back, I don't expect anything to happen, but just in case it does," Dr. Winegren said.

He lowered the torch to the ground where Rance had been digging and with a loud whoosh the flames leaped up in the air about ten feet.

All three men stepped back away from it and Dr. Winegren quickly turned off the torch.

"What does that mean?" Zay asked.

"I'm not sure, other than the substance is flammable, and it rules out spitting cobras. Maybe it is a fire-breathing dragon," Dr. Winegren said.

Buster barely smiled over the sick feeling in his stomach when Dr. Winegren correctly identified the source of the pool.

As the flames reached up and sparks fell, they ignited other parts of the soil where Zay had dug it from the central location.

"So that stuff is flammable," Buster said, trying to act surprised.

"Yes, and it's not oil, but something closely associated to oil, but why would it have the reptilian characteristics?"

"Maybe it's a fossil fuel from young dinosaurs or maybe even a large serpent," Zay answered.

Buster remained stoic at his son's suggestion, but hoped the statement might give more details of the origin of the large serpent he had seen.

"Good thought, but it's not a fossil fuel. It's recent, and I don't think it is coming up from the earth." Dr. Winegren lifted his shovel from digging and found only dry dirt. "It's on the earth as though it has been spilled. This brings up a question of safety too."

After the fire burned itself out, Dr. Winegren took some soil samples. "Mr. Troye, I'm not able to help you out right now, but I would be on the watch for this stuff. If it's coming from underground, we need to know. After all, the largest water table in the nation sits under this land."

"I thought you said it didn't come from beneath," Buster prodded to see how much information the scientist was able to glean from his inspection.

"It doesn't appear to be, but right now, I have more questions than answers," Dr. Winegren said. "I'll be in touch and will be turning this over to the geology department."

The excitement ended as a few dying sparks sizzled and disappeared. The substance that had caused all of the excitement no longer existed.

Buster, Rance, and Zay watched Dr. Winegren drive off, a silence stood between father and sons. Dr. Winegren did prove Buster's encounter real.

"Man, you would think something eerie is going on here the way that guy was acting," Rance said. He then picked up Zay's bike and headed home.

Buster looked at Zay, "Guess you lost your ride."

"It's okay; I really wanted to talk to you about this…whatever it is anyway."

Buster studied his young son and seriously considered telling him everything. He chose not to tell Zay because he was afraid that people, even his family, would think him a bit daffy. But then, if the scientist could prove it first, there would be no one questioning Buster's sanity.

"Dad? What's wrong?"

"Oh, nothing, son, just thinking about possibilities."

"Like a fire-breathing dragon?" Zay said with a smirk.

"Yeah, like a fire-breathing dragon," Buster said with a wink as he put his arm around his young son who had just nailed down the exact cause of the substance. Buster decided it might be time to question the young man.

He looked Zay in his eyes and, in a most serious tone of voice, said, "Zay, what do you know?"

Zay smiled. "I thought you knew more than you were telling."

"But Zay, what do you know?" Buster reiterated.

"Chill, Dad, I don't know anything, but I now know you know more than you're telling. Can you let me in on the secret?"

"I wish I could. You're right, I know more than I am telling and there is a lot more to this mystery than this fluid. Let's keep this our secret, okay?"

"You got it, Dad, my lips are sealed," Zay walked beside his dad with a smug grin on his face, showing the satisfaction of being on the inside of his dad's secret. Even though he didn't know what it was.

Buster looked up in the distance and saw a plume of dust traveling down the road.

"Well, son, looks like your mother's on her way into town. Must be her hair parlor day."

Zay laughed easily with his dad because they both knew she wouldn't miss that for anything, not even a scientific discovery.

"Have you told Mom?" Zay questioned.

"No, and I don't intend to, so keep your mouth shut around her. Not that she would care anyway." Buster let his voice trail off. Unless it would decorate her home or body, Merilee would not be interested. He groaned at the thought of his beautiful wife being so shallow he couldn't share this with her. He yearned to talk to someone.

At the end of the day, Buster followed his usual routine and came in the back door to the mud room, then directly into the bathroom for a shower. Merilee wouldn't allow him into her house until all the dirt had been washed off. He couldn't disagree, but he was extremely thirsty.

He stepped into the shower the water rolled over his head and he drank in the cold water. Shivering with the cold water rolling over his body, his greater need quenched. Ever since that day, he couldn't get enough water. His five-gallon water bucket emptied by noon. His reduced output in spite of drinking more bothered him. In fact, he couldn't remember going to the bathroom all day long and still didn't feel any urgency to go. This was not a good sign. The intense thirst started the moment the horrible creature appeared in the field.

The spirit of evil burned his soul. There would never be enough water to quench it, only the termination of it could satisfy Buster's thirst

6

The Beauty Salon

O generation heed the word of the
Lord. Have I been a wilderness to Israel,
or a land of thick darkness? Why do My
people say, "we are free to roam; We will
no longer come to You?"

—Jeremiah 2:31

MERILEE SANK HER head into the wash bowl while
Karen scrubbed her scalp. She gave wonderful head
massages. This one hour each week helped her maintain
her sanity on the isolated farm in a cheap little
manufactured home. She did her best to keep the home
and yard looking nice and kept. The house looked clean
even though it leaked like a sieve when the dust clouds
rolled in, especially during the off season when the fields
were plowed. At least it would relax a little during the
growing season, but then she suffered from hay fever from

the pollen. There simply was nothing to like about the country and a farm on land as flat as a table.

Karen chitchatted and Merilee tuned in to listen to the latest news around town as the shop filled with other patrons. Mrs. Wallace came into the salon.

"Hello, Merilee, I'm so glad I ran into you."

"Me too, I wanted to tell you how much we enjoyed the visit the other day," Merilee said.

"That is the reason I'm glad I ran into you. I found some more material I thought you and Buster might be interested in."

"That's funny to hear, since Buster doesn't read much, except his Bible and the Farmer's Almanac."

Mrs. Wallace laughed. "It's always the quiet ones that surprise you, but I told him a little about the county's founder, Phillip Donnigan. I found some early history on the man. So I thought Buster might be interested."

"Thank you for remembering?" Merilee said as she organized the material into her oversized purse.

"Yes, that material has several pictures of Donnigan from his childhood to an old man. Buster asked me if I had more pictures. They are rare, but I did find those. I hope they help with his quest."

Merilee turned her interest back to the conversation going on in the salon. Once she entered the tube of reckless air otherwise known as the hair dryer, she would no longer hear the "gossip." Thirty minutes later, when she came out of the dryer, she entered in the middle of another conversation.

"I'm so sorry to hear about Julie Marable," Dorothy Mannering said. "It must be a strange thing to sacrifice so much to do the right thing to come to a point of regret."

"Yes, I guess it's too late to change anything," Janie Engli said. "I hope the Lawson family tries. After all, it's their last heir."

Merilee understood the conversation. Julie's daughter had discovered she was pregnant at age seventeen. Julie and her husband sent their daughter to a home for unwed mothers in Dallas. The baby had been adopted. The rumor flew around town that the father of the baby was Barry Lawson. What once seemed like a problem was now a blessing to the Lawson family. Merilee shook her head but said nothing. The conversation kept plugging along, providing news on all who were newsworthy.

"I heard Dr. Pulling is on his third divorce now."

"Makes you wonder if it's the hours he works or the other women?"

A snicker of laughter floated in the air. Each woman looking at the other with accusing looks. That is, everyone except Merilee who broke the silence by asking a question. "Where does he find these women? I just can't imagine any woman wanting to have an affair with him."

"Well, Merilee, you know some men can be pretty charming in spite of their looks," Karen said. The others nodded in agreement and smiled.

"Well, there's not enough charm in his whole body to make me interested in him."

"Not everyone has a good husband like yours, Merilee," Dorothy chimed in.

"Even if I didn't have a good husband, I wouldn't want another man pawing all over me," Merilee said. "If he tried, I'd chop off his hands."

The shop filled with a strange laughter.

"What do you know about your sister-in-law?" Janie asked.

"What sister-in-law?" Merilee said in all honesty.

"The woman married to your husband's brother."

"Oh, Wylene," Merilee said with a nod of recognition, "What about her?"

"I hear she left him."

"Hum. Don't know. Haven't heard anything."

"I heard she accused him of hitting her one too many times," Dorothy said.

"I don't believe that. Where did you hear such a ridiculous story?"

"From Wylene herself," Dorothy answered with a smug retort that sounded like bragging that she was on the inside scoop and Merilee knew nothing.

"Well, she's just making it up so you'll pay some attention to her," Merilee said. She paid her bill and left. The gossip session continued.

She headed toward the local dress shop, The Enchanted Closet. She needed a gift for a wedding shower.

———◆———

Clara Waithe didn't shop. Yet here she stood in a dress shop with nothing to buy. The Holy Spirit took her by the hand and brought her to this overpriced den of gossip and greed. She stood in front of a dress rack praying, what am

I supposed to do now? The owners of the shop sat in the chatter pit drinking coffee, smoking cigarettes, and chewing up the latest victim of their gossip. One of the owners rose, snuffed out her cigarette, and approached Clara, "May I help you with something?"

Clara thumbed through the blouses. "No, I'm just looking right now." *Looking for why I am here.*

Then the quickening in her stomach happened. The bell on the door tingled. Merilee Troye stepped into the shop. Whatever the reasons for Clara's call here, it concerned Merilee. Clara positioned herself in such a way that she could watch Merilee and know when and if she was to approach her.

As Merilee browsed the gifts section, Gaylene Barrett asked her if she needed some help.

"I'm looking for a wedding gift," Merilee said.

"Oh, did you look at her registry table?" Gaylene responded.

"She isn't registered here," Merilee said as she continued to browse through the bric-a-brac and wall décor.

"What, well we must get her registered."

"She doesn't live here in Church Creek Falls," Merilee said.

"Oh, well, do you have anything in mind, or do you just want to browse?"

"Let me browse for a minute," Merilee said.

Clara glanced over and saw Merilee staring at the curse of Church Creek Falls—a beautiful wall hanging in an alluring turquoise blue with slight orange highlights. It contained a series of geometric shapes overlapping each other leaving gaps like eye holes and a mouth. She pleaded silently, Please, Merilee, don't touch it. She was too late. Merilee picked it up.

Mrs. Waithe approached Merilee. "Hello, Merilee, how are you today?" she said.

"I hope you are going to come see me this week."

"Oh, yes, I wouldn't miss our time together. I learned more from you in those few hours than I ever learn at church," Merilee said.

"That's no surprise. They probably never crack a Bible in that church building."

Mrs. Waithe couldn't look at the dreadful thing Merilee held in her hand. Mrs. Waithe knew what it was and the chaotic evil it produced in a home. She wanted to snatch it out of Merilee's hand while at the same time feeling revulsion at the idea of touching the vile thing.

Merilee smiled at Mrs. Waithe, "I think I will buy this for my den. It's most unusual; don't you think?" Merilee said.

"Yes, yes, it is," Mrs. Waithe said. Internally, she was pleading with the Holy Spirit to show her how to stop Merilee.

"Are you redecorating your home?"

"No, but yes, I am always in a state of redecorating. I have to. The dirt fogs in my house like a sieve. If I don't rearrange, I get mounds of dirt."

"You have a beautiful home and I really don't think that thing will look very good," Mrs. Waithe said as she turned her gaze away from it and frowned.

Merilee stood staring up at the piece and Mrs. Waithe knew her comment went unheard.

"I'm going to buy this, what do you think?"

"Please don't," Mrs. Waithe begged. After all, she had been asked her opinion.

Merilee carried the piece toward the checkout counter.

"I see you found something. This must be a really good friend," Gaylene said with a mischievous smile.

"Yes, she is a close friend."

"That will be $125.00," Gaylene said in a voice loud enough to be heard by the people in the conversation pit.

Mrs. Waithe walked away and whispered another prayer, "Lord, give her endurance." She left the store with a tear crawling down her wrinkled face.

Merilee kept her face straight, but inside she was melting with horror. She thought it would be around twenty dollars. She pulled out her checkbook and wrote the check without flinching. She could feel the other women watching her.

Gaylene wrapped the piece up and put it in one of their more exclusive sacks with the cotton drawstring and the store logo printed across the front. Merilee thought the bags were a symbol of acceptance in the social circle; now she knew it was about money. She graciously accepted the gaudy package and walked from the store with her head held high. Once the door closed behind her, she would most likely be the topic of conversation. She hated that it bothered her.

The trip to the grocery store went faster than planned. Her grocery money had disappeared into her cursed little wall hanging. To top it off, she still didn't have a gift for the shower. She stopped at the local TG&Y and bought some Pyrex pie plates for the shower along with some wrapping paper and ribbon. She hadn't gone over budget too much. Maybe Buster wouldn't even notice the slight dip she made in the budget. He'd been preoccupied the last few days.

Once she arrived at home, the hustle of life engulfed her for a few minutes. Soon everyone would be home for dinner. The wall decoration remained in the trunk of the car. It wasn't vital for the immediate family activities.

Merilee stared at her husband and offspring. She was grateful for their family. Buster was not the richest farmer in the community. In reality he was but a sharecropper, but he gave them a good life, and he was a good man. She looked at him as he listened to Barbara. Her heart skipped a little beat. He was the love of her life and so good-looking with his ocean-blue eyes. Did she really need the social activity that much, or was it the personality of the community demanding it? Yet, she liked the gatherings and the parties. It was almost as important as air, but not quite as important as this scene of her family.

Suddenly, an ungodly roar sounded in the room. She dropped her fork and put her hands over her ears. "Ow!"

"What's wrong, Mom?" Rance said.

Merilee looked at her family, who all looked at her as if she had grown another nose.

"Didn't you hear it?"

"Hear what?" Buster asked.

"That noise, it was almost like the roar of a lion, but louder."

Buster's heart leapt into his throat. He may have seen the monster, but it appeared Merilee could hear it. The whole family sat in quiet as Merilee tried to pop her ears by yawning and swallowing.

"I'm sorry, I must need to have my ears checked, or I am getting an ear infection. It was really weird."

"It's okay, Mom, we'll clean up the kitchen. You go rest," Rance said.

The family began to clear off the table and put away the leftover food.

Merilee went into the living room and lay down on the couch. She knew what she heard was real, and it came from outside her head, not inside it. She was still trembling when Buster came over to her.

"Are you okay?" he asked as he sat on the edge of the couch.

"I think so. I'm just not sure what happened."

"I know what you mean. I've had some strange things happen to me lately," Buster said. Merilee wasn't acting interested, so he didn't say anything more.

"Oh, Buster, I ran into Mrs. Wallace this morning at the beauty shop. She gave me some books to give to you. She said you had asked if she had more about Donnigan."

"Yeah, that's right," Buster said a bit shyly.

"She said he came out of the Irish potato famine so she sent some material." Merilee rose and gathered up the materials. "Are you are interested in that?"

"Yes, I guess because I am Irish. You know my granddad was first generation American and came here because of the famine."

"Oh yeah, that would be interesting. I want to read it when you're through before you take it back to Mrs. Wallace," Merilee said.

Buster was grateful for her interest even if it was not the same interest he had in the famine. He took the magazines from Merilee as she pulled them from her purse.

"You get some rest now," he told her as he took the reading over to his chair. He read a little, but mostly he was looking intently at the pictures of Donnigan.

7

Irish Great Potato Famine 1845–46

> Thus says the Lord, "Do justice and
> righteousness, and deliver the one who
> has been robbed from the power of his
> oppressor. Also do not mistreat or do
> violence to the stranger the orphan, or
> the widow: and do not shed innocent
> blood in this place."
>
> —Jeremiah 22:3

BUSTER CLOSED THE book. There were more pages to be read, but he decided he had enough information about the potato famine. It wasn't really relevant to his quest anyway. He needed to know if Donnigan and the dragon were one and the same. If so, how did it happen? What could be done? And so on. The questions were endless.

The information revealed how the children of the poor Irish parents were often put on the street to beg or take care of themselves when the families couldn't find work to support the family. Mrs. Wallace had alluded to the fact that Donnigan, the founder of Church Creek Falls, had been one of those children. Donnigan learned survival skills at a young age and developed a hardness that stayed with him throughout his life.

Buster thought about the prejudice met by the Irish. They stayed clumped together rather than venturing out into the wide open spaces of America. Which route had been taken by Phillip Donnigan? How had this man ended up in a prisoner of war camp? He would have been a child or a young man during the potato famine. Did he come to America with his family and end up an orphan? But the most pressing question in Buster's mind was how this information connected to the monster. There were no facts to support his theory. He had started looking into sink holes, and now becoming a student of local history. However, his quest was not about local history but rather the eyes of the man who founded the town. Ever since he saw the photo with the vertical pupil set in a yellow iris in Donnigan's eyes, Buster knew he needed to discover how this creature and Donnigan were connected. Was Donnigan truly related to the reptile incident, or was it trick photography? The few pictures Mrs. Wallace had brought of Donnigan didn't show his eyes clearly, only the one he saw in the museum. She had brought it too. Buster was glad because it confirmed he had seen the same eyes in Donnigan as in the monster. Buster took the picture and stared at the eyes for a few seconds. He was afraid to look too long. But he needed every detail of this picture before he returned it to Mrs. Wallace.

To get his mind off the hideous picture, Buster reopened the book and finished reading about the potato famine then filed it away to ask Mrs. Wallace about Donnigan's history. Maybe this would be the easiest way to satisfy his curiosity so he could return to the real problem at hand—a giant reptile.

◆

With the kitchen clean, the family sat down in the den to watch television. Tonight *Gunsmoke* came on. Barbara knew about a program on the other channel, which they didn't get. It was a show called *Peyton Place*. Barbara would hear the plot line the next day at school. It was a hoot to hear about the escapades of the main characters and then to match those characters antics to real life people in her own *Peyton Place*, otherwise known as Church Creek Falls. In fact, it seemed the shenanigans that took place in real life were much more interesting than a silly television show.

The family retired for the night. Barbara didn't keep her radio on. It served up more static than music. But she soon overheard her parents talking. She put her book down when she heard her dad raise his voice to her mother. He had never done this and it caused her some worry.

"What do you mean you spent $125 on this…this…whatever it is," Daddy said. His voice was loud, but he sounded more confused than angry.

"I know; I should have looked at the price. I really thought it would go nice in here. I haven't had a chance to really decorate since we finished the house," Mother began to explain.

"But why did you spend so much?

"That's a mystery to me too. I didn't even look at the price tag. I always look before I buy, but there was something about it that…," her voice trailed off as if she were looking for the right words.

"You're right. There's something about it that feels…eerie."

"Yeah, I know. I am going to take it back tomorrow. I liked it in the store, but now, it just seems gaudy."

Barbara strained her ear to hear more. Nothing came for a moment, and she wondered what had happened.

"It's okay," her daddy said in a calmer tone. We can manage, if you want to keep it. I'm sorry I yelled at you."

Barbara quietly got out of bed and peeked out the door. She could see them staring at something. She opened the door.

"What are you guys talking about?" she asked.

Her mother turned toward her. "Oh, this wall hanging I bought today."

Barbara gazed at the turquoise and brassy-looking object. "Looks like a tribal mask to me," she said rather matter-of-factly.

Her dad looked at it. "I think you're right, sweetie."

"No," Mother said, "it's geometrical shapes. The holes just make it look like a mask. It doesn't matter anyway; I'm taking it back."

"Well, why don't you hang it up over the couch and see?" Barbara suggested. "You may be surprised. It may look pretty good."

"Okay, but I doubt it." Her mom rose and walked into the kitchen to get nails and a hammer from her all-purpose drawer.

After hanging the sculpture, they all three stood back and looked at it.

"It kinda grows on you," Daddy said and Mother nodded.

"Doesn't look bad, Mom, you may have done well after all."

Daddy turned to Barbara and said, "You really like it?"

"Oh, for some reason it feels like it belongs here. Not sure I like it. It feels like the strange relative in the attic."

Barbara woke up from a nightmare slinking through her sleep. She pulled the bedcovers up under her chin. She felt like a small child wanting to go get in bed with Mom and Dad. She talked herself into getting up and checking out the glow peeking under her bedroom door and find its source. It's probably just moonlight.

As she opened her door, horror grasped the sound in her throat and would not let it escape. The sculpture her family had hung on the wall glowed with a blue strobe light effect. The light pulsated from the shape of the openings in the piece. Barbara took a quick glance at the window to check for full-moon light. It wasn't there. She slammed her bedroom door shut and jumped in bed. This time she pulled the covers over her head. All she knew to do was pray and she did.

With her eyes wide open and focused on her door, Barbara didn't find sleep until the early morning hours.

Exhausted from her encounter, she dragged herself up out of bed. When she arrived at the breakfast table, her mother frowned and said, "Barbara, do you feel okay?"

"Mom, I changed my mind. I think you should take it back."

Rance looked up. "I like it."

Zay shrugged his shoulders and said, "It makes for an interesting conversation."

Mom stood and stared at it for a few minutes. "I just can't make up my mind. Then I think of the money and decide there is nothing worth $125 to hang on my wall."

"Good choice, Mom," Barbara said as she rose from the table and started gathering her things. She wasn't ready to share her adventure from the night before because…well, nothing really happened. She saw some light or thought she saw light. It all seemed so foolish now.

"You guys ready?" she asked her brothers. They pushed in the last mouthfuls of food; they knew Barbara wouldn't wait and they'd have to ride the dreaded school bus.

While Rance gathered his books, he turned to his mother, "How are your ears this morning?"

"Oh, you mean the loud noise? Haven't heard it again."

"Good, because I did in the middle of the night. It was painful."

"Hey look, Mom, the thing looks like it's changed shape," Rance said as he passed by the wall hanging on his way out of the house to Barbara's car.

Barbara followed behind Rance and looked at the wall hanging as she passed by it. Rance was right, the holes were in different places; they were more symmetrical and the eye holes were slanted.

Mom said, "That is some optical illusion."

Merilee was now alone with the awful thing. She tried to ignore it, but she kept seeking it out. As she stood staring into the eye sockets she heard a noise, but this time it wasn't loud. It was smooth and soothing and calmness overcame her. The calmness did not give her peace but rather felt suffocating, overpowering, as if she was being willed to be calmed rather than actually being calm. The voice whispered loving words to her, but at the same time, the words shamed her.

Carlos Martinez stood and stretched before kissing his young pregnant wife good-bye. "Are you sure it is okay to take Rachel with you?" she asked him.

"It'll be okay; she can play while I work. She can come home at lunchtime and rest with you," Carlos said as he kissed his wife good-bye and left with their young daughter.

The doctor told her to stay in bed as much as possible, which was never easy with an active toddler. Her church family took turns keeping the active toddler. Some days no one volunteered. Today turned out to be one of those days. Being a high-demand landscaper, Carlos worked many long hours. His ability to take Rachel with him to work due to his outdoor activity depended upon his customer. The Newton's spoiled little Rachel and seemed disappointed when she didn't come with her daddy to their house. Mr. Newton often played ball with her in the front yard.

The phone rang. Merilee answered, knowing every neighbor on the party-line heard it also. Some would listen to her conversation, and she knew who they would be. Even though there was no privacy, it was nice to have a telephone so far out in the country. It served as a common source of gossip and news. The gossip came when someone filled in missing details in the conversation.

"Hello," Merilee said.

The voice on the other end belonged to Mrs. Cathey, the county peace officer.

"There's been an accident in town," Mrs. Cathey began.

"One of my kids…" Merilee knew her voice was quivering.

"Barbara has been in an accident, but she is okay. We just need you or Mr. Troye to come to the courthouse."

8

The Beginning of Tragedy

> Perhaps they will listen and everyone
> will turn from his evil way, that I may
> repent of the calamity which I am
> planning to do to them because of the
> evil of their deeds.
>
> —Jeremiah 26:3 (NASB)

MERILEE PLACED THE receiver back in the cradle. Barbara's okay. I need to go get her, probably means her car's not running. She grabbed her purse to go find Buster and get to Barbara. With her mind a blur, she found herself needing to verbalize every step she took. Her heart racing and her hands felt clammy. She stopped and took a deep breath before she left the house. If only Buster was here to help her cope. Her emotions were in turmoil as she imagined every raw scenario that could have happened to Barbara. The question of Barbara's safety, health, and state of being traveled through her head.

Eeeii. A loud shrill noise made Merilee put her hands over her ears and double over. It didn't help. The pain in her head and stomach grew with the same intensity of the sound. She screamed out loud, or so she thought she did, she wasn't sure.

Then as suddenly as it started, it stopped.

"Tragedy will come and I will be here."

The words she heard seemed comforting, but there was a tonal quality that belied the comfort. It felt like hot liquid being poured over her body on a cold day. At first comforting, then painful, and finally frightful because she couldn't get away from it; it was everywhere. The words were smooth and soft, but didn't make any sense.

Merilee realized she had been standing in front of the reviled wall hanging and looked up at it. She knew the words were coming from it. It smiled at her. Even in the midst of fear, she didn't get alarmed at the inanimate object speaking to her.

She screamed back at it, "Oh no you won't."

As she said the words, a stab pierced her chest. That thing is giving me a heart attack or a stroke!

The voice spoke again, "No, just a reminder of what I can do."

The pain continued, until Merilee called out in a broken voice as she fell to her knees.

"Jesus, help me." The pain stopped instantly. The last thing Merilee heard was his words coming from a growling throat.

"Noooo, you can't do that."

With trembling hands and wobbly legs, Merilee drove toward the road. She looked for Buster's truck. She found it in the same location the strange liquid was found. As she drove the half mile to the spot, she prayed Buster would be close by. Merilee breathed a sigh of relief when she saw him looking up in the sky and talking. He looked angry, sad, and scared all at the same time. She walked up behind him. Buster turned and grabbed her arm, hard. She jerked away from him with the unexpected movement.

"Let's go," he said.

"Where?" Merilee said. She felt anxious to get to Barbara.

"It's that…," Buster stopped in mid-sentence. "I think Barbara is in trouble. We have to go to town."

"How do you know?" Merilee asked bewildered as Buster guided her toward the car.

He calmed himself. The monster told him Barbara was in jail for killing a child. He didn't believe anything the vile thing told him. Nonetheless, the monster achieved its goal by making him anxious to check it out. When the two of them were speeding down a dirt road at highway speeds, Merilee finally spoke up. "Do you know where we are going?

"Yes, we're going to get Barbara, she's in jail," Buster said.

"Jail?" Merilee screamed. "What are you talking about?"

"They told me that since a child died, there has to be an investigation."

"A child died?" Merilee turned white.

"What is going on? I got a call from the justice of the peace telling me there's been an accident, but Barbara's alright. We just need to come get her. And when I find you, you claim to know this...wild story about a dead child and Barbara in jail. What are you drinking?"

"I'll tell you all about it when we get Barbara home, okay? But trust me, I have not been drinking," Buster said in an effort to comfort her.

Merilee looked out the window and wept. Buster knew this was a dire situation. He hoped it could be settled before it became fodder for the gossip mill. The fifteen-mile trip to town felt as if it were the first time he traveled it. Silence pervaded the car. He mulled over the words of the creature. Could the dragon in his field be that same serpent of old, the devil described in Revelation as a dragon?

Was God's Word identifying the creature for him? Buster pondered the things he knew about the devil from the Bible. He realized he knew very little. This disturbed him, but his mind was on Barbara. He then realized a critical point about the dragon. In that moment of panic over Barbara's situation, the dragon was not a hallucination or a vision of madness but a spiritual vision. He's seen that serpent of old that deceives the whole world. And in that moment, he didn't need to worry about his own sanity; he needed to discover why—not what.

Why had this thing appeared to him, and what could he do to protect his family? He reached over and took Merilee's hand and sighed. "We must stay strong in our faith."

Merilee wiped the tears from her eyes and nodded as she squeezed Buster's hand. "I love you so very much," she said. "Even with your white farmer's brow, I love you."

They smiled at each other as the joke relieved the tension. They would endure this trial together. When they arrived, they saw Sheriff Johnson, a longtime friend, coming out of the jail area.

"Where is she?" Buster asked.

The sheriff pointed to the door and said, "I'm so sorry."

"Can you tell us what happened?"

"As far as we can tell, it was an accident and nothing more. The child ran out into the street."

"Whose child?" Merilee asked.

"That's the kicker. We don't know. She looks familiar to me, but she's a toddler. They all look a lot alike except to their mothers. She ran out of the Newton's yard."

"The Newtons?" Buster exclaimed. "There are no small children living in that area."

"We know. We're looking for the child's parents by canvassing the neighborhood. Maybe someone is visiting in the area."

"Can I go see my daughter?"

"You can go see her and take her home. We were only keeping her till we got all the facts. She's pretty shook up."

Buster took Merilee by the hand and pulled open the heavy metal door that led to the jail cells. Barbara sat at a table on the other side, staring into space with her brothers on each side of her.

"Daddy, Mother!" The boys jumped up at the sight of their parents.

Barbara turned her tear-stained face toward her parents when she heard the boys call out to them. She fell into her father's arms and sobbed. Buster caught a few words through the sobs.

"Nowhere…and I didn't see… it was a noise…nobody there… Where did she come from…I killed her! Daddy! I killed a baby!" Barbara said plainly as she looked into his face. Buster stroked her hair as memories flooded him of his little girl with a scratched knee jumping upon his lap for comfort and help. He couldn't fix this. Not this time. But he knew the One who could give them endurance. The family would put their faith in Him.

Merilee patted Barbara on the back. Barbara reached out to her mother but didn't say anything. She didn't let go of her father. She turned to him, and while wiping away tears, she said, "What is going to happen to me?"

"We are all going home," Buster announced. "Mom will drive your car and you can go with me."

Barbara nodded in agreement and the family left the sheriff's office just as another man walked in.

"Where is she?" The man shouted. This had to be the father of the child. Barbara stopped. She wanted to apologize, but Buster pulled her out. "Now's not the time," He whispered to his daughter. The man needed to be alone with his baby girl."

Carlos Martinez focused on his task at hand. He didn't even stop when he heard the sirens wailing. It wasn't until the activity slowed down that he went over to the play area to check on Rachel. She wasn't there. He began a search knowing that she may have gone after another toy.

When he couldn't find Rachel, the awful truth hit him. He ran to the front of the house that faced Main Street and saw a small group of people gathered in the street. They informed him of the horrible thing that had happened. Carlos dropped his tools. He ran to his pickup and drove wildly to the sheriff's office. He'd seen the sheriff's car that he had seen in front of the Newton's house; the sheriff would know where his Rachel had been taken.

Sheriff Johnson recognized Carlos the moment he walked into the door and suddenly the entire scene made sense to him. He walked toward Carlos and motioned for Buster to keep going.

"Carlos, your baby Rachel is over at Montgomery's." Sheriff Johnson informed the man of the most important piece of information he needed, but also the worst information he could receive. Carlos' knees buckled and took him to the floor. He began to wail in moans painful to hear.

"Come on and I will drive you over there," Sheriff Johnson said.

———◆———

Once outside, Barbara said, "It was his child?"

"Probably," Buster said as gently as he could. We'll let the sheriff handle it."

The wail of grief pierced through the door, and Barbara clutched her father's side as her tears fell. Buster became misty-eyed as he felt her body being racked by the emotional pain of the loss.

When Buster and the family arrived home, Buster noticed a dust devil in the field. This one was a normal size swirl of dust; the difference this time was Buster's demeanor. He was not afraid, he was angry. Buster walked over to the field near the dust devil.

"If you are here, show yourself," Buster cried out to the swirling dust. In just a few seconds, a huge head emerged from the dust. The wings closed around the serpent's body and the dust settled.

"Do not attempt to summon me," it said verbally, "I summoned you." The serpent's huge yellow eye focused on Buster. Buster clenched his jaw and ground his teeth as he made a tight fist with both hands. He wanted to lash out at the creature and punch him hard in the face. Yet he also knew it would be a worthless gesture. It might break his own hand and probably would give the creature a good laugh. So with clenched teeth, Buster screamed. "What is going on?"

The head moved around and scanned Buster. He felt him crawling around in his mind again like a snake looking for a rat.

"Get out of my head," Buster screamed.

"Would you rather I go into the head of your wife?" The head smirked and then let out a loud laugh. "I was there this afternoon. She is quite innocent and beautiful."

"No." Buster conceded and became compliant to the reptilian nightmare. "What do you want?"

"From you? I want you to see my handiwork," The reptile replied in mental telepathy.

"Why me?" Buster said as he ducked his head and tried to get the creepy thing away from him.

"Why not you?" Came the reply with a wicked little snicker. "I want you to see what I can do because you are the only one capable of seeing what I do."

"What? I don't understand."

"You will, in time, but the events have just begun. Oh, and thanks for allowing me to use your daughter today. She did a really bang up job." The serpent laughed at his own wicked pun.

Then the head and the dust devil disappeared back into the ground. Buster sat on the ground thinking over the words the serpent said. The mention of getting into Merilee's head now registered on him. He wondered if the serpent could do that. Merilee hadn't mentioned seeing the serpent, only hearing it. Could it talk to her too? He asked a question of the creature out loud, even though the creature was gone. "Why me? I'm a nobody. Why are you wasting your time on me instead of heads of state where you can do some real damage to many more people?" Even though the creature was no longer visible, Buster heard the laugh as it said, "You're so funny, you think you know so much, but you are so stupid and so easy to maneuver you almost take away the challenge."

"So I'm a challenge?" Buster retorted.

"Humph, a little, but not much, as you will see." This time the Doppler sound of the creature leaving assured

Buster that he was truly gone. How much of his thoughts had this creature discerned?

Buster returned home to find Barbara collapsed into an exhaustive sleep. In the master bedroom, Merilee was talking to the boys about what happened. She was calm and reassuring. He didn't interrupt them but went to the kitchen instead. Buster poured himself a glass of water, added a few cubes of ice, and turned toward the den to sit and ponder the events of the day. As he turned, he saw that hideous sculpture Merilee had bought. It was still the same bronze, gold, and turquoise, but the shape seemed different. It almost seemed to be smirking at him and he nearly dropped his glass when he realized that smirk was familiar. It was the same look upon the face of the reptile only a few minutes ago. Buster went over to the wall and reached out to the lightweight metal to take it down. But strangely, it was much heavier now, and he couldn't budge it. It was attached in several places, almost as if it had grown into the wall.

Buster was tired and needed to think, so he pulled a towel out of the laundry basket of folded clothes and put it over the wall-hanging. Then he sat down in his chair, leaned his head back, and sighed. There's a dragon in my field and the only information I can get is the history of Phillip Donnigan.

When Merilee joined him, she calmly looked at him and said, "Spill it."

Buster knew what she meant. "Spill what?" he said in an attempt to delay the discussion.

"How did you know?"

"Merilee, there is something evil in our field and it talks to me," Buster ducked his head in shame. Having said it aloud made it sound as if he were evil.

"I thought so. It's talking to me too." Merilee took a sip of her ice tea and leaned back. She saw the towel over the sculpture.

"I don't know who did that, but my thanks go to them."

"I did," Buster said, "and you're welcome."

"How do you hear him?"

Merilee didn't speak. She just pointed to the towel. Buster's heart leapt in his chest.

"That's why I can't get it off the wall. It's how he gets to you."

Merilee nodded. "The loud piercing sound I hear is when that thing wants my attention." She sighed and shook her head as if saying it out loud was foreign to her ears, just as it had been to Buster.

"What about you?" she asked him.

"I see him," Buster said.

"How?"

"I don't know, but he told me tonight I was the only one who could see him."

"Did he tell you about Barbara tonight?"

"He told me and took credit for it," he replied with scorn toward the "thing."

"Is he going to kill us?" Merilee asked.

"I don't think he can, but I'm sure he's going to torment us."

"How do we get rid of it?"

"That's the reason I've been going to the museum."

Merilee chuckled. "So we need to feed him rotten potatoes?"

Buster gave her a puzzled look.

"You know, the great potato famine."

"Oh," they laughed, weakly, but still it felt good as a release of the tension.

"I'm not sure why or how, but the history of this town—and especially Donnigan—has something to do with that creature. I have to know all I can about Donnigan to understand the creature," Buster explained.

Merilee nodded as if she understood. Buster leaned on the edge of his chair and took Merilee's hand. "This is a spiritual battle. We need to learn all we can about the devil from the Bible."

Merilee nodded in agreement. "How do we start?"

"I guess we read. Does the Bible have an index so we can look up devil?" Buster said with a slight grin.

"No, but it does have a concordance," Merilee said

Merilee looked at the clock as she put on her shoes. She would arrive a few minutes late to her Bible study with Mrs. Waithe. Once she explained family breakfast time extended a little longer, Mrs. Waithe would understand.

Merilee knocked on Mrs. Waithe's door. She waited a few minutes before knocking again. Even though the woman was almost always at home, she did go out now and then, but she should be expecting Merilee today. She looked around the yard and the surrounding houses.

Something didn't look right, although she couldn't name what was different or out of place. Absent mindedly she knocked again showing her frustration with her fists as she banged on the old screen door. Without waiting for an answer, she opened the screen and began banging. When she did, the wooden entrance gave a bit. It wasn't closed all the way. She stepped closer and heard a low moan coming from inside.

Merilee called out to the elderly woman she knew as her best friend. She found her slumped over the kitchen table.

"Mrs. Waithe, what happened?" Merilee called as she hurried toward the ailing woman. She looked up at Merilee and smiled.

"It's okay, dear, I was praying."

Merilee felt foolish as she noticed the woman had been lying upon her open Bible.

"Sit down, we have much to talk about," Mrs. Waithe said.

Merilee went to the coffee pot and poured herself a cup of coffee and then picked up Mrs. Waithe's cup to refill it. The house was small but neat with a 1930's style kitchen with a low thirty-inch counter. She had to bend over to put the coffee pot back in its place. That was when she noticed the huge ugly rattlesnake curled up behind the coffee pot. She screamed and dropped her cup on the floor.

"Mrs. Waithe!" she yelled in a terrified voice. She backed up looking for something to kill the snake, but the elderly woman stood up and toddled over toward the cabinet. She watched the snake for a few minutes, and then quick as lighting, she grabbed it behind the head and carried it outside. She pulled a hunting knife from her apron pocket and sliced its head off. She then deposited the head and body in a nearby trash can. Merilee watched in horrified wonder and secret admiration at the scene.

Mrs. Waithe came back into the kitchen, washed the snake blood from her knife and placed it back in its sheath attached to her apron pocket.

"I never know when one of those nasty critters is going to show up," she said. Merilee stood by the counter with her mouth agape.

"Close your mouth, dearie, he's gone," Mrs. Waithe said as she cleaned up the spilled coffee and broken cup.

"Is there enough for another cup, or do we need to make another pot?" she asked Merilee, as if nothing had happened.

"How…how can you do that and be so calm? That was a rattlesnake?"

"I know. They are always poisonous; which is why I get them behind the head."

"You need an exterminator," Merilee said.

"Only one kind of exterminator for these critters. They show up for a spiritual battle. That one was the biggest one I've seen. I guess time is getting close."

"Time for what?" Merilee asked.

"Time for trouble, disaster, accountability." She answered Merilee and poured her a new cup of coffee and motioned for her to sit down. "Don't worry there won't be any more. They are the messengers of the devil to warn me to back down. Been gettin' 'em for years now."

"Back down?"

"Yeah, there must be justice you know."

"Uh-huh." Merilee had no idea what her friend was talking about.

"Let's get to our study, shall we?"

"Yes," Merilee said as she pulled her Bible out of her bag and opened it to the book of Jeremiah chapter six.

"This will be most interesting for you my dear."

"First tell me what you mean by justice."

"It's the same in Jeremiah, God kept warning the people, 'you are not listening to my words but choosing to disobey them.' God gave them the law to show them how to live a holy life and be God's people but they chose to live by their own standards and as such they ignored the words of God. Now think about it, they ignored the words of God. Since they disobeyed God must punish them in order for there to be justice." Mrs. Waithe paused a minute watching Merilee's face.

"Yes." Merilee nodded as she attempted to follow her mentor's reasoning.

"When people disobey God, they ignore Him and mistreat other people. That is what God's word is about, loving Him and each other. In order for there to be justice, the wicked have to be punished so that the good people can be safe, otherwise the bad wins."

Merilee smiled. "I think I'm beginning to understand. When one steals from another, the thief has to be punished otherwise he will continue to steal and encourage others to do the same. Is that right?"

"Yes, my dear that is right. That is why Jesus went to the cross. He took on the punishment for all our wrong doing so there would be justice for all. The sin occurs when we do not accept His justice, then we must each bear our own punishment for our wickedness," Mrs. Waithe said. "But God didn't want anyone to perish in hell so He gave us the Bible to show us how to live a justified life," Mrs. Waithe said as she patted Merilee on the hand. She continued.

"The people of Church Creek Falls have been disobeying God's law since the town was formed, the elderly and wise woman continued. There has to be justice so judgment will come. I think the snakes are a sign that judgment is here."

"Do you think our town will be overrun with poisonous snakes?"

"No, the snakes only appear as warnings so I'll stop praying and teaching."

Merilee nodded her head. She didn't completely understand but she did trust this woman. Mrs. Waithe opened her Bible to Jeremiah 6. She pulled her finger down the page. "Ah, here we are verse 27." She laughed out loud. "My dear, these verses will answer some of your questions." They read them together.

"I have made you an assayer and a tester among My people, that you may know and assay their way. All of them are stubbornly rebellious, going about as a talebearer. They are bronze and iron; they, all of them, are corrupt. The bellows blow fiercely, the lead is consumed by the fire; In vain the refining goes on, but the wicked are not separated. They call them rejected silver, because the LORD has rejected them."

"An assayer is one who determines the purity of a metal," Mrs. Waithe said as she began the lesson. "They judge the quality of the metal. So it is with Jeremiah whom God called to assay the people of Israel, so it is with me. God has called me to be a judge over Church Creek Falls."

"How do you know?" Merilee questioned.

"When preacher Dan stood in the pulpit at church, He spewed a social mores sermon based on his own opinion. That was when I started praying 'cause I knew we were in trouble. That was the first snake I saw."

"You saw a snake at church?" Merilee asked.

"Yes, curled around the preacher's feet, a cobra with its hood spread. I watched three people get bit. They were totally unaware of the serpent much less the sting of its bite. A few weeks or months those people died dreadful and early deaths. I recognized my calling as a prophet."

"You mean…" Merilee stammered. "You were the only one to see this?"

"I'm not through yet. You've got his image in your possession."

"I don't understand." Merilee said. She pondered the statement and gasped. "The mask!"

"Yes," Mrs. Waithe responded. "Did you hang it up?" Merilee nodded.

Mrs. Waithe sighed, "I'm so sorry, I couldn't talk you out of it that day in the Enchanted Cottage."

"I don't understand," Merilee felt like crying. "I can't get it down now." She ducked her head in shame.

"Don't feel bad, I did my time with the hideous thing."

"You did?" Merilee felt some comfort in knowing Mrs. Waithe had been in her shoes.

"How did you get rid of it?"

"I didn't hang it. I took it back to the store the next day. I ask them not to put it on the shelf. Didn't help any; they did anyway," Mrs. Waithe said.

"Let's get back to your husband's task."

"My husband?" Merilee questioned.

"Now God doesn't need your husband to judge the people. He needs your husband to be assured that what is about to happen is a result of the character of the people and their rebellious disobedience to God's Word. God needs Buster to know the events will be taking place are justified."

"But why?" Merilee asked.

"So he can warn them and maybe the people will listen and change their ways."

"Why Buster?"

"God equipped Buster. He is known as an honest, just man. God chose Buster Troye because of his character and his genealogy."

The genealogy remark escaped Merilee.

"If he begins to tell the townspeople about their character flaws, they will grow to hate him," Merilee countered.

"Those who reprove need to be strong as fortresses."

Merilee's heart turned from fear to great love for the man she married.

"What is your role in all this?" she asked Mrs. Waithe.

"I will support him in prayer and action through all the trials as long as I live. You see in verse twenty-eight where it says all of them are stubbornly rebellious as a talebearer."

Merilee shook her head, "That certainly fits Church Creek Falls, the most gossiping and bullying town I ever saw. No one is exempt, not even Buster."

Mrs. Waithe waited for a few minutes before she continued.

"God rejected Israel, his own, because of rebelliousness. God will not let the impurity of the character of the people in Church Creek Falls infect other communities. He will destroy it first in order to show others there must be justice. The evil of that dragon serves as a tool of judgment. The serpent of old knows he is about to have a big party in Church Creek Falls, and he is enjoying the anticipation as much as he will enjoy the party. That is why he sends his little minions to me, to taunt me, that I cannot defeat him." Mrs. Waithe leaned back in her chair and ran her wrinkled fingers through her thick snow-white hair. She sighed.

"He will have his party."

Merilee stared at this woman she loved so deeply and saw her many years in the crevices of her face. The battle was not new. It had been fought by this lady, not to win, but to prepare. The devil would have his party of destruction unless people listened to Buster and repent.

"There must be justice," Merilee replied quietly

9

Mask of Innovation—Everything Changes

> But this people has a stubborn and
> rebellious heart; They have turned aside
> and departed.
>
> —Jeremiah 5:23

HE SAID HE was going to show me what he could do.
The thought marched through Buster's head as he plowed.
Buster pushed the old tractor hard so he could get away
quickly from the area where the hideous thing appears.
That serpent slithered in his brain bringing back the
memory of those words. The words felt like a curse placed
upon his family. It caused Buster's gut to tighten in a knot.
Buster found himself neglecting his prayer life and Bible
study now. Just thinking about his helplessness in the face
of the creature caused sweat beads to form over his upper
lip and forehead. His stomach roiled with the thought of

losing any of his family. They were his support, his rock, and his security.

Why would God allow this hideous creature to show himself? Buster looked up and asked the question aloud.

"Why is this creature tormenting me?"

He didn't expect an answer, but he received one. It came from his study of John; each time Jesus met someone possessed by a demon they would declare Jesus to be the Holy One. Jesus would silence them. On occasions when Jesus performed healing, he admonished the healed one not to tell anyone. Things begin to clear in Buster's mind as he could feel a piece of knowledge working its way through his thought processes like a raging river banging on an unrelenting dam. The knowledge was there.

Zay had an intelligent mind but a short lease on his own worth. It would only take one wise crack to make Zay roll up in a ball and hide anywhere. He so easily felt shame. The creature almost felt sorry for the lad and future events he planned for him. They were so simple, and yet…would be so devastating to the boy and his father. The creature laughed as he gave Buster a little glimpse of the tragedy awaiting him. It was all so delicious. Buster was lapping it up as the creature fed his anger with taunts about his mistreatment. He knew that if Buster ever completed his thought, it would be the end of this game. He had to keep his mind closed to the truth Buster was so desperately reaching to obtain.

Merilee hammered at the ugly thing on the wall. She did her best to pull the awful thing off the wall. Why won't it let go? It grew in size, ugliness, and strength with each blow she landed. She knew Buster hated it, but she hated it worse. It presented a continual sneer at her and her stupidity. Covering it had become the best they could do. How could I have ever thought the thing was beautiful? It attracted her in the store until its purchase used up her grocery budget then it became a curse. Since the thing had been hung on the wall, nothing but sorrow lived with her family.

A tear crept down Merilee's cheek as she accused herself of destroying her family by wasting their money. Next time, she wouldn't pay for something so extravagant and hideous. Why had Gayle and the other ladies at the store even bought the thing at market? She had been in the store many times but never saw it. In fact, she couldn't remember seeing "it" in the store before, and she had been in there the day before.

She sat down in Buster's chair to catch her breath and to reassess her plan of removal. There had to be a way. Laying the hammer on top of the table next to the chair, she stared at the wall for a few seconds. It bothered her to look at the horrible thing long enough to reason a method of removal.

She reached for her hammer again, and as she picked it up, she noticed a book under it. On the front was a picture of the very mask she was trying to remove from her wall. She dropped the hammer to the floor and picked up the book. It was titled, *Mask of Innovation*. Buster had bought it at the museum, but she had not noticed the front cover until now. Opening the book to the front, she scanned the index but could find nothing that would tell how to remove the thing. She sat back and started reading the first page.

"Phillip Donnigan considered himself an artist among other things. In truth he excelled in trickery, still he tried many different things. Perhaps searching for his talent or skill he produced a menagerie of work. Some of which is still around. In particular, one piece he called the mask of innovation. The title of the mask resulted from rumors the mask could change shape."

Merilee gasped as she sat up straight from the slump she had fallen into when she landed in the recliner. She looked at the front again and began scanning the pages for pictures. She went back to the front pages and began reading again but she couldn't find her place. The last sentence she had read about changing shape was not there. Instead she read, "The mask was called the mask of innovation because Donnigan had to change the shape of it so many times."

Merilee felt as if she had been pulled into a whirlpool, her head wouldn't stop spinning with all the crazy thoughts whirling around in it. At the same time, she heard the voice in her head again. This time it spoke softly, although there were no words, merely sounds as a brook babbling down a steep hill or the wind blowing through the trees. The sound lulled her into a stupor. A terrible awful scream pulled her out of the reverie. She prayed the scream was not real because it shrouded her in a breath of icy cold air.

Glancing out the window, she saw the source of the scream: Rance.

◆

Mrs. Paul looked over her list of things to do and take on her fantasy flight to Dallas. She felt satisfied with the results of her packing and closed the suitcase. When she picked up the picture from her desk, long forgotten, she saw the look on Jason Hamlin's face. She realized he must truly have feelings for her. She studied the picture for a couple of months before she called him. He sounded both surprised and excited to hear from her. Soon they were making arrangements to meet. He was the one that suggested she fly to Dallas to meet him. She realized in that moment she didn't know where he actually lived. But obviously it would be close to Dallas.

She felt a bit giddy; they were in for a weekend of delight. She couldn't wait to get on the road. She had decided to drive to nearby Lubbock and then take a plane to Dallas. Even though it was a short one-hour flight, it would add to the fantasy to be picked up at a large airport by a handsome man. Then she imagined how he would take her to the finest restaurant in Dallas and to an exclusive getaway for their evening of a sexual feast. Even though it would be short-lived, it would be worth it.

———◆———

Dr. McCoy sat in the café sipping a cup of coffee with Jim Lawson sitting across from him. There was a long silence, but it wasn't awkward; it was the silence between lifetime friends. McCoy felt comfortable telling Jim about Barry on school property in the act of sex with his girlfriend. McCoy wanted to bring it up but knew it would be moot and hurtful to apologize for his action. Instead, he took a sip of the dark brew, set the coffee cup down, and looked at Jim. "What now?" he asked Jim.

"That's my question too," Jim answered.

"Even though Barry's death happened in July, it's only a month since I heard about it. I watch all the Halloween decorations go up and I see skeletons and I think, that is what my boy is now. Then I think, I wonder if his bones burned up too." Once Jim started talking, he didn't stop, one horrible thought following another. McCoy listened even though it made his skin crawl, but that's what friends do. When Jim paused from his soliloquy, McCoy asked about his wife Joan.

"She floats through one day to the next. She carries a dust rag around with her and dusts the furniture all day. I had to get out of the house, I couldn't bear to watch her another minute." Jim pulled his coffee mug to his lips and took a big swallow of the now-cooled liquid.

"She asked me the other day about the baby."

McCoy paused, wondering what baby she was referring to.

"You know, the baby conceived the night you caught them on school property," Jim explained after seeing the look of confusion on McCoy's face.

"Oh, yeah." McCoy didn't elaborate.

"She wants us to find that baby so we can be a part of his life."

"Have you tried?" McCoy asked.

"Yes, we called the adoption agency," Jim said. "But they didn't give us any hope. In fact, they basically told us, no way."

"Did they know your circumstances?" McCoy asked.

"Yeah, and that was probably one of the things that worked against us," Jim answered then lifted his coffee mug to his lips. McCoy caught a faint hint of alcohol as the steam from the brew wafted toward him. He knew then why it took Jim so long at the condiments table. Jim confessed to nipping a drink here and there until his baby boy was born. He loved that boy with all his heart and soul from the day he entered the world. The bond Jim had with Barry displayed itself around town. Even as a teenager, Barry often said he liked spending time with his dad as much as with his friends. Barry was handsome, smart, genius level, and going places.

McCoy sighed with the last thought; he put the stop sign in Barry Lawson's future. Even a baby conceived before marriage would not have slowed Barry down; he would have been a good daddy and he truly did love the baby's mother.

Jim put his coffee cup down and continued, "We offered to find a doctor to do an abortion and to pay for it." Jim stared out into space as he said it. "Abortion is a terrible thing. It makes you think it's an easy answer, and now I would give my right arm to hold that precious baby for just a minute."

McCoy said nothing. What could he say, except to nod his head in sympathy?

"Her parents sent her to Ft. Worth to a home for unwed mothers. We took Barry to see her before he shipped out. I think he loved that woman the same way I loved his mother. I wonder why I couldn't see it then. I guess I was just too afraid of gossip."

"Hmmm," McCoy responded.

"Gossip don't mean a thing," Jim said. "I don't care what others say no more. It just doesn't matter."

McCoy noticed Jim's eyes filling with water, and he wondered if the welling of tears showed in his own. His tears were not from the loss of a son but from shame. He and his wife had aborted their first child…conceived before they married. She never got over it and now they slept in separate rooms and never touched each other, seldom even speaking. The abortion prevented future children.

It was that baby that had sent Barry to the military recruiter's office instead of the college registrar. That baby! McCoy thought with agony in his soul. If he had only stayed out of it, Jim may not be suffering so much loss now.

"You know, he's about six months old now," Jim said, with a wistful look in his eye.

Jim Lawson found the letter in his mailbox when he arrived home. With shaking hands, he slumped to the floor and read it to his wife. "Due to the mitigating circumstances of your son's death, the adoptive family of your biological grandchild has determined it would be a positive influence on the child to have you as a part of their child's life. This is due to the lack of grandparents in the child's life. They request a formal meeting first at the adoptive home and then further arrangements can be made from there."

He laughed a little through the misty eyes as he related the good news to Joan. "See, dear, we will be able to see our grandson and know him." ---If only---" Jim stopped and touched the hand of his precious wife as she lay on the couch, wrapped in her favorite afghan. He slid to the floor and wept. Hours later he finally called the ambulance to come get the body of his wife. At least this time he had a body, he knew without a doubt, he was alone.

The death certificate Jim received listed heart failure as cause of death. The family doctor said he felt she literally died of a broken heart. Jim wondered why he was still alive, but now he knew; he had to continue on for their precious grandson. He wished that Joan could have lived long enough to hear the news. After the first letter from the adoption home stating the adoption was closed, meaning that the child would never know or have any contact with his biological family. Joan had given up on life. Jim came home from work to find her lying on the couch as if she were taking a nap. Only when he approached her and saw the paleness of her face did he realized she was not napping but had left her body.

———•———

Wylene Troye walked from the courtroom in broken silence. Her divorce was final.

———•———

Zay slowly stood and faced his brother, Rance, who picked up a two-by-four and swung the board with all his might emitting a loud guttural scream as the board connected squarely with Zay's head.

10

Zay and Rance

Let everyone be on guard against his neighbor, and do not trust any brother; Because every brother deals craftily, And every neighbor goes about as a slanderer. Everyone deceives his neighbor And does not speak the truth, They have taught their tongue to speak lies; They weary themselves committing iniquity. "Your dwelling is in the midst of deceit; through deceit they refuse to know Me," declares the LORD.

—Jeremiah 9:4–6 (NASB)

BUSTER WALKED AROUND the hospital room, muttering, "How could this happen?" Merilee looked up at him. She ignored him. This was his way of coping with this latest tragedy in their family. Merilee held Zay's pasty white hand and stared at the bruised and swollen face of her youngest child. While she ached for him to get better, she yearned more for an explanation.

When Barbara walked into the hospital room, Buster put his arm around her and squeezed her with a powerful hug. Even though it left little room for her to breath, she loved his mighty and comforting hugs. He'd been giving them to her more frequently since she had…killed…the little girl. Her blood still ran cold even though the police, her parents and even her counselor told her there was nothing she could have done to prevent the accident. The little girl was running downhill and couldn't stop. Barbara was going below the speed limit and wasn't breaking any laws when the fragile child stepped in front of her car. The one blessing, —if it could be called that Barbara was driving slow enough that the child lived for a few minutes and her body remained intact, with not a scratch on her. It looked as though she could brush the dirt off her dress and get up, except for the impact had done irreparable damage to many of her main organs.

Barbara never saw the girl. She saw the ball. Even when she stopped for fear a child would follow the ball, she was still unaware of the child lying beneath the bumper of her car. The driver of a passing car had seen the incident and called the police. The driver was a friend of her mother's, and she had taken Barbara aside so that she never saw the body of the child. That was such a small thing at the time, but Barbara felt grateful; it helped her to overcome the trauma. That along with the forgiveness of the child's parents. Carlos now worked on the farm. He and Barbara often ate lunch together and recalled the joy of Rachel. They prayed together and often asked Jesus to tell Rachel how much they missed her. Still, Daddy's hugs were the best healing medicine. Even her counselor agreed. He held this hug just a little longer as if hugging his daughter helped him recover from the trauma of his son lying in the hospital bed so brutally beaten…by his own brother.

—◆—

Rance never felt as alone as he did now. He knew his parents were at the hospital and if Zay were not there they would be here by his side. He clung to this knowledge and prayed he would see his family again. He rocked back and forth saying "I'm so sorry…I was wrong… I just…I just…."

But no one listened and no one cared. The people who processed him were friends and neighbors, and they treated him as a nonentity. No one looked at him, except in anger. Never had Rance felt this alone in a group of people. Even as a juvenile admission, it was rough. No, it wasn't rough…no, it wasn't rough. It was unbearable.

"How is my brother?" he asked the lady taking his fingerprints.

She looked at him with contempt and answered, "Why do you care?"

"Because I love him. He's my brother."

11

Describing a Dragon

For wicked men are found among
My people, They watch like fowlers lying
in wait; They set a trap, They catch men.
—Jeremiah 5:26 (NASB)

BUSTER HEADED TO the police station. He needed to see Rance. Anger at Rance boiled inside him.

"Buster, remember that Rance is our son too," Merilee said quietly, "wait for an explanation."

Buster nodded at her as she continued. "Rance is aware of his dilemma, Zay isn't."

Well into the night Buster was finally allowed to see Rance. The moment he saw him; it broke his heart.

Rance was a defeated young man with lack of sleep and nourishment—both physical and mental. Buster walked up to him. It took Rance a moment for his foggy mind to register that his father was standing before him. Buster knew the exact moment when the boy knew he was there because he jumped into his dad's arms and wept.

It took several minutes of body-wracking weeping before Rance's energy was spent. Buster had tears pooling in his eyes—pools that would never leave his eyes, for behind the sadness rested an anger that balanced it. He wanted to both love and beat the boy.

When Rance recovered, Buster asked him the question on everyone's mind, but no one asked, "Why?"

Rance sat down at the table in the bare room. Buster set down the bottle of water and sandwich he'd been allowed to bring him. There was some leniency with Rance since he was a minor, but Buster knew there were others listening.

The words of the dragon raced through his mind, "See what harm I can do you." For the first time Buster realized that this could be the work of that dreadful serpent instead of Rance.

Rance opened his mouth to spill it out. Buster took his hand and attempted to communicate without words. He nodded as he said, "This is going to be bigger than your rattlesnake story?" Buster said as he winked. Rance understood and nodded. "Yeah, a snake can cause a lot of mayhem and damage."

Buster knew then it wasn't Rance wielding the board that hit Zay, it was that evil serpent. But Buster knew the others wanted to know the reason behind this unexplained assault by two brothers as close as a newborn calf to its mother.

"We were talking about the sinkhole in the field," Rance said.

Buster understood. This would be code word for the dragon.

"We decided to go look at it."

Again Buster nodded that he understood. They had seen the dragon.

"When we were there, the ground starting moving and Zay started slipping. I picked up the board for him to grab so I could pull him away from the sinkhole." Rance began to weep again, and Buster reached out and took his hand. He understood now that the dragon had attempted to attack Zay, and Rance wanted to kill the serpent, not his brother.

"It's okay, son, I know. I've seen the hole come and go too. It appears solid and then starts sinking. So what happened next?"

"Zay looked down behind him at the hole. I was aiming at…" Rance stopped. He didn't know how to complete the sentence. Buster nodded and tried to find a word that would satisfy the listeners.

"You were aiming at Zay to grab the board?" Buster asked giving Rance a foothold.

"Yes, but when Zay looked away his hands dropped and so did his head. That was when I hit him."

Buster nodded. He knew exactly what had happened, but he needed to make it plausible to the listeners so he could take his son home.

"Rance, why were you swinging it so hard?" Buster asked but winked and squeezed Rance's hand.

"I didn't know I was. I think I was excited and I didn't know the strength I had behind my throw. How's Zay?" he asked.

Buster let out a sigh of relief. Rance's story lined up exactly as Buster thought it might. He'd seen the monster devour a full-grown bull. The monster probably would not have devoured Zay but instead wanted Rance to think that he would. It was a carefully laid plot by the monster to cause a visible fight between the boys and to cause one to kill the other and the one to suffer at the hands of the justice system. The cleverness of the monster couldn't be underestimated. He also saw the monster's goal first hand. The monster wanted to kill them. The question was why?

In a few minutes the sheriff came in and looked at Buster. "What do you think?"

"I think I need to take my son home. This was clearly an accident and there's no need for legal intervention." The sheriff laid a bag on the table containing Rance's street clothing. "I agree. But why didn't he tell us this before?"

"Because he's a kid and was scared out of his wits," Buster replied with a controlled tone of sarcasm.

"Yeah, I don't guess any of us ever gave him an opportunity. He can go as soon as he gets dressed. You can leave the jumpsuit and flip-flops on the table. Come into my office, I need you to sign some papers."

Buster nodded and turned toward Rance who was already getting into his clothes. Buster smiled at him. They'd be able to talk about what really happened in a few minutes.

The drive over to the hospital was short, so they decided to wait until after Rance saw Zay before they would discuss the details. When Rance arrived at the room, Merilee and Barbara jumped up and hugged him.

She didn't need to be told that it had been an accident. It had been a well-planned disaster. Before each disaster, she heard the mask speaking or screaming at her. It gave her notice or mocked her. Merilee suspected the latter. Rance leaned over the bedside of Zay and picked up his hand.

"They have him in a drug-induced coma waiting for the brain swelling to go down. Doc says he has a chance of being fine with no problems."

She didn't tell him it was a fifty-fifty chance of no problems. Rance needed hope and that was what she was going to give her son. She wouldn't lose both of them tonight. The family sat quietly all night around the bed of their beloved brother and son, each praying silently and sometimes aloud. They gave thanks for the quick release of Rance. At least that part of the plan had failed. Zay was still alive and in the hands of Jesus no matter what happened.

The morning sun peeked in the blinds at 6:35 a.m. Not an early hour for a family of farmers but an early hour for a family sleeping in makeshift beds of hospital chairs. The empty bed had been given to Rance, and the sound of the boys sleeping was music to the ears of their parents and sister. The family opted to go to the cafeteria for breakfast together, leaving Zay in the care of his nurses. It was a good decision.

As they sat around the table eating their breakfast, they spoke in code in case anyone was listening.

"The sinkhole must be huge or in different places," Rance said. The family knew the code, sinkhole referred to the monster.

"When I first saw it behind Zay, it was a sandstorm moving slowly, but then I saw the full extent of it and it was going to swallow Zay."

In this way Rance was able to share with them that the monster had risen from behind Zay. The family knew where the incident took place; it was nowhere near the original sinkhole in the field. This incident revealed to them that the monster was not limited to his place of appearance and seemed incapable of inflicting harm on the family himself. He used other weapons such as fear, deceit, and lies to harm them. The family knew they would get the exact details in the privacy of their own home. They prayed together for Zay's healing and swift return home.

When the family arrived back at Zay's room, they were met with a most pleasant surprise. Zay was sitting up in bed, eating a hardy breakfast and flirting with his nurse. Merilee smiled and said, "Looks like you are doing better."

The doctor stepped into the room. "Hello."

"Good morning," Buster responded with a start.

"It appears there is no damage and the boy can go home whenever you wish. He will have the bruises for a while, but other than that, there is no damage."

The trip home was a joyous occasion. The family began to recall all the events that had plagued their family in just one week and how any one of them could have been devastating, but the Lord had brought them through it all. The tragedy turned into a time of praise for a family who saw evil in its full ugliness.

12

Joan's Funeral

> Behold you are trusting in deceptive
> words to no avail.
> —Jeremiah 7:8 (NASB)

BUSTER AND MERILEE entered a full church. Ironically, they found empty seats halfway down the aisle, almost as if they'd been reserved for them. While the people were there to remember Joan Lawson's life, the memory for her only son, Barry, lingered in their minds. The only remaining family member, Jim Lawson, had reason to doubt the reality of a good God. Sadly, the only prayer being offered to God today would probably be a bit slanderous and ill-spoken as each member of the congregation would say, "Thank God this isn't me."

Buster wondered how one could endure so much pain, especially for a man of weak character such as Jim. He was a hardworking, honest man but didn't possess the temperament to survive so much sorrow. Jim's history of alcoholism dogged his footsteps through each trauma he suffered. Buster watched Jim sitting in front by the simple casket surrounded by multitudes of flower baskets. The flowers represented the heart of the town. The people did care. Few of the people sitting in the pews really knew Joan Lawson. Nonetheless, the townspeople noted her funeral as this week's top social event.

The scent of fresh flowers both overwhelmed and comforted in the sweet aroma that would most likely serve Jim as a haunting memory for the rest of his days. Jim slumped over looking at his hands.

With all this show of support, not one person is reaching out to Jim, including me. Buster felt the ache of his loneliness. He rose from his seat to sit by Jim. A few minutes later several other men followed. Jim was no longer alone.

Dr. McCoy and Jim Lawson shared high school football teammate memories so Buster moved over and let Dr. McCoy sit next to his friend. Because of the difference in social standing between the two men, not everyone present was aware of the lifelong friendship. A friendship between the esteemed educated head of the school system and the former alcoholic blue-collar worker seemed unlikely. Although Jim worked his way up from an entry level worker to the ranks of an accountant supervisor at the ammonia plant, it still seemed an unlikely friendship. Buster wondered about the story of shared joy or tragedy between them. Someday, maybe, he would ask one of them.

As he listened to the strains of "Nearer My God to Thee" played by the organist he bowed his head to pray for Jim.

But he couldn't. The horrible slithering of the creature's voice in his brain and spirit rose in him. Why would he be here in church? This was supposed to be a sanctuary against evil. How crude, he screamed in his head. Leave me alone. Buster shouted in his head in the same way it spoke to him, through telepathic thoughts.

The roar of the dragon snickered and said, it is my favorite place. There is more evil in this building every Sunday morning than anywhere else in the whole town. Right now, all the evil of Church Creek Falls sits in these pews. The creature laughed. Buster ducked his head not in prayer but in shame.

Buster didn't answer but instead looked around at the people crowded into the church. His thoughts didn't go unheeded by the dragon. *I know* was all he could think. Each Sunday morning, Buster saw Deborah Mullaney come in with her two small children followed by her inattentive husband. The one he often saw across the state border with other women. He watched Sybil, a new widow, flirt with all the men only a year after she buried her husband. Granted Sybil became a widow at the tender young age of thirty-eight. Still her bold flirtations disturbed the sensibilities of the town. Mostly, because she didn't respect the boundaries of marriage; any man served as a target for her. Sybil had a reputation for her loose moral compass. She spent her Saturday nights at the dance hall and her Sunday mornings at church. Buster often smelled booze on her breath as she entered the sanctuary. Her early attempts to tease Buster troubled him. Merilee held the honor of the most beautiful woman in the world to him.

He found himself just being stupid around her because of her dazzling beauty. When she fell in love with him, Buster knew he would never risk losing her. Although Merilee proved to be extremely naive and maybe even stupid in the ways of the world, that was one of the things he loved most about her, her innocence. She couldn't conceive of the way men viewed her and desired her, but Buster knew. He dedicated his life to protecting her from the ugliness of sexual impurity. It started with his fidelity toward her.

Still he knew the people with their sensual desires weren't the worst among this crowd. Charlie Pepperdine sat with his head held high. He demanded and expected to be honored frequently by the townspeople since he was a successful businessman who contributed to community and school fund-raisers that were public. His picture appeared in the local newspaper at least once a month. Yet, unknown to most of the community, Pepperdine's life read more like a professional cheat and scoundrel wrapped in a fluffy ball of flattery. Pepperdine hid his thieving well.

Buster saw the greed and called his hand on his shady business practices—Charlie reimbursed Buster for the several thousand dollars he'd absconded from Buster, but not without an attempt to ruin Buster's reputation by spreading rumors of Buster meeting at the hotel with Sybil. The hotel across the street from Pepperdine's office gave credence to the rumor of the two at the hotel. Pepperdine conveniently forgot to say that it was Merilee meeting with Sybil, not Buster. After the incident, Buster never did business with him again and the two men never spoke, even though both men served on the church deacon board.

Then there's the man Buster labeled the devil himself and that was Don Miller. He had the million-dollar smile of a shyster with the handshake of a politician and the most messed up gospel message ever given in a church pulpit. Don was the pastor of the church.

As the singer finished the song, Dan Mullaney rose to offer the eulogy. Buster leaned back in his seat and sighed. The evil was so strong on him he couldn't pray, he couldn't leave, and he couldn't change it. Buster glanced over at Merilee. Gazing at her beautiful heart-shaped face with her flawless olive complexion and perfectly straight white teeth, he thanked the Lord for her naiveté and innocence. At least the creature couldn't touch her.

Instantly Buster heard a wicked snicker. He quickly turned his head to see if he could find the source of the sound he'd heard. He felt the evil slither out of his mind with the snicker growing into a full-blown laugh. Buster ducked his head, for he recognized the laugh growing stronger. The plotter of evil and malice had just let Buster know that Merilee would be the next tragedy. He knew he was helpless to stop it. He couldn't even pray for guidance. But he did say, "Lord, bring her through it stronger and closer to you."

As Pastor Miller completed the message, the organ began the mournful strains of song to allow the guests to come and pay their last respects to the deceased. The evil had left him but Buster could feel its bold presence still in the surrounding area. Even though the creature may be out of sight and sound, his sensitivity to it seemed to be growing. A sense of darkness let him know the creature lurked within the building. Prayers lay hindered on the floor when he could feel the creature.

Still, he felt there must be a way, so he decided he would pray no matter what. Even in the midst of evil, God stood stronger than the creature. Almighty God, please give me wisdom with understanding and help me protect my wife, my children, and if at all possible my community from this retched creature.

Heaven's window opened and heard Buster's prayer. Mercy and peace fell upon the head of God's servant.

As Buster approached the casket, he could hear Jim sobbing out loud. He felt a stab of pain since there was no one else with him; the other men on the row with Jim stood around the casket to fulfill their role as pall bearers. Buster looked behind Jim and saw a few strange faces that could have been family. However, they weren't mourning; it was almost as if they were hired attendees to the funeral. Nonetheless, this apparently was all Jim's family.

Buster turned to Merilee and whispered in her ear that he would meet her at the car. Then he turned toward Jim, sat beside him, and put his arm around him. Jim looked at him and then melted into Buster's side and let the tears roll freely. Buster and Jim weren't close friends, but at that moment, Buster cloaked a wounded man with the peace that passes understanding.

When the church emptied, Jim approached the casket. The preacher looked at the clock on the back wall and fidgeted. The funeral director did his job of offering direction and comfort. The pall bearers stood stock still on either side of the casket. Jim picked up the cold hand of his beloved wife and kissed it. He held it for a few minutes while he told her good-bye. While Jim spoke in a low voice, Buster attempted not to listen to the final private conversation between husband and wife, but he could not help but overhear one line. "Soon, baby, justice will come and we will be together again."

Buster held Jim up as he escorted him toward the family limousine that would follow the casket to the cemetery for burial. Buster wondered how Jim would endure the rest of the day.

13

Finding Mrs. Waithe

If you have run with footmen and they have tired you out, Then how can you compete with horses? If you fall down in a land of peace, How will you do in the thicket of the Jordan? For even your brothers and the household of your father, Even they have dealt treacherously with you, Even they have cried aloud after you. Do not believe them, although they may say nice things to you.

—Jeremiah 12:5–6 (NASB)

AS BUSTER ARRIVED at the car, he found it empty with a note attached to the steering wheel. "We went with the Overstreets to get something to eat then they will take us home. You did a good thing today. Stay with Jim as long as you need. I love you. Merilee."

After the cemetery services, Buster drove Jim home. Jim's heart overflowed with bitterness as sour as rotten kraut. Buster had prayed for God to help him protect his community as well as his family. He needed to start with Jim Lawson. It would take some talking and some loving to get through to him. Buster had a plan.

———◆———

When Merilee and the children arrived home, they changed clothing and met back in the kitchen; each one gathering a snack or drink. They all sat in the den. Barbara and Rance sat on the couch underneath the towel that covered the hideous mask.

"Ow! What is that?" Barbara jumped off the couch screaming. Cautiously she crept toward the back of the couch to discover what sharp object had pierced her back. She expected to find a spring poking through the couch and she was a bit fearful it might explode from its fabric covering. She gasped.

She saw a tapered piece of turquoise shimmering metal waving in the air. Barbara dropped her glass of milk and cookies and screamed while backing away. After she regained her sensibility, she crept back toward the couch and reached out to touch the strange object and discover its source. As she grabbed it and moved it back and forth, it broke off in her hand. She recognized it as the same metal as the wall hanging. In fear she said in a loud voice, "Stupid thing. Surely there is a way to get that thing down," Barbara said as she looked at her mother staring the beast down. Barbara wondered if she were frozen in fear or communicating with it.

"Mom!"

"Oh, sorry, I think the thing has grown since we have been gone," Merilee said as she dipped her cookies into her glass of milk. Barbara watched her mother and pondered her reaction to the anomaly. Before Barbara could question her mother, Zay interrupted.

"Yeah, it grows every time we leave the house. I have been measuring it. It never grows when we are here, just when we are gone."

The conversation changed from one of fearful surprise to an engineering discussion. Barbara determined each family member was reacting within their own coping mechanisms. For Barbara, this was not easy, because there was something that touched her and she felt it drip into her soul. She couldn't explain it, but she knew there was something very much alive in that piece of metal.

"How much has it grown?" Rance asked.

"About three feet, but that's not all."

"Oh, a metal wall hanging that we can't get down has grown three feet and you say that's not all. How much worse could it be, and why are we sitting around it like growing metal is a natural thing?" Barbara said.

Zay ignored her and continued with his discovery. "It's changed appearance too. I took pictures of it on a regular basis." He pulled the desk drawer open and took out a pack of recently developed pictures. He sorted them on the kitchen table. "Come look."

As the family gathered around the table, they stared and gasped. The change was gradual, but it was changing shape as if it was malleable. Rance ran over to the towel and pulled it down. The family looked full face into the metal sculpture with open mouth and what appeared to be blue metal flames coming from its mouth. It emitted a humming sound as if it had become electrified.

"Mom, can we go visit grandma?" Barbara said in a shaky voice. Merilee nodded her head as she stared at the horrible thing with her mouth agape.

"Yes," she said without taking her eyes from it as she moved around it.

"Mom, are you hearing that?" Zay asked, referring to the steady hum.

"Yes, and I don't like what it's saying."

Zay was not listening, instead he studied it from all angles; it had become three-dimensional and almost looked alive. He reached out to touch it, and when he did, the rest of the family squealed in horror. Zay ignored them.

"I agree with Barbara that this is a good time to visit grandma." He then walked around the wall into the entryway and opened the bathroom door behind the wall. The family followed him. There in the bathroom was the body of the large serpent draped in the sink and over the shower stall wall.

Each of them was frozen by the eerie and unearthly sight, except Zay. Instead, he walked up to it and inspected it. "Zay, what are you doing?" Barbara asked as she hovered behind her mother.

Zay was deep in thought.

"He is fascinated by it and looking for the cause," Merilee said as she backed away from it. "Zay, we need to go," she quietly begged him.

"It's okay, Mom, it can't hurt us."

"I know but there is more to that thing than metal, and whatever that is can hurt you."

Zay finally saw the fear in his family's face and realized they could not see the object as a scientific anomaly but rather as something to fear. He took one last look at the growing tail and thought to himself, it really is beautiful. He looked at the claws on the feet and saw them twitch. He then shut the door. "Where are we going?"

"To Grandma's," Barbara said with growing anxiety.

"We can't go until Dad gets home," Merilee said.

"Oh yes we can. Remember, we have two cars now and I'm getting out of here," Barbara said as she practically ran to the kitchen to get the keys. They all agreed and each hurriedly packed an overnight bag.

Merilee called Jim Lawson's house hoping Buster would still be there. He was. She told him they were going to his mother's. She would explain when he arrived. She had his clothes, no need to come by the house.

"It's that horrifying mask isn't it?" Buster asked.

"Yes.' It is so hideous we can't stay there."

"Okay, I'll meet you at Mom's. And Meri, I'm glad you're going over there."

She hung up the phone, grabbed her purse, and started to walk out the door when she stopped and picked up the book open to the page she had been reading earlier.

"What's that?" Zay asked her.

"Answers, I hope."

Merilee and the kids arrived at Buster's mother's house thirty minutes later, a bit calmer. They told her their house needed some repairs, so they needed a place to stay for a few days.

——◆——

A few days later, Buster and Merilee found a furnished apartment in town. Still they had need of personal items, and Buster and Merilee decided to go back to the farmhouse and pick up some of these things. They wished there was someone they could take with them. Someone who…someone strong in their faith. They didn't need a muscle man, they needed a prayer warrior.

Buster dropped his head and moaned. "Is there anyone in this town who is a prayer warrior?" Buster asked.

"I can only think of one person I would trust to share the horror and to pray," Merilee said.

"Who?" Buster asked.

"Mrs. Waithe."

Buster smiled. "You're right."

Mrs. Waithe was a ninety-three-year-old woman who had been an active original member of the church but then just disappeared. For a while people would visit her, but when pastor Miller told the secretary to take her off the prayer and birthday list, she soon was forgotten. People forget. But Merilee didn't forget. She still went to see her once a week for Bible study and lunch. Merilee said she learned more from that old woman than she ever learned in church. She had taught her how to study her Bible for herself and discover the jewels of truth in the words that had to be mined out.

"Why did she drop out of church? Was it her health?" Buster asked.

"Oh, gosh no, she can still run circles around me—healthiest woman I know, although she is slowing down some. She dropped out because she said the pastor, you know Bro. Miller, preached apostasy and the devil is stronger in that building than God."

Buster laughed out loud. It felt good. He had not laughed that hard since…well, he couldn't remember when. Merilee joined him. "You know she is right. I could feel that awful evil thing in the church at Mrs. Lawson's funeral," Merilee said.

Buster stopped laughing, "Did you hear it?" he asked Merilee.

"No, but I could feel it crawling all over my skin." She shuddered at the thought. "Did you feel it?" she asked Buster.

He nodded and said, "I felt it and heard it. He said church was his favorite place to be, more evil there than anywhere else in town."

"Now you know why Mrs. Waithe left." Merilee smiled. "But you know she only left it physically. She told me yesterday she had been praying for something to shake up the church and she knew it's coming soon. She told me a great tragedy will strike this community and bring them to their knees, for they'll have no other place to go…" Merilee let her voice trail off in a whisper.

This monster did not appear to torment Buster's family. It revealed itself to Buster before it tormented and destroyed the community. The big question was why it chose Buster and Merilee and their children?

"Why do you think he exposed himself to you and nobody else?" Merilee asked.

"How do we know we are the only ones? I haven't told anyone else and I am pretty certain if there is anyone else that has seen the monster, they wouldn't be telling anyone."

"Wow, didn't think of that. He could be tormenting everyone in town and no one will speak up. Maybe that is why we need to say something," Merilee said in her "fix it" quick thinking.

"Not sure. Give me time to think this over and pray about it," Buster answered.

They sat in silence for several minutes in the driveway of their newly rented apartment.

"Buster, if we are the only ones, why do you think the monster would pick our family?"

"I'm not sure, but it is almost as if he wants us to know he is here and show us what great evil he can accomplish."

"He sure has been attacking us," Merilee responded. She sat quietly for a few moments. "Let's go get that precious woman. We need her and so does this community." Buster agreed and they headed toward Mrs. Waithe's house continuing their conversation.

"Attacking but not winning. Think about it, Merilee, the tragedies that have hit our family have been a nuisance, not a tragedy, but look at the Lawson's. That is a tragedy."

"You're right, and your brother and Wylene," Merilee said. "By the way, did you hear about Mrs. Paul?"

"No, what?"

"She was murdered."

"What?" Buster exclaimed.

Apparently, she flew to Dallas for a vacation. Her body was found in a hotel room. It appeared her death was painful and brutal."

"Sounds personal too." Buster shook his head in disbelief.

"I hear Dr. McCoy was admitted to the hospital with deep depression, seems he tried to kill himself," Merilee said.

"Where do you hear all this stuff?" Buster asked.

She definitely has his attention now. "The beauty shop, it's better than a newspaper. Of course more than half of it is gossip, but you get more details than with a newspaper." Merilee smiled at the irony of it.

"How is Karen?" Buster realized the evil could be attacking her too.

"She is a hardworking woman and she loves the Lord. She tries to stop the gossip. Sometimes she just turns on all the dryers so nobody can hear. She's a good woman."

"Has she suffered anything?" Buster inquired.

"She lost a child, but that was several years ago," Merilee answered.

He turned the car into Mrs. Waithe's driveway. "Are we going to tell her about ..."

"The dragon?" Merilee finished his sentence and continued, "Yes, we are. If we're going to ask her to pray for our protection, she needs to know against what, and trust me she will recognize him even if we don't tell her. She has discerning eyes."

"I'm glad." Buster felt relief for the first time since he'd seen the dragon out in the field. He had learned a lot about it, more than he ever wanted to know about evil and the large serpent of Revelation twelve. He learned what he thought was myth or deception was a cleaver ruse to keep him from knowing the truth. If one believes the truth is fantasy, then they cannot see truth and will be easily deceived. Oh, thought Buster, we have a whole community that has been deceived, and the deception is using God's church to blind us. Good people slimed with evil. They can't escape it, so they succumb to the impure thoughts the slime instills in their fooled brains.

"No wonder Church Creek Falls is a little Peyton Place," Buster said out loud.

"What?" Merilee responded.

"It's something Barbara says about our town. She said there is a television show called *Peyton Place* and it is all about the immorality and greed of the people and how they use each other to gain their own desires."

Merilee smiled at Buster's knowledge of the show. "Well, now you know what the beauty shop is like. It's like watching the show."

Mrs. Waithe opened the door. Buster noticed her straight stature for a woman of advanced years and her snow-white coiffured hair, her eyes as bright as a teenager's, and her skin smooth and vibrant. She looked more like sixty than ninety.

"Hello, my good friend," she greeted Merilee and swung the door open. When she saw Buster, she reached out and grabbed him for a hug. "Welcome, my dear warrior."

"You know?"

"I don't know details, but I know you are being trained for a battle of the ages," Mrs. Waithe answered.

"I told you she was discerning." Merilee smiled as they sat on the couch opposite her recliner.

"Tell me what I need to know."

She looked at Buster and so did Merilee. So he began to tell her about the first encounter and the things that had happened since then.

She smiled. "You don't have to describe him, I have seen him too, and he has been in this town for many years."

"When did you see him?" Buster felt relief that someone else had seen the same thing.

"I saw him in 1958. He came in a blue suit, shiny smile, full head of hair, and we called him Brother Don."

Buster sat back and let her words sink in. "You mean…"

"Yes, when the man came, I looked up in the pulpit and saw a huge slithering fire-breathing snake dripping acid of deception on every member in the congregation. I looked around and no one else was alarmed. Then he turned to me and looked me straight in the eye and said, 'You don't belong here. Get out!' So I did. But I should have stayed and fought for my church. I was a wimp, but you…you are a warrior. You have not backed down."

"Well, in a way we have." Merilee began. "We've moved into an apartment because the mask took over our house."

She asked Mrs. Waithe to pray for their protection while they removed thing from the house. Mrs. Waithe sat silent as though she were listening to something else.

"No, don't move into the apartment, you need to stay in command of your home."

"How do we do that?" Buster asked, "The thing has taken over our home."

"Yeah, but without you there, he doesn't care. He will just follow you to your new apartment. You will have to face him wherever you are."

Buster knew she was right, and his heart sank to his work boots.

"What do you think of going out there with us and helping us fight this thing? Merilee says you are a great prayer warrior." Buster pleaded.

"I will fight with you but I want you to know two things. First, there is great tragedy coming, and it will have an impact on all of us. And second, I will not live through it. God has promised He will take me home before the tragedy arrives, so when the hard part comes, I will not be with you in body, but I will be with our Father. There I will plead your case face-to-face, but you will fight alone as a family," Mrs. Waithe sighed.

"Is there anyone else to fight with us?"

"No. Like Dietrich Bonhoeffer, you will be fighting this great evil alone." Mrs. Waithe pulled a book off her bookshelf. "Read this as quickly as possible, it will give you courage."

Buster nodded and took the book about Bonhoeffer, along with a small biography of the man who stood against Hitler.

"Oh, and one other thing." Mrs. Waithe said. "You need to acquaint yourself with the founding of our community."

Buster looked up at her. "That's strange."

"It will give you the answer to the question of why this community is the source of the tragedy and how long this evil has been here."

"I said that's strange because when I first saw this thing, I found myself on a quest to learn about Donnigan, the founder of our community," Buster said.

Mrs. Waithe nodded, "This proves you are the one the Lord has chosen."

Merilee turned toward Mrs. Waithe, and a question lingered on her mind. "Mrs. Waithe," Merilee said in a slow drawl, causing the three of them to stop in their tracks.

"Yes."

"Have you ever heard of a book called The Mask of—"

"The Mask of Deception, humph, I mean innovation?"

"Yes."

"Do you have it in your possession?" Mrs. Waithe asked, looking over the top of her glasses like a stern school teacher.

"Yes" Merilee answered with hesitation.

"It goes with the hideous thing hanging on your wall. It was written by Donnigan, the one who made the mask."

"But it—" Merilee started.

"Changes its story?" Mrs. Waithe finished her sentence.

"Yes. What's going on?"

"I'm not sure. I know the book cannot be destroyed and whoever buys that hideous mask will somehow end up with the book."

"I thought it might give answers. Have you ever seen it?"

"Oh yes, I did my time with the mask. I tried to read the book. It was the most gosh awful piece of trash I ever tried to read. I gave up on it because nothing in it made any sense, and as you said, it kept changing its story."

"I guess that is the innovation," Buster said as he headed toward the door. "Shall we go ladies? It looks like a battlefield is waiting for us." Buster then turned to Mrs. Waithe as Merilee stepped past him.

"Mrs. Waithe, please pray for Merilee's protection from this evil thing," he pleaded.

Mrs. Waithe answered with a pat on his hand and smile, "I will as I will pray for you."

"Ready to go face this ugly thing?" Buster asked as he opened the door for the two women. Under his breath, he pleaded for courage, "O God, there is no other God but you. There is no power greater than You."

14

Trouble Breeds Terror

> Therefore, thus says the LORD,
> "Behold I am bringing disaster on them
> which they will not be able to escape;
> though they will cry to Me, yet I will not
> listen to them."
> —Jeremiah 11:11 (NASB)

A COLLECTIVE GASP came from the trio as they pulled up in front of the farmhouse. "Do you see that?" Buster asked. The two women didn't speak but nodded their heads as they stared at the green farmhouse. When they had left, it was white, but this green was not a new paint job but rather a slime covering the house.

"What's going on?" Buster said as he put the car into park and opened the door.

Merilee shuddered. "Oh, I don't want to go in there, let's just go."

Mrs. Waithe grabbed her arm, "Pray for true vision."

"What?" Merilee looked at Mrs. Waithe in shock. "What do you mean true vision? Are you saying I am not seeing green slime all over my house I only left three days ago?"

"I guess that is exactly what I am saying. Remember we are dealing with a liar—and a vicious hateful liar at that." Mrs. Waithe said almost through clenched teeth. Still her sweetness came over to Merilee as Mrs. Waithe put her arm around Merilee.

"How can he do this?" Merilee cried while attempting to choke back tears of anger, frustration, and fear.

"He can't, it is an illusion for your benefit. Do you have a camera handy?" Mrs. Waithe asked.

Merilee laughed at the absurdity of having a camera. "No, I don't carry one with me."

"Well, I do," Mrs. Waithe said as she fished around in her purse.

"Why would you carry a camera?" Merilee's tears had almost dried up and her fears gave way to curiosity.

Mrs. Waithe laughed, "I guess it is pretty weird to carry a camera all the time, but I discovered about ten years ago that the camera will not capture the illusion. In other words, the camera can only show what is really there."

"Wow, I don't suppose your camera is a Polaroid, is it?" Merilee asked.

"Well, yes, it works best for proving my theory." Mrs. Waithe said with a sarcastic smile as she snapped a picture of the house and then one of Buster and Merilee as they stood together looking at the house.

"Uh oh, I may be in trouble, if that camera destroys illusions and shows me without my makeup." Merilee said comically as she wiped the last of the tear away; even if Mrs. Waithe's theory proved to be wrong, she certainly knew how to remove worry and fear.

The sixty-second development process seemed longer than normal to Merilee. Meanwhile, Buster continued on his quest and slowly walked around the house, occasionally touching it with a stick or his pocket knife. Merilee thought he looked as if he was scrapping the slime off the house.

"What are you doing?" she called to Buster seconds before he rounded the corner in the back of the house. She didn't want to get close but followed him. The slime changed as she neared the back of the house, to a pink mold much like she had seen on the top of cottage cheese. It was the mold Buster had on his pocket knife.

"Strange it changes from the back to the front," Buster said when he saw her. "I can't scrape any of the green off, because it disappears when I touch it, but the pink stays on my knife." He pulled a small magnifying glass from his shirt pocket. As he gazed through the glass, he dropped the stick with the pink mold on it and cried out.

"What is it?" Merilee shouted to him.

"It's people!"

"Huh?"

"Tiny little people, crying out with looks of pain on their face."

"Did you know any of them," Merilee asked in a state between laughter and horror.

"No. It was just my imagination," Buster replied.

"The pictures are ready," Mrs. Waithe called.

The first picture she gave to Merilee was the one of her and Buster staring at the house. It was actually a good picture. Then she handed them the other picture. Merilee took it, looked at it, and then she handed it to Buster.

The white house stood in the middle of the picture, which proved the green slime to be nothing more than an illusion. As they looked again, the green on the house disappeared, the pink stayed the same. Again Mrs. Waithe snapped a picture. The sixty seconds went by and the pink mold remained in the picture.

"I don't understand," Buster said to Mrs. Waithe.

"I think the green is the illusion of the dragon, while the pink is a vision of the truth," Mrs. Waithe answered.

"But why show it if we can't change it?" Buster pleaded with Mrs. Waithe for the answer he desperately needed.

"It is not for you to correct. It is for you to warn." Mrs. Waithe replied. "It's what I have been doing for years. The sad thing is that few will listen."

Buster nodded in agreement.

"Consider it part of your education and preparation," Mrs. Waithe said and then she opened the door and went inside.

"Right now we have greater things to do," Merilee said as she and Buster followed her.

They didn't see any changes inside the house. Even the growth of the hideous metal thing had gone back to its original size.

"He's not here. He has no reason to be here. He moved with you," Mrs. Waithe said.

"Buster, we need to get the kids back out here. That thing is with them," Merilee said as her voice raised an octave. Buster was already on the phone, telling Barbara to pack up their clothes, leave the apartment, and come back to the farmhouse-they were not moving.

On the other end, Barbara threw a dozen or more questions at Buster, but he persisted with the urgency of his insistence. Barbara was not too happy with the anxious feeling of expediency, but she complied. Then Buster called and canceled the apartment. He turned to Mrs. Waithe, "Do you think—"

"You bet," she said. "Show me where to sleep and I will stay with you until this thing is over. I've been waiting for something to happen and it doesn't surprise me that God appointed Buster Troye as the one to make it happen."

"What do you mean?" Buster asked her.

"Remember how you said you felt that the history of our community had something to do with the present situation?" Mrs. Waithe asked.

"Yes."

"You're right, and it is not just the history of the community but your family history as well," Mrs. Waite said as she proceeded toward the mask on the wall.

"Remember I'll die before the final battle comes. I have arrangements made for my body, so just call Mike at Montgomery's funeral home, and he will take care of the rest. Remember, my death will be the signal that the worst is coming but that the end is near."

"Will...we...be...joining you?" Merilee asked.

"I don't know, but I would consider it a possibility. Remember his ultimate goal is death."

Buster watched her as she toddled off to her room, a ninety-year-old gray-haired warrior, stronger than any soldier he had served with during WWII. Then his curiosity caused him to look at the wall. The metal wall hanging was nothing. It had shrunk to its original size and Mrs. Waithe held it in her hands.

"How did you get it off?' Buster asked her.

"I lifted it off. I have history with this ugly thing too." She turned to Merilee and handed it to her, "Only you can rid your family of this thing because it is after you. Take it back to the shop."

"But will they take it back?" Merilee asked as she took the thing and held it as if it was hot to the touch.

"Yes, they have dealt with this thing for many years. They expect you to bring it back." Mrs. Waithe said casually.

"I want to take it back to the shop and get my money back," Merilee conceded.

"But we know what it is and that it is evil," Merilee said.

"It's not evil. We gave it the power of evil with our imaginations. I'm going to take it back." Merilee found a new courage that helped her stand up straight with resolve.

Mrs. Waithe smiled and said, "Sounds like a plan to me."

When Merilee entered the store, Gaylene said, "You kept it longer than anyone."

Merilee gave a weak smile. "You mean this is not the first time it has been returned?"

"We found this thing in the back of the store when we opened it and it has been purchased numerous times and always brought back." Gaylene opened the cash drawer and removed the $125.00 and handed it back to Merilee without asking for a receipt.

"What will you do with it now?" Merilee asked as she put the money into her purse.

"The same as we always do. Throw it in the trash in the backroom, until we see it hanging again, unable to remove it until someone comes to purchase it," Gaylene said.

"Why do you charge so much?" Merilee asks.

"The thing sets the price. Sometimes it is five dollars and other times it is one thousand dollars, but it seems the one who buys it pays without any question, just like you did."

"You knew I couldn't afford it." Merilee said as her head drooped in shame.

"It's okay, we knew you would be back in time, at least we hoped so. Really glad to see you got it off your wall."

"What do you mean?" Merilee probed.

"Everyone who buys it says it becomes stuck to the wall where they put it. It seems it comes back just as there is someone else ready to buy it."

"I don't want anyone else to buy it. Is there any way we can stop it?"

"I guess if you keep it." Gaylene said.

"Okay." Merilee pulls the money out of her pocket.

"No, keep your money," Gaylene said. "If you are willing to try to get rid of it, we should pay you. We do much better business when the thing is gone."

"I know this is a strange request but could you give me a list of people who have owned it before and maybe whatever history you have on it?"

"Sure." Gaylene pulled out a sheet of paper from beneath the cash register and handed it to Merilee.

"You have it ready?" Merilee asks in astonishment.

"Yes, everyone who has ever bought it asked for the same information."

"What do you think they do with it?"

"I've wondered that too, so I ask one lady one time. She just shrugged her shoulders and said, 'I was curious.'"

Merilee folded the paper, thanked Gaylene and left the store, heading for home still holding the hideous mask in a store sack, but this time the simple brown paper sack. Merilee had no idea what she was going to do with the thing. Then an idea occurred to her.

She returned home shortly after the encounter at the store and saw the family back together in their own home, enjoying a cup of hot cocoa and cookies and laughing easily with one another. It had been a long time. They all had Bibles open in their laps or near them. She knew then that Mrs. Waithe was answering their questions by taking them to Bible Scriptures. There was a peace in the house very similar to the peace she always felt at Mrs. Waithe's house. Deep down Merilee knew that Mrs. Waithe was their drill sergeant preparing them for their battle, and as long as they were in training camp, all would be calm.

"Hi, Mom, isn't it nice to have the thing gone?" Rance said.

Merilee smiled at him and kissed him on top of his head. "Yes, son, it is. BUT…"

"BUT what?" they all asked.

"I brought it back with me."

"Why?" Buster said as he shot up out of his seat.

Merilee turned and looked at Mrs. Waithe who was smiling.

"You know don't you?" she asked the dear woman.

"I hoped for it--, I prayed for it."

"I don't understand," Zay said, "why you would pray for her to bring the hideous thing back."

"It's simple really. Since we have the answer about how to control it, as long as it is in our possession it cannot hurt another." Merilee answered.

Mrs. Waithe patted her hand and smiled. "Very good, my daughter," she whispered.

"Where are we going to keep it?" Barbara asked.

"Truthfully, I don't think it will be a problem. I am throwing it in the incinerator."

"Good place for it, hope it stays." Barbara said with doubt in her voice.

"I think it will. After all it is only a reflection of the reality in our lives," Merilee said. "It's the idol of the dragon. If we don't worship it with fear, then it has no power over us." Then she swept her hands around the room and what is going on in our home right now is peace that cannot be explained or understood." The family all nodded and smiled in agreement.

"Mom?" Zay asked with a pondering note to his voice. "Yes."

"Do you think that thing growing was real or did we just imagine it?"

Merilee sighed out loud. Her youngest had just asked the question that had been plaguing her own mind.

"I've asked the same question but why would we all see it?"

"Dad never saw it." Rance inserted.

"Yeah, but he wasn't here when...we...you know," Barbara said, unable to complete her sentence.

Mrs. Waithe had been quietly listening to the conversation.

"Did all of you see the same thing?"

"Yes...well, I'm not sure, we never talked about what we saw," Merilee said.

"Maybe that is your starting point. See if you all saw the same thing. Each of you write down a complete description and then compare them."

Each of them nodded their heads.

"That sounds like a good idea except...," Barbara let her voice trail off.

"Except we don't want to think about it." Rance finished the sentence with his bold and harsh voice.

"I agree, Rance," Merilee said to console her children." "But at the same time, I think it would answer a lot of questions for us."

"And what if nothing comes of it?" Barbara asked. "All we would've done is dredge up the scary thing again. It still has us in its grip."

"She's right." Zay resounded.

"I know," Merilee said as she handed out pencils and paper." "But I truly think we should each make a brief description. Remember, all we are doing is checking out if the thing we saw was the same for each of us. It doesn't have to be detailed, just enough for comparison."

"But, Mom, I took pictures and we all looked at them. We all agreed then," Zay reminded them.

Mrs. Waithe said, "You all saw pictures and didn't disagree, so you must have all seen the same thing."

"What does that mean?" Barbara pleaded.

"It means you all saw the same thing," Mrs. Waite said.

"I don't understand the importance of us all seeing the same thing," Zay said.

"That thing is the image of the dragon. That means the mask is his idol." Mrs. Waithe said and left the room. The three children turned toward their mother and looked at her with bewilderment on their faces.

"I guess it means what we saw was real, and it scares us but didn't own us," Merilee said with a shrug.

"So what did that little exercise proves?"" Zay whined.

"It proved we are not going crazy as individuals but as a family, and I guess the family that goes crazy together stays together." They all laughed a slight little snicker. It helped relieve the growing tension.

"Dad, have you told Mom how you saw it in the field?" Zay said.

"What?" Merilee exclaimed.

"Not the metal thing, but the real thing. He saw it in the field," Zay chimed in with a smile and grateful to release the secret he had been holding.

"When?" Merilee finally managed to ask.

"The same morning we saw the upside down mirage in the sky," Buster answered.

"That's been months ago," Merilee whispered.

Buster put his hand over Merilee's. "There is more to this thing than we know, and as Mrs. Waithe pointed out, there is a connection between the sculpture and the reptile residing in our field."

Merilee shuddered. "Is it big?" She asked timidly, not really wanting to know the answer.

Buster knew she didn't want to know, so he played it down. "It is pretty good size, but it only appears at certain times. I don't think you will ever see it."

"Why not?"

"I think the sculpture was the only way he could approach you."

Merilee didn't ask any more questions but took Buster's word for it. Then she changed the subject by telling him about her experience in the shop when she took the sculpture back. She went to the bedroom and pulled the slip of paper from her purse and perused the names. They went all the way back to 1887. The records of that piece were detailed with descriptions of the people who purchased it. It told of their activities, mostly involving sexual immorality or greedy business practices. Occasionally, there would be a name that would have a simple statement by it: Protected. The notes also told of the trails and demise of the former owners. The ones noted with protected would say... restored. She took the paper to Buster and handed it to him.

Buster felt his stomach lurch as he read the first name Donnigan, Phillip, the founder of the community. But it was the last name, Merilee Troye, and the words beside that name that caused both of them to stare with mouths agape.

15

1867 – Church Creek Falls

> Do not trust in deceptive words For if you truly amend your ways and your deeds, if you truly practice justice between a man and his neighbor, if you do not oppress the alien, the orphan, or the widow, and do not shed innocent blood in this place, nor walk after other gods to your own ruin, then I will let you dwell in this place, in the land that I gave to your fathers forever and ever.
>
> —Jeremiah 7:4–7

PHILLIP DONNIGAN HAPPENED upon a small pond, and both he and the horse drank deeply after their difficult ride through high hills, mesquite trees, and lots of sticky brush. They had encountered a few critters on the way, including a big horn sheep that tried to wipe them out with a head butt. But the horse stopped and ducked its head and remained in the submissive position until the sheep became tired of waiting for a fight and walked away. Donnigan owed that horse a barn full of oats, but all he could find was this stream. With their thirst satisfied, hunger hit his stomach with a vengeance. He wiped the sweat from his forehead and looked around. There were a few trees here and there, but the most amazing thing was how far he could see. The land was almost a table top. The trek up to the top of the mesa had been arduous and hot, but once they reached the top, the temperature cooled and the distance stretched forever. His eyes had never seen such stark plainness with such beauty. The sun was set over the horizon that stretched over the plains. Donnigan stood in awe until the last dose of color drained from the sky and melted into the horizon.

"We are home," Donnigan said as he stroked the muzzle of his newly acquired horse. It looked as though he had landed on another planet alone. He surveyed the land for shelter and firewood. But in this landscape there was neither, only brush. The sky would be his roof and the prickly bushes kindling for a fire. It appeared the pickings would be few for that too. With determination, he picked up the prickly bushes and broke them up until he had enough to make a fire. His rough hands suffered small puncture wounds letting his blood run freely over his hand. It took a little while, but he had a fire by nightfall. It burned big and bright with a short lifespan. So he gathered up the straw growing around him and twisted it into ropes, then twisting the ropes into bigger ropes he finally wove himself some logs. The straw logs burned long enough for him to cook the rabbit he had caught for dinner. He tied the horse close to his tent formed from his coat. There he would spend the first night on his newly acquired land.

Donnigan lived in his chosen spot alone for several weeks living on whatever critter he could find. Occasionally, he would catch a wild turkey or a prairie chicken. Those nights were feast nights. He had learned as a small child how to survive on little and bring his body under subjection.

As a small child in Ireland during the years of the potato blight, Donnigan had known nothing but hard times most of his life. He had more security and belongings at this moment than he had ever had in his life.

He remembered those blight years in Ireland. They were bad and each year was worse than the year before. So many people died of starvation that the family would leave bodies alongside the road or in the fields where they fell. Homes were filled with bodies as well. Partly because there was no place to bury them but mainly because the survivors didn't have enough strength to dig graves in the unforgiving hard rocky ground.

Phillip could still remember when his Da decided to leave Ireland. He took him and his brother out of their little shanty with few belongings. They kissed their mother good-bye and stayed with her until the life passed out of her eyes. She was gone in less than an hour after they decided to leave. Mr. and Mrs. Donnigan had already formulated their plan in the event one of them died. Mr. Donnigan carried out the plan. They left her body there in the shanty knowing wild animals would feed upon it. But it would be a disgrace to her for them to stay there and join her in death by starvation. Mr. Donnigan found passage for the three of them to America, the Promised Land.

The phrase made Phillip laugh. It was the promise land alright, but not for the starving Irish. His da, weakened by years of hard work, worry, and starvation passed within three months after they landed on Ellis Island. He couldn't find work and he had so little strength to overcome the sadness. Phillip took care of his younger brother by theft and deceit. They both learned to beg. That was how Phillip's younger brother found a compassionate home at the age of four. Phillip started fighting over cardboard boxes at the age of seven when he found himself totally alone in the "promised land."

The brothers grew up on opposite sides of the same law. Phillip's brother, Sean, became a policeman while he became the leader of one of the meanest gangs in New York. He learned survival skills in the streets, including how to carry himself to make people trust him and how to put on a good front to make people interested in him. Phillip Donnigan was a tough bird and heartless.

Dismissing the painful memories, he turned his attention to his current dilemma: building shelter. He used the prairie straw and dirt to make bricks. He built a nice little one-room hut. He kept improving it while at the same time building other huts. The people traveling through were weary of outdoor sleeping and long treks of nothingness. The huts looked like mansions to many of the wanderers.

Donnigan knew how to manipulate people. He didn't know how to plot a business plan, but he knew how to survive. His schemes came quickly. He acquired the land as far as he could see through homesteading. Soon he began to woo settlers and carpetbaggers to settle in his little straw village. He needed a work crew to help him build his kingdom.

The sight of shelter tempted many people as they strode weary and broken across an endless prairie with long nights under a merciless sky punctuated by the terrifying sounds of night creatures. The creatures often claimed the lives of children and livestock and would break into meager food reserves either stealing or destroying the only sustenance the wanderers possessed.

Next to a need for shelter, the wanderers wanted land to settle upon and plant their seeds. During the spring and summer months, Donnigan's village grew to about ten families, each with a home, an outhouse, a smokehouse, and a handsome parcel of land. He allowed his horse to be used for planting, and all he asked in return was food for sustenance and labor to continue building his village. The village grew both in population and produce.

Soon merchants came and set up shops, and horsemen with a fresh batch of wild horses were always a welcome sight to the townspeople. The plan worked. The people were given an opportunity to claim their own land with a home already on it, and Donnigan gained fame and renown while building fortune. People called the place Phillip's Place, which was derived by telling new people to go to Phillip's place. The name stuck during the building stage.

After all, everyone in town knew that Phillip Donnigan was the premier leader of this little village. Or at least they should know, not because of his good nature but because of his demand of the king's price from each family. A tradition understood to carry the severe penalty of forfeiting one's land and home to Donnigan if disregarded. Fathers let their daughters be seduced and young husbands gave their wives to this nefarious man.

He knew he was a handsome man with charm and he knew how to use it, especially against young girls in unsuspecting families. He wooed and impregnated most every young girl in the village within a year. He smiled at his work, for this would imprint the villagers to him. A few families packed up and left rather than allow Donnigan such immoral entrance into their families. One man in the village, known as Robert, kept his three daughters from Donnigan and taught his four sons to protect their sisters. Robert's wife was a stout woman of high moral standard. No man would be allowed to shame their children, no matter what the threat. Robert and his wife stood firm, they kept their land and they did not move. Of all the families that came to Phillip's Place, only Robert's remained untouched by the worthless seed of the village creator.

Robert and his family built a small hut in the center of the village. As the building began to take shape, the other families felt sorry for Robert, for they knew as soon as it was finished, Donnigan would claim it for his own. Still Robert and his family built, until one Sunday morning they nailed a large wooden cross on the wall by the front door. The family stood there and sang hymns inviting others to join them. Within an hour the entire village sat in the home of Robert's family which served as the completed church of Phillip's Place, that is all but one, Donnigan himself.

As Donnigan sat on his front porch and watched the people flock to the church which was directly in his line of sight, he could feel the anger building within him. He knew he had to stop this nonsense or he would lose his grip on the entire town. During Donnigan's angry reverie a snakelike creature slithered under his porch and hissed. At the same time, he smiled and squinted his eyes. When he opened them, they gleamed a yellow-green color with a thin vertical pupil. The anger became a perpetual slow simmer. The snakelike creature was no longer under Donnigan's porch but residing in the person of Phillip Donnigan. The entity had watched this man from his birth, and with each blow of tragedy suffered by Phillip Donnigan the dragon spirit became more pronounced in him. Today, the entity took over the body, mind, and spirit of Phillip Donnigan.

The entity was patient, and that patience always gave him what he wanted. Right now he wanted the death of Robert and all his family. It couldn't be just any death, there had to be shame poured upon the family first.

That first Sunday morning as the people gathered, hope sprang forth from the villagers. After a period of worship, Robert stood and informed the people he felt they needed to organize the community. With everyone in agreement, the first order of business was to name their town. It had been called Phillip's Place long enough and it wasn't his village but rather the town belonged to these settlers. The decision was made to call the town Church Creek Falls. It was a strange name for the area, but it came after much discussion.

The church was the only meeting place in town and was the one building that belonged to no one. Robert had built it on the one spot Donnigan had not claimed in the Homestead Act. Robert had claimed the parcel for the community and as such they needed a community organization. So Church was the first name the community chose for a name.

Creek came because of the small creek that flowed through the area. It had been the lifesaver of most of the residents, so it was decided it needed to be part of the name too. The final word, Falls, was added as an indication of the wicked influence that had permeated every home in the village. As this word was added almost every family held a newborn. They made a sincere promise that day they would not let the man's offspring be influenced by the worthless deeds of their father. Every family held one of Donnigan's offspring, except the Robert Troye family. So it was that Church Creek Falls was born with Robert as the first mayor and pastor of Church Creek Falls, Texas. Robert and his family were the only people not indebted to Phillip Donnigan.

16

A Mask or an Idol?

But they are altogether stupid and
foolish In their discipline of delusion —
their idol is wood! Beaten silver is
brought from Tarshish, and gold from
Uphaz, The work of a craftsman and of
the hands of a goldsmith; Violet and
purple are their clothing; They are all the
work of skilled men.

—Jeremiah 10:8–9 (NASB)

"WHAT DO YOU think of this, Merilee?" Buster asked as
he held the paper with the history of the sculpture.

"Those words and my name were not on there when I
took the thing back. How did it get there?" Merilee sat
down trembling.

Buster read "Merilee Troye – final victim. Result---
victory!"

"Do you remember when I was doing research into the community history?"

"Yes."

"I ran across this fellow Donnigan. He was from Ireland, came here as a child from the great potato famine, fought in the civil war, and ended up in Anderson. Then he came out here to fight Indians and this is where he landed."

"Do you think that has anything to do with this...dragon?"

"I'm not sure, but I remember reading about how he was in a feud with the local preacher."

"At least they had a preacher," Merilee said.

"This Donnigan decided he would try to make friends with the preacher, so he made a sculpture and gave it to the preacher. But the preacher refused it, said he didn't want anything from the hands of the devil."

"Sounds mean," Merilee stated.

"I'm not so sure, it may have been smart because that sculpture was the one you just took back."

"Where did Donnigan put it, since the preacher refused it?" Merilee queried Buster as she poured them both a cup of coffee and sat down across the dining table from him.

"He built a courthouse and put the sculpture over the doorway. Said he wanted people to know he built the place and he would be the mayor, instead of the preacher," Buster replied as he sipped the hot coffee, then got up and went to the refrigerator and poured a little evaporated milk into the coffee. He sat back down as he stirred the coffee.

"Is Robert Troye related to us?" Zay asked.

"I think he may be my grandfather, your great-grandfather," Buster replied as he mused over the history he had just read. He pondered this in his mind.

"What does it say about it on the paper?" Merilee asked Buster as he sat down.

"There are some pretty strange things here. Look."

"What am I looking at?" Merilee wanted to know as she looked at the list of names.

"The date. It has been exactly one hundred years since he made the thing and offered it to the preacher," Buster pointed out to Merilee.

"Do you think that is anything significant?"

"I don't know, but it feels important... not sure why, other than it would have been about the same time my grandfather disappeared. By the way, where are the kids?"

"I don't know? They were here a few minutes ago." Merilee responded as she and Buster rose from their chairs and started looking for the kids.

"And where is Mrs. Waithe?" Buster added.

"She left after our discussion about what we saw in the mask, and she didn't say anything."

Buster went back to the table where he had left the list; he picked it up and began reading. "Look!" he exclaimed as he handed it to Merilee and pointed to a name. "Mrs. Waithe owned the thing back in 1920, the year I was born." Buster said. "Look what it says beside her name."

Merilee took the paper and read the short blurb beside Mrs. Waithe's name. 'Protected.'

"Do you think there is any significance to the dates, or is that just coincidence?" Merilee asked as she handed the paper back to Buster. He folded it and put it in his shirt pocket.

"I don't know, but I think we need to go find Mrs. Waithe and ask her about it." Buster grabbed his hat and jacket.

"Where are you going?" Merilee asked as she too grabbed her coat and purse and followed.

"To the field," Buster replied.

"But what about the kids?" Merilee asked.

"I think they may be in the field with Mrs. Waithe."

"Why?"

"Because that's where I saw the thing. I think they have gone down there to see it. Hurry! We have to get to them before the thing shows its ugly head!" He grabbed Merilee by the hand and they ran to the pickup.

Merilee followed reluctantly. She didn't like snakes, and she had a sneaky suspicion that a dragon would be worse. In other words, she was afraid, terribly afraid. It was Buster's attitude that scare her for the safety of her family. She knew her mother instinct would overpower her fear. Nonetheless, it didn't stop her from shaking.

"Buster, are you telling me everything?" she finally asked in almost a whisper because she really didn't want to know. She appreciated the protection Buster provided by keeping some things from her, however, this was a time she needed all the information he could give her. Whether she wanted it or not.

Buster looked at her. "No, but I will."

This was enough for Merilee. She turned her face toward the road as she steeled herself for the view she would find. In her mind she whispered a prayer for courage and for her children's safety.

The narrow turn row between fields proved to be a bumpy road due to recent rains. But Merilee barely felt the bumps in the road. The bumps in her spirit kept knocking around in her head and heart; along with her fear for her children, her gratefulness that Mrs. Waithe would be with them. The anxiety coursed through her veins at the mere thought of facing the real thing behind the hideous mask.

Then she saw them. The four of them stood still as if they were statues facing the same direction.

"There!" Merilee shouted as Buster turned the pickup into the plowed field without a second thought. The bumps now became full scale rolls and tumbles. But neither Buster nor Merilee complained. They pulled up as close as they dared. Merilee was afraid but forced herself to look at the ground. She didn't see any snakes or reptiles of any kind.

Then she followed the eyes of her children and Mrs. Waithe, and they stared up into the sky. Merilee could see nothing. She turned to Buster. He was staring at the same place with a tear rolling down his cheek.

Merilee went over to him and spoke to him, but he seemed oblivious to her. It was if they were all in a spell and she was the only one not captured by it. She walked up to Barbara and screamed her name and waved her hand in front of Barbara's face. Her gaze solidly fixed on the sky. She didn't respond. Merilee walked to each of her beloved family members and tried to gain their attention, all to no avail.

Finally, she approached elderly Mrs. Waithe. She stood up straight with strong shoulders and her face appeared much younger. She shook Mrs. Waithe by the shoulders, and then either Mrs. Waithe or something else knocked her to the side. Merilee looked up at her and saw her arm extended as though she had been the one that pushed her aside. This gave Merilee some hope. She stood in front of Mrs. Waithe again, to get her attention. Mrs. Waithe started speaking in words Merilee could not understand. Then blood appeared on Mrs. Waithe's shoulder and a grimace of pain upon her face. Mrs. Waithe fell to the ground in a heap.

Buster and the children gasped at the same time. Merilee screamed out of fear.

At that moment, Buster and the three children collapsed on the ground. They looked at each other with horror etched on their faces.

"Dad, did you see...?" Zay asked, but didn't finish his thought.

Buster was still looking at the sky and shouted, "Why did you do that?" A deep look of intense hatred and anger clouded Buster's face as he picked up a huge clod of dirt and threw it. He was yelling but his words were unintelligible. The children joined him by throwing rocks and anything they could find at the point they had been staring. Rance was the first to stop and collapsed onto the ground next to an unconscious Mrs. Waithe and Merilee who was holding her and attempting to stop the flow of blood from the gaping wound on her shoulder.

"Oh Mom," Rance said before he began wailing in deep gulping sobs. Soon the rest of the family was sitting on the ground wrapped around each other. They all sobbed with groans so deep Merilee couldn't understand their words. She shouted, breaking the scene of terror that had gripped them all so fiercely.

Buster finally stood, picked up the frail bleeding woman, and put her in the pickup. Merilee called to him, "Go straight to the hospital! The kids and I will be behind you."

While the family sat in the surgery waiting room at the hospital, Buster said, "Remember, she said she would not live through the tragedy, but when she was gone, it would arrive soon." Merilee nodded in remembrance.

The doctor came out. "Mrs. Waithe is okay but the wound is serious. Can you tell me how it occurred?"

Buster stood and faced the doctor, "It was a snake." He made the deadpan statement, because all the tears of grief were gone and they were replaced by the growing steadfast anger of a warrior. Merilee and the kids nodded in agreement.

"Wow, it was one heck of a snake! Can you tell me what kind so we can get some anti-venom?" The doctor said.

Zay whispered it in his dad's ears. "Remember what the herpetologist said about the slime being similar to a cobra?"

"We think it could have been a cobra," Buster said.

"Okay, I'll get on it." The doctor said, shaking his head. "I wonder how a cobra could get into this part of the country?" It doesn't look good for her. If I were you I would be preparing for the worse case." He said and then headed toward the swinging double doors.

Buster stopped him, "Can we see her?"

The doctor nodded and pointed down the hall. "She's in the second room."

The family went to Mrs. Waithe's room. When they entered her room they saw an alert woman smiling. "I injured him more than he injured me," she said with a smirk.

The family smiled. "How are you feeling?"

"I feel fine but I probably will not recover from this wound. The doctor thinks it's a snake bite, so he wants to give me anti-venom."

"Yeah, he asked us what kind of snake," Zay said, "I told him a cobra."

"Good choice. It'll take some time to get that kind of venom," Mrs. Waite said. "Won't make any difference, but it'll make him feel like he's done something. Now we have to get to business, time is short. First thing you need to do is get me out of here soon. We have work to do at the farm and my time is short."

"What happened back there?" Merilee asked as she put her hand on Buster's shoulder.

Buster looked over at Merilee, "Where?"

"The field."

"Oh, just what you saw."

"Buster, I didn't see anything except all of you staring at the sky and then blood on Mrs. Waithe," Merilee said.

"We were looking at the dragon," Buster said.

She gasped in horror. "But what caused the wound on Mrs. Waithe?"

"The dragon bit her."

Merilee sat still with her mouth agape and whispered, "The snakes kept getting bigger until…"

"What are you saying?" Buster asked Merilee.

"Remember when I told you about the snake at Mrs. Waithe's house when I was there for Bible study?"

"Yeah."

"She said they were getting bigger and they were coming to intimidate her."

"So are you saying she is going to get better?" Zay asked.

"No, I am saying she faced each one as it came, and each time it was bigger, but she was stronger," Merilee said.

"I don't understand," Zay said.

"Neither do I." Buster reached over and took Merilee's hand and squeezed it. "But I know we are not going to fight this thing alone or unarmed."

"Buster, what are we going to do?"

"We are going to pray, stand firm, and just like Mrs. Waithe, we will put on the whole armor of God."

"Read, read, read," Mrs. Waithe tuned in. "The Word of God is what makes you strong. When you know the truth, a lie can't hurt you."

"We need to discover all we can about the history of our land," Buster said. History holds the key to understand the present and the plans for the future."

"Because for some reason, that horrible large serpent belongs to this land. I want to know why."

"Dad, what do you mean by the whole armor?" Rance asked.

"It's from Ephesians 6:10. It says put on the whole armor so you may stand firm against the schemes of the devil."

"So you are saying this is a scheme of the devil?" Zay asked.

"Do any of you have a better explanation for a dragon in the middle of our field?" Buster said in an incredulous voice, giving reality to the unreality they were living. "And what about that mask?"

The children nodded as they thought about it. When the family arrived back at the farmhouse, Buster picked up the family Bible from the living room coffee table. "Come here, and I will explain about the full armor." Buster waited as the family each took their place in the family room.

"Paul wrote this passage based on the uniform of the Roman soldier to make a point of the armor of God. The first thing is the belt of truth. The belt would hold everything together, much like a policeman's belt holds all of his paraphernalia. So no matter what happens we have to be truthful…in all details… no matter how minor they may seem or how much we don't want to tell something. Understand?" Buster looked around the room at his children and observed their faces. He knew that each of them probably had some piece of information they hadn't shared yet.

"The second piece of the uniform is the helmet of salvation. This protects the head from the deathblow. Don't ever forget that the devil's scheme is filled with lies and deceptions, but the ultimate desire of his heart is murder. He has been a murderer from the beginning. The helmet of salvation keeps his deathblow away from you. He cannot kill your soul."

"Then what about Mrs. Waithe?" Barbara asked almost in anger.

"Good question. Anyone think they may know the answer?" Buster asked. Everyone shook their head no.

"I can't say for sure either," he continued, "but I know the creature only injured Mrs. Waithe's body, he did not take her soul. Plus, her injury most likely serves a purpose we cannot see. Her death will be her homecoming to heaven."

Mrs. Waithe nodded in agreement and added, "I have been battling this thing for many years and he hasn't killed me yet. And this is not the first time he's bitten me. The one consolation I have is that he'll suffer more than I."

"The next piece of the armor is the breastplate of righteousness. This means that the heart is protected by Christ. We know this because it says in Philippians that the 'peace that cannot be understood will protect the heart and mind through Christ Jesus.' In other words, it's our heart and mind that the enemy will seek to deceive, and our trust in Christ Jesus will protect us from that deception. Jesus is righteousness, because He only does the will of His Father, God.

"The shield of faith will put out the fiery darts of the enemy. This means that when the dragon or the devil throws these deceptions at you, they may hit you directly but if you are carrying your shield of faith, then the darts will be put out."

Mrs. Waithe was listening, and as Buster added this last part, she removed the bandage from her wound.

"Don't do that." Merilee said as she stood to rewrap the wound.

"No, I want you to see the fiery dart that thing threw at me." Merilee sat down and waited. The family stared at her shoulder as she unwrapped it and revealed only a small red mark on her flesh.

"See, that fiery dart was put out."

Rance stood up and touched her shoulder. "How?"

"I'm not sure but as I said, this isn't the first time this thing has bitten me. But each time it heals, it makes me weaker in the flesh but stronger in the spirit."

"So each time a fiery dart hits us, it makes our faith stronger," Rance said in confirmation of Mrs. Waithe.

"Good point, Rance," Buster said.

"Finally, we put on the boots of peace. This means we have to let our friends and neighbors know what's happening, and when they are struck by the deceptions of this fearsome creature, we must be hands-on to give them faith and strengthen the truth to them."

Merilee nodded in agreement. Buster motioned for her to finish the lesson, and she nodded again. Buster was grateful for the rest. He knew what he spoke was the truth, but like his family, he needed to meditate on the concepts for a few minutes. Reading them as a Sunday school lesson was easy, but actually having to live them in battle was a different scenario.

"Our weapon against the devil is called the sword of the spirit or God's Holy Word."

Merilee picked up where Buster left off. "In other words, the Bible is our sword. In fact, in Hebrews 4:12, it says the Word is sharper than a two-edged sword. Two-edged means it cuts going out and cuts coming in. It will cut the truth from the lie and the evil from the righteous. Therefore, the knowledge of the Word is our defensive weapons."

"So what do you do? Start wielding this book around, swish, swish, swish." Zay stood up and made swashbuckling movements and noises as he flung his Bible through the air. The family laughed at his antics.

"I think that's the idea, but it is the words in that book you use." Buster said. "That means you better be reading it every chance you get so you have the words in your mind when the time comes for you to do battle with the dragon."

"Dad, we can't win against that dragon," Zay whined.

"Then why hasn't he eaten any of us yet?" Buster asked his youngest son.

"I don't know; I hadn't thought about it."

"It's because he can't. He can only lie, deceive and scare us. If he keeps us in a state of fear he can control us."

"Wow!" Barbara said. "He has sure been controlling me."

The rest of the family nodded.

"There is one final piece to this armor and it is your only offensive weapon against him." Buster said.

"What is it?" Rance asked.

"Prayer." He cannot stand against your prayers because he has no defense against them." Buster looked in the face at each of his teenage children. Each of them ready to do battle and yet not realizing how intense the battle would be. Nor did they realize that each of them would fight a personal battle with the creature.

"From this moment on, we are the family of the Troye Musketeers, out to do battle with the devil." Merilee said as she extended her arm.

Mrs. Waithe added, "To Robert and Buster Troye."

The family all joined hands and shouted together: "To God be the glory!"

17

Neighbor Demands Restitution

> Thus will each of you say to his neighbor and to his brother, "What has the LORD answered?" or, "What has the LORD spoken?" For you will no longer remember the oracle of the LORD, because every man's own word will become the oracle, and you have perverted the words of the living God, the LORD of hosts, our God.
>
> —Jeremiah 23:35–36 (NASB)

"THERE IS LITTLE one can do..." the preacher droned on.

Buster had listened as long as he could manage. Coming to church was getting more difficult. Buster opened his Bible and looked at the paper he had slipped inside of it. The paper Merilee had brought home. Maybe the descriptions on that page held a clue to ridding his community of the dragon. Most were one-word descriptions, which didn't make much sense. Maybe if he knew the people better, the words would seem more appropriate. Buster placed the list of names back in his Bible and endured the rest of the service. His brain kept struggling for something to make sense of the notations. He could almost feel the explanation coming to his cognitive thinking but it just wouldn't quite reach out enough for him to grasp it.

The voice in his head spoke; Buster had come to expect it. He let out an audible gasp. He stared into the normal human-size face of his nemesis, the serpent. It was coiled up on the pulpit with part of its body wrapped around Pastor Dan. There was the wicked poisonous face staring directly into Buster's eyes. Buster leaned as far back in his seat as he could to get away from the sneering vile thing. It laughed with the forked tongue flicking with each evil laugh. *See Buster*, it said.

Buster sat up straight and stared back at the dragon. "See what?" He sneered under his breath, aware that he was sitting in church attempting to listen to a preacher. Buster wondered if anyone else could see the fire-breathing serpent, now in control of both the pulpit and the message.

See how they worship me--The dragon said with a satisfactory glance over the congregation. Buster took a look at the same congregation and saw the people's faces looking at the pulpit with admiration and…worship.

They aren't worshiping you, they are listening. Buster argued in his mind.

Oh, but who do you think is speaking, it's certainly not this imbecile I am using. He couldn't spout the ABCs correctly. The dragon morphed into a man that looked like the photos Buster had seen of Phillip Donnigan.

See I have been here since the beginning. This was my first host and worshipper. You should have seen him when I took over his body and soul.

Buster swallowed hard, both due to the dryness of his mouth and his inability to think of anything to say. Donnigan was not just the bad guy in this event; he was the first victim. His reputation in history lauded the progress and victories the serpent of old enjoyed in the community.

What's the matter Buster, are you having a few memories of your own?

The serpent said to Buster but the statement also came out to the audience as, "Right now, you may be beginning to have a few memories of your own." Buster realized the serpent, in the form of Donnigan and occupying the body of Pastor Dan, was speaking to the audience the same words Buster was hearing but it seemed only Buster could make sense of them.

Buster moved his eyes from Donnigan and looked at Merilee. He prayed she was not in the same trance as the rest of the congregation. She looked back at him with a tear rolling down her cheek.

She leaned over to him and said, "I'm sorry."

Buster responded, "For what?"

Merilee responded, "All the things I have done to you." Buster realized she too was mesmerized by the smooth words of Donnigan.

Buster ducked his head so as not to witness the heartbreak of all those in the room being sucked into this diatribe.

You may as well give up, came the voice of Donnigan. *After all, when these people learn the truth about you, they will not have any respect for you.*

Buster did not respond, instead he allowed the strains of the music to run through his head. The voice of the serpent went silent. The music continued to play inside Buster's head but the words he put to the music were prayer. The dragon could not hear the prayer.

Father, I haven't always followed you. You know my wickedness and all of it was committed against you and no one else. You have forgiven and renewed me; therefore, those things no longer have strength for injury to another. Lord, I pray those will be kept hidden in your heart.

Buster looked up and saw that Merilee was no longer in the trance. She almost looked angry. Buster patted her hand, "Are you okay?"

She said, "No, I hate that man, who claims to be a servant of God but speaks like the devil." Then she got up and started walking out of the church. Buster did not know what was going on in her mind, but he was certain she wasn't fooled by the smooth-sounding words of a man whose soul belonged to the dragon.

◆

The Troye family neared the end of their noon meal. They heard a forceful knock on their front door. It caught the attention of the family but none moved. It was unusual to have uninvited visitors at their home. It went unheeded for a few minutes until Merilee answered.

Buster became vaguely aware of voices at the front door. It was Merilee talking to someone and it was a deep male voice. Buster placed his napkin on the table and rose to join Merilee. She had answered the door by herself. He saw Deputy Sheriff Anderson dwarfing Merilee in his shadow as he held a piece of paper toward her.

"Hey, Glenn," Buster said as he approached the huge man with the deep voice. Noticing the stunned look on Merilee's face, he knew they were in for another ride. He wondered how many more of these tragedies his family could endure. They were never-ending and always a surprise. Buster reached out and took the paper and looked over it briefly as Sheriff Johnson spoke.

"I'm sorry, Buster, I didn't want to do this, but I have to." The big man said with a soft apologetic tone. "It was like I was telling Merilee, I'm just the messenger."

Buster continued to read and nodded. "It's okay, Glenn, this is not a big surprise. After all we did find the body of his prize bull on my land." Glenn nodded a grateful nod. "Buster, I know you didn't kill that bull. But I can't figure out what did."

"I know, it was really strange," Buster agreed.

"It was as if it had been speared yet in the shape of a bite. I have seen a bite that looked like that once before," Glenn pondered.

Buster heard *bite* and his ears perked up. "When? Where?" Buster prodded while trying to contain his excitement.

"Oh, don't get me wrong, it wasn't anything like that one, if that was a bite. This was on a dog, and it was a snake bite," Glenn said. Buster knew the bite on the bull was from a snake—a large dragon snake. But he couldn't tell Glenn. He might arrest him for insanity.

"Thank you, Glenn, I guess I better get busy and find a lawyer," he responded as he tipped his hat and turned away. Buster shut the door and stood there for a few minutes, wondering how he would handle this.

Buster offered to pay his neighbor for the bull the day after the serpent laid it at his feet, although he had no idea how he would do it. The neighbor knew Buster couldn't pay him in one lump sum. Buster wondered if that was why the neighbor had filed this lawsuit. Buster folded the summons and placed it in his coat pocket. He then picked up his hat and headed to the house of his neighbor, Garrett Boseley.

"Hi, Garrett," Buster called out as he walked up behind Garrett in the field.

Boseley turned and saw Buster. Garrett ducked his head and in a sheepish voice answered, "Hi, Buster. I guess you got that paper."

"Yeah, a few minutes ago. I don't understand, I told you I would pay for that bull. You don't have to sue me. Let's settle on an amount and put this behind us."

"I can't." Garrett pulled his gloves from his hands and removed a handkerchief from his pocket and wiped his brow. A common action in the summer, but it was close to thirty-eight degrees. Garrett was not sweating from the weather, but he was sweating.

"You want to explain, the only thing you can win in court is my paying for the bull and I am here right now to do that," Buster pleaded. Nonetheless, he noticed the normally tall and arrogant man sitting on the pickup tailgate with his head and shoulders slumped. Buster joined him.

"You wanta' talk about it?" Buster asked, offering an opening.

"I need...I need...to know...what killed that bull?"

"Garrett, do you think you know?" Garrett nodded his head.

Buster continued. "Have you seen the creature that killed it?" Buster asked.

Again Garrett nodded and wiped his forehead. "It told me to sue you, and if I didn't, he would...would...do the same thing to me and my family."

Buster put his arm around Garrett. "He's ugly, isn't he?" Buster said.

Garrett nodded and sighed a breath of relief. "What happened, Buster?"

"I don't know. When I first saw the monster, he had the bull in his mouth. He dropped it at my feet as if he was giving me a prize. But I knew he did not regard me as his master."

"Did he threaten you?" Garrett asked.

"No, he didn't threaten, but he sure has been causing havoc in my family and all those around me." Buster stood up and looked up at the sky.

"See that Garrett" Buster said.

Garrett looked up. "No, I don't see anything."

"Well, I do. I see the monster watching us."

Garrett jumped back. "For real?"

"Yep, he is always there. He may go away for a while, but he has been visible in my life for four months now. He is getting bigger every day too. He could swallow up this whole town in one gulp."

"Can he hear us?"

"Yes, he listens to everything we are saying."

"Does this mean…" Garrett couldn't finish his statement.

"I don't know. He has caused my family a lot of hassle, but this is one hassle he is not going to get either one of us in. You drop this lawsuit and we will fight him together." Buster stood up defiantly.

"I'm not that strong, Buster, I'm afraid."

"That's okay, I understand. I'm not that strong either, but I am learning to trust the One who is that strong," Buster said.

Garrett looked at Buster and said, "You mean…God?"

"Yes. He is definitely bigger than we are, but Garrett, look at me, he hasn't touched me or caused any permanent injury to my family. He has hassled us, but he hasn't really harmed us," Buster responded.

"So you think if I drop the lawsuit, he won't harm us?" Garrett asked.

"I can't say that. I don't know why he hasn't injured me or any of the family, but he has injured and killed others. I do know there is much more to this dilemma than we know," Buster said.

"What do you mean?"

"I mean this goes deeper and further than we can imagine. In fact, I am not sure, but I think our town's founder, Phillip Donnigan, may have something to do with this."

"You're kidding! What would a historical character have to do with us?" Garrett said, looking at Buster as if he had lost his mind.

"Can't say right now, all I know is this thing has been around since that time."

"You sure?"

"Yep, I've found evidence, and somehow there is something in our community history that if we can find out the details it will help us get rid of this evil."

"Buster…you called it evil. How do you know it is evil and not a friend?"

Buster just chuckled. "I guess you are going to have to figure that one out for yourself, Garrett. But what about this lawsuit, can we at least drop it and save ourselves this hassle?"

"I'm afraid. I think it may cause injury to my family," Garrett said in a low voice with his head ducked. "I don't really want to, I'm just afraid not to."

"Can we still be friends?" Garret asked rather sheepishly.

"Of course." Buster smiled and turned and looked at the monster.

You seem to be shrinking? Buster thought as he looked the monster in the eye. Buster gave the creature a victory smile, the monster turned away.

Buster had found a way to diminish the power of the creature; so simple and yet so hard to do. It was a matter of not believing his lies and not acting in accordance to the deceptive tricks he played. Even though the monster seemed to be shrinking, Buster could tell the comment made the monster extremely mad. Even if it did diminish his power, there was still a mighty force of power behind that evil calloused eye; a power with the ability to destroy and kill. Buster knew he would have to be careful.

By calling out the lie of the monster, Buster saw his full armor at work. Buster put his faith in the breastplate of righteousness, Jesus Christ.

"Garrett, I want you and your family to come over to our house for dinner tonight," Buster said as he winked at Garrett.

"Okay," Garrett answered with a shaky voice. "I guess we could do that. But why?"

"I have an idea I want to share with you, and I think it would be good for us to be able to discuss what is happening."

Garrett gave a slight crooked grin and nodded, "Yea, it would be."

—◆—

As Merilee prepared dinner for their guests, she listened as Buster revealed his plan for overpowering the huge monster.

"Do you think it will work?"

"It has great possibility, if the people will just…"

"That's the problem, isn't it, the people?" Merilee stated the obvious.

"Yeah, if we can convince Garrett and his family, maybe they can convince someone else and our defense will keep growing."

"The kids?" Merilee asked.

"They can do the same with their classmates. The more the better."

Buster, Merilee, and their three children felt more at peace now than they had in months. They were thankful for the presence of Mrs. Waithe and her spiritual strength.

After dinner, the family all moved to the living room with their coffee and dessert; the kids had a bottle of cola, a rare treat. Merilee thought the colas would make the atmosphere more relaxed for the children. She was right. They wanted to go to the garage and play their records. Pat Boone and Patti Page were relegated to the old folks listening while Barbara and her friends danced to the sound of a ratty-looking group of British boys with strange haircuts. They called themselves the Beatles. Merilee thought they looked like beetles too.

Merilee knew what the kids were doing out in the garage, and she suspected that Buster knew too but wouldn't say anything. He really didn't approve of dancing, but after seeing some of the dances on a rare glimpse of *American Bandstand*, he hadn't said much about Barbara dancing.

In the meantime, Buster outlined his plan to Garret to defeat the monster in their community.

"I don't know, Buster, the plan sounds good, but...," Garrett paused.

"What's the matter, Garrett? Give us your ideas?" Buster inched closer to the edge of his seat and took his cake plate from the coffee table. He truly felt that if they would stand up to the demon snake it would lose its power, because Buster felt the power of the dragon flowed from fear in the hearts of those who heard the threats. It was a trial-and-error plan, but at least it was a plan to fight back rather than give the monster their town.

"You say you have seen this thing, but I have only heard him and that was enough. All he ever tells me is how you are going to use me and then leave me holding the bag for a bad idea," Garrett said with a trembling voice. He reached over and took his wife's hand.

Buster attempted to swallow the piece of cake he had put in his mouth in order to answer Garrett, but Merilee stepped in before he had a chance.

"Garrett, have you read John 8:44?" Merilee began.

"I'm sure I have, but I can't recall what it says."

Merilee pulled a Bible off the bookshelf behind her and turned to the passage she had just asked Garrett about. "Look, it says he is a murderer and has been from the beginning, and it says he is a liar and the father of all lies, and when he speaks, he is speaking a lie because he can do nothing else but speak lies." She hands the Bible to Garrett.

"But that means you are saying this monster is the devil," Garrett said as he held the open Bible but did not look at it.

"Do you have a better idea?" Buster asked. "Even if it's not the devil, it's a tool of the devil to spread lies and deception. Why, even the monster may be a visible deception I'm experiencing. But you can't deny the things that have happened on our community the last few months."

"That's true but…" Garrett stopped and looked around the room. He took his wife's dishes to the sink in the kitchen. "I don't know what is going on but I know I can't do what you are asking." He walked to the garage and opened the door to get his children. "Son." He emerged with a sullen and red-faced young man.

Buster stepped into the garage and saw Barbara buttoning her blouse, her hair mussed, and her face red, not from embarrassment but from a young man's prickly beard.

"See, it's even infecting our young people," Garrett exclaimed in anger as he grabbed his son's arm.

After the Bosleys left, Barbara went to her room and shut the door. Buster started back there, but Merilee grabbed his arm and stopped him.

"Give her some time," Merilee said.

"I can't do that. I need to address the situation."

"No, you don't. She is already embarrassed, and if you go in there, she will not be able to speak to you again. Let me talk to her." Merilee said. "But it won't be tonight. She is defensive right now."

Buster didn't like it but he agreed. Besides, his plan to overcome the creature had just been defeated and he could hear the vile thing laughing at him. He wanted to lash out at something. If he went into Barbara, it would probably be her. He was glad Merilee stopped him and thankful she volunteered to handle the inappropriate behavior in his teenage daughter. An interruption occurred in his thought process; he wondered how much of the behavior was prompted by the creature.

The presence of the creature clouded his thinking in all areas of life. He could not defeat the thing alone. The time had come to bring in someone else, and Buster knew in whom he would confide.

18

History Tells the Future

The LORD said, "Because they have forsaken My law which I set before them, and have not obeyed My voice nor walked according to it, but have walked after the stubbornness of their heart and after the Baals, as their fathers taught them," therefore thus says the LORD of hosts, the God of Israel, "behold, I will feed them, this people, with wormwood and give them poisoned water to drink. I will scatter them among the nations, whom neither they nor their fathers have known; and I will send the sword after them until I have annihilated them."

—Jeremiah 9:13–16 (NASB)

MRS. WALLACE DIDN'T say a word as she stared at Buster and contemplated his story. Buster waited for her response, holding his breath, hoping she would not think him a lunatic. Finally, she spoke.

"Buster, why did you bring this to me?"

"I know it sounds strange, but I believe there is something in our town's history that holds the key to this thing."

"I don't understand why you think the answer is in history?"

"No, the answer is not in the history, but the history of this community is the key to understanding it and to get rid of it," Buster reiterated.

"Mrs. Wallace, I really believe this thing is building up to a horrendous calamity, and it has been building up for years," Buster said.

"What kind of calamity?" Mrs. Wallace asked with wide eyes and a face more pale than usual.

"I'm not sure, but—"

"You feel it?" she interrupted him.

"Yeah, I guess you could say that, but it's really more. He crawls around in my thinking, I can feel him, I can hear him, he is always in my head, it's driving me insane. I see him almost all the time now."

"Do you see him now?" Mrs. Wallace asked.

"Yes."

"What is he doing?"

"Just staring."

"But if he is so big, how does he fit into a building like this one?"

"He is more like an apparition than the actual sense of seeing him. And it is only his head that I see all the time." Buster felt foolish as he tried to explain to her.

Mrs. Wallace rose from her seat and walked over to a counter near the opposite wall from where she and Buster had been sitting. Buster watched her gray head bobbing above some of the items keeping her always in sight. It was her ease with the many artifacts that impressed him. She knew the town's history and the story behind every artifact. Buster wondered if he should follow her or wait. He didn't like moving around in the museum because he might knock something over or muss something important. He could tell by her movement that she was searching for something.

"Aha!" she exclaimed. She returned with a big smile and an object in her hands. She sat a heavy old book on the table near Buster. She didn't say anything; she just scurried back among her antique treasures picking up items here and there, for a few moments she would disappear into another room. She returned with two more big books and more items.

Most were indiscernible to Buster but appeared interesting. Especially, the small sculpture similar to the one Merilee had brought home. He picked it up and began to finger it as Mrs. Wallace returned. She saw him holding the small piece and laughed. "I see you are acquainted with that little trinket." She said with a laugh.

"How did you know?" Buster asked as he quickly dropped it on the table as if he had been caught stealing.

"The look of horror on your face, there are two expressions that thing evokes. One is wonder what it is and the other is fear. Don't be afraid, this one is not the real thing. It's a copy and does absolutely nothing. I wouldn't have the horrid real thing in my presence."

Buster knew he had made the right choice. This knowledgeable woman would be a great resource to him. She could possibly collaborate his story. He pulled his Bible out of his pocket where he always kept it. When he did, Mrs. Wallace laughed and pulled a Bible from her jacket pocket. "At least we are looking the same place for answers." They both laughed as they placed their Bibles on the table with all the other artifacts. Buster opened his and pulled out the list. He handed it to her.

"Do you know anything about this?" he asked.

Mrs. Wallace looked it over and nodded. She pulled a similar list from her Bible. "Interesting that we both keep them in our Bibles."

"I found that it made a noise like many people talking until I put it in my Bible," Buster explained.

"Me too," She said.

"Do you have any idea what it means?" Buster asked.

"I think I might know, but I also suspect that you have part of the answer too."

"Really!" Buster said. It had not occurred to him that there could be other people with parts of the puzzle.

"Is there anyone else that has a piece of this puzzle?" Buster asked her.

"Most everyone in town. Where do you think I got all this stuff? It came from people wanting to get rid of it."

"Has anyone else ever told you a story like mine?" Buster asked hopefully.

"No, you are the first who has seen the creature. Many people have heard it, in fact most everyone in town has heard it, but you are the first to actually see it." Mrs. Wallace said. This is what brought you to me in the first place isn't it?"

"Yes, but…I had no idea I would learn so much history."

"Buster, have you ever had a genealogy done of your family?"

"No, can't say I have."

"How far back can you go?"

"Only to my father. My grandfather disappeared when my father was a young boy."

Mrs. Wallace looked at him intently without saying anything for a long minute. Finally, she said, "Disappeared?"

"Yes, the story I have heard is that he went to sell the cotton, he was never seen again. His wagon and horse was found along with the receipt for the cotton."

"How old was your father?"

"Young, maybe four to ten years old."

"What did your father tell you about your grandfather?" Mrs. Wallace asked.

"My father couldn't remember much. He said no one talked about my grandfather. He sensed there was some shame in his disappearance. I think my father thought he left my grandmother for another woman."

"How do you think he ended up in Texas?" Mrs. Wallace probed further.

"He came from North Carolina searching for opportunity, I think. Not sure of the circumstances."

"Do you think this is where he landed?"

"I know it is. That was the one fact my father was sure about. He was born here and was the oldest child, when grandfather went missing."

"What do you know about your father?"

"Again, not much, I was young when he died, but my mother talked about him. She really loved him, and in her eyes he could do no wrong. Guess I always thought of him as the perfect parent," Buster smiled.

"Okay, Buster, give me the names of your parents and grandparents, and I am going to do some digging into your past with your permission."

"Oh, okay."

"Now let's look at some of these items. Other than the ugly mask, do you recognize anything?" she asked him.

Buster stared at the table, occasionally asking about an item. Before him lay an inkwell and several quill pens, buttons of all sorts and sizes, a pocket watch, a couple of knives, a jar with a lid, which closed with a wire clasp, a handsaw, a bridle, a small smudge pot of some sort, a blanket, and what appeared to be a piece of leather with some kind of markings barely visible through the burns. He looked at a coffee pot and several pieces of different kinds of metals, including some pieces that resembled silver, a few old coins, and a dangerous-looking hatpin. Several ladies' bonnets, bows, and hats and a couple of men's hats, both straw and leather.

"I know what some of them are, but I don't know anything about them," Buster answered as he fingered some of the pieces most carefully.

"I don't understand what this has to do with my story."

"These are all belongings of Phillip Donnigan," Mrs. Wallace said.

Buster looked again. "So what is the connection between these and my monster?"

"The people who brought these in to me knew they belonged to Donnigan, and they said they felt they brought evil into their homes. There is a story behind each piece, and each story involves some version of your monster."

She told Buster a few of the stories. While they were interesting and served to confirm the character of Donnigan, they did little to enlighten Buster to the coming tragedy or how to stop it. In fact, each piece seemed to be a repetition of the same story: tragedy is coming to Church Creek Falls, and there is nothing anyone can do to stop it.

The Holy Bible of the God of Israel had offered the only viable solution to ridding his community of this thing, and in all practicality it was nothing. "Trust in the Lord with all your heart and lean not on your on understanding." That seemed to be the theme. Still there was something that burned inside Buster, urging him to keep exploring the history of the community. Somewhere there is an answer to the eradication of this horrid thing on his farm and a practical way for life in Church Creek Falls to return to normal.

Buster left the museum more confused than when he entered, even though he had gained small pieces of information. He was grateful for the pictures of the items Mrs. Wallace copied for him. Although they were black-and-white and had streaks through them, the pictures were enough to remind him of each piece and relate it to the stories. Again, Mrs. Wallace had been thorough and had handwritten each story. She gave these stories to Buster. This proved to be an interesting concept, for in the grammar and language could be found fear and trembling. These were things the written word usually could not convey, but in these words, the fear encompassed the words. Buster took the neatly tied package, aware that it was the only one in existence. He would ask Barbara, the super speed typist, to copy them for him. Mrs. Wallace stopped him at the door. "Did you notice anything from the stories?" she asked him.

"They were all interesting," he responded with puzzlement in his voice. "Was there something I was supposed to notice?" he asked. Mrs. Wallace picked up the piece of leather with the burned marks and handed it to Buster.

"This piece should have significance to you. Do you remember the story behind it?" she asked Buster.

"It was found after the church in the center of town burned up on April 25, 1918. Does that date mean anything to you?" Mrs. Wallace queried Buster.

"Yes, it was the day I was born."

Mrs. Wallace smiled, "There may be some connection." She said as she closed the door behind Buster, leaving him standing on the porch thinking about what she had just said.

As Buster crawled into his 1966 green—and--white Chevy pickup, he pondered the piece of leather in his hand and his next move. It seemed the closer he got to answers the more mysterious they became. Buster had seen the creature take on the form of Donnigan in the pulpit at church. Maybe there was a connection between them. But he wondered, what could that connection be between the monster and the artifacts belonging to Donnigan? If this piece of leather came from the burned church, then it would never have belonged to Donnigan. How did it get into Mrs. Wallace's box of artifacts? A bigger question in Buster's mind loomed. Why was he the only person to see the thing, yet all had heard it? Buster saw that with Garret, but… Buster paused. Mrs. Waithe had seen it, obviously many times, for she had said it had bitten her before. She also said it had grown. What did he and Mrs. Waithe have in common that would allow them to see it while the rest of the town stood blind to it? It was time to start a community investigation and start talking about this thing.

Buster went by the city square courthouse in the center of town. On the east side of the courthouse was a row of pickups in varying ages, colors, and models. Buster smiled to himself as he thought of the spit and whittle club inside Anne's Café. These were the old-timers, the men who had fought the dustbowl days with a firm character, and they endured through the hard winters and dry summers. These were the men who made this land productive and desirable. These were the men responsible for causing the price of land to rise from five dollars an acre to more than five thousand an acre. They were the tired and retired farmers.

A few of them were farmers who decided to hire out the work and serve as managers. This time at Anne's Café was part of their management schooling.

An idea hit him; these were the men who had seen and experienced many of the incidents written in Mrs. Wallace's little book. Buster made a left hand turn and headed toward Anne's Café. There might be some answers there. Today would be his induction into this elite group of farmers.

Buster walked in and took off his cap. While hanging it on the hat tree near the door, he looked around for the best prospects; he was looking for the group of the oldest and wisest men there. It didn't take him long to spot a table full of white heads with one bald pate in the middle. He walked over to the table and called the men by name. The four men looked at Buster as though they were seeing a ghost.

"Well, what brings you here, Mr. Troye?" Kearney Williams asked.

"Looking for some wise company," Buster said as he patted the old man on the back. He knew Kearney was as crooked as they come, and he usually had little to do with the man. Kearney had the reputation of the old man for a little poker and a girl in the basement of the Olde Towne Inn, along with a few drinks considered illegal in an all dry county. He was a scoundrel, and most people felt fear at his slick style of cheating. He could rob a man of a week's wages before the man knew it was payday. Buster remembered to pray for wisdom and protection before approaching what he considered the devil's playground.

"You come to the wrong place, son, not much wisdom here even though we got pert near four thousand years of living between us." Kearney laughed at his joke all the while chewing on an unlit cigar.

"It is a surprise to see you Buster. Don't think I've ever seen you pass'n time around here," said Joe Martin, the mayor of Church Creek Falls.

"No, Joe, I guess this is the first time I ever stopped here mid-morning."

"All right, son, what you got on your mind?" asked the final bald-headed fellow, Marshall Baker.

Buster pulled up a chair and ordered a cup of coffee from the waitress, a woman known as Kate to the locals, because most people did not know her real name or where she lived. Buster knew her real name was Kathryn Martinez and she was the mother of three children, one whom died under Barbara's car. Her husband had been a successful landscaper until the gossip of incompetence ruined him. Now he was a farm laborer part-time and a drunk full-time, which was the reason Kate had to work as a waitress. Buster had come into the café with his family. She had been friendly and helpful to them and kind to the kids, in spite of their painful history. Buster had later seen her walking the bar ditches picking up coke bottle for resale. It was then he put her name in for financial assistance from the church benevolence. The pitiful assistance they gave her made him ashamed and he had taken it upon himself to pay her electric bill every month since then. She didn't know because the electric company sent him the bill. Merilee and the kids knew, and sometimes he knew it was hard for them to keep from bragging, but Buster held them to a strict code of silence. Now all he had done for this hard-working woman would be forgotten as he would be included with this group of lusting, cheating, greedy old reprobates. That didn't bother Buster, because it wasn't this group of men Buster sought to please.

Buster smiled at Kathryn as he ordered. He was careful to treat her with respect.

"Buster, you sweet on that ole Mexican woman?" Kearney asked after she had left.

Buster didn't acknowledge the comment but turned toward Joe. "Joe, I am here on a mission of discovery, rather than a social call." Buster began his speech toward the mayor, also a sign of respect of his position in the town.

"Not sure there is much to discover here, but tell us what you are looking for and we will make something up if we don't know the answer."

All three men hee-hawed and Buster gave a weak grin. It would have been funnier if not so true. This made him wonder if this was a good idea. Even if Buster gained information from this group of men, would he dare believe them? He wouldn't believe everything they said; nonetheless any information he gleaned from them would have a germ of truth and could help lead to further "truthful" research as to the origin and source of the monster that had invaded his life; a monster that had brought hassle to his life and tragedy to others.

Buster could see the face of the monster. He noticed it would flick it's forked tongue out over the group of men and they would all burst into laughter, usually over a sick joke or injurious comment about a fellow citizen. It appeared the monster controlled the group. Buster wondered how many times he had been the object of conversation in this group.

"I want to know about the origin of our town." Buster began his inquiry.

"Oh, not only is that easy but it's a fun topic," Joe said. "But why you asking us. Just go read the plague on the courthouse cornerstone, it tells the whole story."

"I know." Buster responded. "But, I want to know the details that are not on that plague, I want to know the things that were not suitable for printing." Buster smiled a crooked smile that conveyed a message that these men understood.

After a quiet chuckle, Joe continued. "You want to know the character of the man who founded this town and why there was a gunfight over the land?" The apparition of the monster wrapped himself around the shoulders of the three guys sitting opposite Buster.

"More or less." Buster answered, hoping to keep the topic open.

"Phillip Donnigan plotted our town—quite a colorful history if you know all the tall tales told about the ornery critter."

"So I've heard. I guess it is the unwritten I want to know."

Kearney became quite serious as he turned to Buster and asked, "Why?"

"Why what?" Buster responded.

"Why do you want to know?" The look on Kearney's face told Buster this light conversation had just taken a right turn from serious to conspiratorial.

"I have to respond with another question, why so serious?" Buster asked.

"You are treading on dangerous ground." Marshall said.

Buster felt a cold chill as Marshall spoke. The monster raised his head in an arch and stared directly at Buster. The look of malice in the eye of the monster translated through the eyes of Marshall.

But in Buster's head, a voice of reason and truth spoke, and it said, " 'They bend their tongue like their bow; lies and not truth prevail in the land; For they proceed from evil to evil, And they do not know Me,' declares the LORD. 'Let everyone be on guard against his neighbor, and do not trust any brother; because every brother deals craftily, And every neighbor goes about as a slanderer. 'Everyone deceives his neighbor and does not speak the truth, they have taught their tongue to speak lies; They weary themselves committing iniquity.' 'Your dwelling is in the midst of deceit; through deceit they refuse to know Me,' 'I am the Lord your God.'"

The words came from the Bible, but he couldn't tell exactly where, but at the time that didn't matter, he could look it up later. The important thing was that he was hearing the words of the Lord, and they perfectly fit this situation. He was in the midst of evil-doers and liars, they didn't tell jokes, they plotted crafty plans against everyone in the town. He saw the fear the disciples of the monster had instilled in them. These men held notes on Garrett's land. They knew the tricks to legally rob a man of all his possessions. Garrett had no choice in the kingdom of these rulers.

Buster then realized the monster was gone. He began to look for him, and then once again Buster heard the comforting words of God from the book of James, "Submit therefore to God. Resist the devil and he will flee from you." The little wimp had to run when the powerful words of God entered into the group.

Buster let a knowing smile curl the corner of his mouth. Kearney opened his mouth but nothing came out.

"Buster, do you really want to know," Joe asked shaking and almost pleading for Buster to listen to their story.

With the monster gone, Buster saw a group of broken and fearful men. He felt sorry for them. They were actually looking to him for hope.

"I know this is dangerous ground," Buster said as he ducked his head and, in a whispered prayer, repeated himself, "I know."

The four men seem to soften with some understanding and even what appeared to be sympathy.

"When I was a young man, I set my sights on conquering my little corner of the world by being the best farmer in the county or the state. Then…" Marshal choked up and couldn't continue.

Buster knew he had come to the right place. He decided to reveal his hand. He pulled out the paper Merilee had received from the clerk in the store with the listings of owners of the mask on it.

"I see you had possession of the mask for a while, the one that was supposedly forged by Donnigan himself." Buster pushed the paper toward Marshall; the other three leaned over to see.

"You get this from the shop or museum?" Joe asked.

"I don't want to get anyone in trouble," Buster responded, feeling as though this had some legal implications.

"It won't, there's a copy of it in my office too. We know where the copies are, each person on this list has a copy, so if your name is on there, you have been touched…by…"

"By what?" Buster urged Joe to continue.

"By…we don't know; the best description is pure evil!"

Buster leaned back and looked at the misty eyes of each man as they stared at the paper. They too had seen the monster and he knew it. He wondered if they were touched by the same experience as he. Would he become a curmudgeon like them in his old age?

He decided to be straightforward with them. "Did any of you see it?"

They all looked at him with sad eyes and nodded.

Joe looked at the other three men, "Should we tell him?" They all shrugged.

"We saw that mask change and it grew."

"Anything else besides the mask?" Buster asked and looked hopefully into the faces of these men who held pieces of the puzzle. He finally decided to help them loosen their tongues.

"I understand. I am afraid to tell people what I saw too because they…well…they might think I'm crazy."

"Yeah." Marshall chimed in. "I don't think any of us have ever told anyone what we knew. Once you've heard the voice, you know when others have heard it too."

All the other men nodded.

"You mean you only heard it?" Buster prodded.

"Yes, isn't that what you meant?" Joe said.

"Guys, I'm going to put it on the table—because I want answers and solutions. I saw the thing on my land. Have any of you seen it?"

The men all leaned back in their chairs as if they had gained a new respect for Buster. "You have seen it?"

"Yes, and it appears this thing has been around since Donnigan."

"Humph, I think it is Donnigan," Kearney said. "And now I am just like him."

For the first time Buster felt sorry for Kearney.

"I saw a huge reptile," Buster said flatly, hoping to sound as normal as possible.

"Big enough to lift a large bull and lay it at my feet."

The other four men put their coffee cups down and stared at Buster. He now knew he had made a colossal mistake.

"It made a sacrifice to you," Joe said almost in a whisper. "Come on guys, let's go to the dungeon. We need privacy."

Kearney took the bill and paid it. He also bought sweet rolls for everyone. While not a big gesture, it was out of character for Kearney who usually stiffed the bill. One of the favorite tales of how he became wealthy was that he never paid for anything. Buster was already amazed at the turn of events. He was surprised at the way the four men took him by the arms and swept him out of the restaurant.

In only a few minutes, the five men sat in an unknown room in the basement of the courthouse.

Joe stared at Buster as he said, "Okay, men, its truth time. It looks like we may have a chance to defeat this thing."

Buster stared at the vault doors they had just walked through and watched as Joe secured them. He then looked around the room generously furnished like an English Gentleman's club. Kearney walked over to a cupboard and pulled out some small glasses, while Marshall lit a fire to warm the room. The old-fashioned fireplace took a few minutes to start producing heat. Buster wondered where the smoke went; he didn't remember seeing a chimney on the courthouse.

"How long has this been here?" Buster asked as he looked around the room.

"Not sure. We accidentally found it around 1950 when we were upgrading the court-house," the mayor said. "This may be one of the most critical meetings this room has ever seen. And it's completely free of roving eyes and ears."

The men pulled up an extra wingback plush chair and offered it to Buster. As he sank into the chair, Kearney handed him a glass of fresh iced-tea. Four intense old gentlemen crowded around him and the mayor said, "It's time to lay all our cards on the table." Buster knew they were not talking about poker.

The room itself had been a big surprise, but Buster's biggest surprise came as these men's demeanor changed.

They were known as blow-hard cheats, but in here they were all business of the highest degree—no foolishness or cheating. Each man was deadly honest and forthcoming about his experience with the voice of evil.

"Before I tell you my story, I want to know more about this room." Buster said as he looked around for a doorway. They had taken an elevator to the basement. They had entered that through a door virtually unseen behind the filing cabinets in the court clerk's storage office, then down an unadorned winding tunnel except for a faded abstract painting on the concrete walls. Buster wasn't even sure if they were still in the court-house building.

Kearney leaned back and took a long drag of his cigar; "Darnest thing we ever saw, couldn't believe what we found." He looked up at the corner of the ceiling as if he was recalling that day.

"It was the four of us that found it," Joe took up the lament. "And it was about the same time that dreaded mask came into each of our possessions." Joe shook his head as he stared at the floor and drifted off into his thoughts.

Kearney came back and pushed himself to the edge of the chair getting as close to Buster as he could without invading his space.

"Buster, we found a man in here, and we think he had been here his whole life," Kearney said in a tone of sadness.

"Was he alive?" Buster asked, hardly believing what he'd heard.

"No, he was just a skeleton, but the skeleton was completely intact in what looked to be his final position of life."

Kearney moved back in his seat. Buster could tell this was a difficult piece of information for these men to tell, but he couldn't understand why they all seemed so emotionally involved and even a bit "spaced out" as his kids would say. Marshall pushed to the edge of his seat and got close to Buster. "I don't think they can tell it unless they're close to me."

"The room was nicely furnished," Marshall said. "In fact these chairs were found here as was all the furniture, but there was a four-poster bed over there." He pointed to the corner near the opening where they had entered. Marshall leaned back.

On cue, Kearney leaned forward and put his face close to Buster's ear as if he were telling him a secret. "The skeleton was on his knees, with his head bowed resting on his clasped hands. How did a skeleton stay in that position long enough for a body to decay? The room smelled as fresh as washday and not a speck of dust anywhere." Then Kearney leaned back in his chair. The four men looked at Buster as if he would have an explanation.

"This is the only place on earth we have found that the monster cannot speak to us," Joe finally spoke up. "We don't think he can hear us either." Buster now understood the reasons for the secretive actions. They were still fearful of the monster.

"Who was he?"

"We don't know." Buster realized the mystery of this room and the peace and comfort it held was a mystery to all of them. "What did you do with the bed and the skeleton?"

Joe got up from his seat and walked over to the wall where they had pointed out the bed. - He reached down to the floor and put his fingers under the wall, then he rose and pulled back the wall partition to reveal a beautiful bed adorned by a praying skeleton. "We hid it."

19

Meet Phillip Donnigan

> Blessed is the man who trusts in the
> LORD And whose trust is the LORD.
> For he will be like a tree planted by the
> water, that extends its roots by a stream
> And will not fear when the heat comes;
> But its leaves will be green, And it will
> not be anxious in a year of drought Nor
> cease to yield fruit.
>
> —Jeremiah 17:7–8 (NASB)

THE FIVE MEN released themselves from the chamber of peace where tales of horror had been exchanged. The truths revealed overshadowed the luxurious and peaceful surroundings of the hidden chamber. It was a veil of evil exposed to Buster unlike anything he had ever heard. When the cool night air hit him, he shuddered. They'd been there all afternoon. He looked at Joe who still stood beside him and saw him shudder too.

"What do you think?" Joe asked Buster as he put his hand on his shoulder.

"I think we do have a chance if we are true to the Word of God." Again Buster shuddered, not from cold but from icy fear he felt as the discussion in the room verified his theory. Church Creek Falls was in the midst of idolatry. The community worshipped a creature with their lives and fear in their souls. A relationship so strong it felt like a lover's grip on the heart of the community, an evil abusive lover.

Buster had offered the leaders of the community a solution—the same one God offered to Israel in the book of Jeremiah, chapter 11: "Listen to My voice and do according to all which I command you: so you shall be My people, and I will be your God."

"I truly believe that only obedience to the one true God of Israel will banish this thing. I think the people allowed it to grow when they began to follow Donnigan and his wicked ways, and each generation has become more wicked than the one before. If we stop the wickedness, not only do we stop the tragedy, but we also stop the continual idolatry of this man Donnigan."

"I know," Joe said. I feel the same way. Come on, let's travel home together at least the majority of the way. There's comfort in numbers." Joe said. "I'll follow you." He lived close to Buster's farm.

Buster nodded. While Buster felt a sense of success he was also plagued with apprehension as to whether the men would fulfill their part of the plan. Would they become frightened again once they left the safety of their vault?

Buster had not seen, felt, or heard the monster, but that did not mean he was not waiting for them. Could a praying skeleton be the reason there was peace in the room? Either the living man spent his life praying or the position of a praying man was more than the monster could endure.

The journey home filled Buster's head with the images the men had painted for him with words. He knew he was the key to the plan working, and that filled him with dread. What if they failed?

"You will fail you know." A voice filled with an Irish brough spoke up.

Buster saw a man sitting with him in his pickup. The presence of the man startled him enough he swerved toward the bar ditch.

"Careful." the man mocked him. "You may kill yourself before you have a chance to be a hero and save your community." Then he laughed, not an evil laugh but a knowing, gentle snicker that sent goose bumps up Buster's scalp.

"What's the matter, can't talk. I know you know who I am."

Buster finally found his voice though it was weak. "Phillip Donnigan?" he said.

"Yep, in the flesh, or so to speak."

"Are you a ghost?" Buster muttered as he slowed down his vehicle hoping that Joe would see the man sitting beside him.

"No." The man reached over and pinched Buster. "See, and you are not dreaming."

"But, I don't understand?"

"I don't expect you to. I'm not really Donnigan, although I have taken on his body for public appearances."

"Then who are you?"

The man looked long and deep into Buster's eyes with yellow eyes, the monster.

"Can you take on any form?"

"I can take on the form of my followers and innocents." With that the monster changed into the shape of Mrs. Paul and gave Buster a most beguiling seductive look. But Mrs. Paul had been murdered in Dallas.

"So, I guess you can't do it on a living person?" Buster said with a mocking tone.

At that moment the monster took on the shape of Merilee. Buster lost control of the pickup, but since he was going so slowly, he was able to stop it on the side of the road. Then the monster spoke in Merilee's voice.

"Please don't hurt her?"

The monster that looked like Merilee laughed. "Don't worry, I don't have to. You can do that all by yourself."

"What do you mean?"

"Figure it out," the monster said and then changed back to Donnigan.

"So you heard the whole story tonight?" Donnigan said.

"I heard everything those men had to tell me, I don't believe it is the whole story."

"You're right, you haven't heard the whole story yet because you have been so busy researching my history you forgot your own."

"And what does that mean?" Buster said as he attempted to start the pickup and pull back onto the road. Joe was nowhere to be seen, and the pickup would not start.

"It means there is more to yourself than you know, and before you start putting that little wimpy plan into action, you better get all the facts about yourself and your grandpappy."

Buster didn't have anything to say, and even if he did, he was shaking too much to say it. Without any defense against this monster, Buster began to sing, "I know that my redeemer lives."

"Oh crap!" cried Donnigan as he put his hands over his ears. Then he was gone.

"Buster! Buster!" He looked to his left to see Joe banging on the pickup window. "Open the door!"

Buster rolled down the window. "Where did you go?"

"Right behind you. I've been here the whole time. I saw him with you." Joe reached in, unlocked the door, and pulled it open.

"But I couldn't see you," Buster said. He noticed a look of confusion on his friend's face. "Joe, it's okay, he's gone, I'm all right."

"I figured that. Come on, I will drive you home. We will come back and get your pickup in the morning," Joe said almost in a panic.

"Joe, what did you see?"

"I saw Donnigan in the pickup with you, and I know what he can do." Buster knew the help he thought he had enlisted would all soon abandon him.

"It's okay, Joe, I can drive home. I'm thinking maybe I better drive you home, you seem more upset than me."

Joe didn't answer but nodded as he walked over to the passenger side of Buster's pickup and cautiously pulled himself into it. Joe looked at Buster and with genuine concern and asked, "Are you okay?"

Buster nodded.

"I remembered how it was the first time I saw Donnigan. I can't believe how unruffled you are by the man's appearance."

"I believe God is big enough to conquer this guy," Buster replied, surprising himself with the new level of faith that had taken over his heart."

Joe gave a nervous chuckle as they drove down the road. "Buster, are you naive enough to think God can conquer this guy?"

"What's funny?" Buster asked.

"Just thinking about the plans we made earlier, they sounded good back then but now, we can't win," Joe said.

—◆—

The loud incessant ringing continued. Buster opened his eyes and realized it was Merilee sitting under the hairdryer. Thankfully, he couldn't remember the dream he'd just been having, other than the feeling he had been or was being tortured and somehow the ringing figured into that scenario.

Buster lay in bed watching Merilee as she dressed for the day. His dream terror melted with the comfort of her presence. While their marriage was probably not perfect, it was as near perfect as he could imagine. Merilee was without a doubt as naive as a child, and had experienced little of life's tragedies, that is until now. It was her innocence that had brought the ugly sculpture into their home and her innocence that could never reconcile the evil it represented with the ways of the world.

Buster knew the world. He served three years in the military during the height of World War II. He knew the evil that lurked in the hearts of men. While the worst evil was definitely the killing of another human being, he had also learned that there were many ways to kill a human. Among those included death to the human heart through infidelity in marriage. This is why he felt their marriage was near perfect because he knew there was no infidelity. Buster had watched his friends' life crumble into an act of suicide after he discovered his wife with another man. He had listened to the inhuman ways men referred to women easily deceived into a bedroom tryst. He knew the evil that lurked in the world. Last night in his pickup, Buster had looked that evil in the eyes. It was the same evil that told him Merilee would get hurt.

His whole body shuttered with the memory and he hoped the whole thing had been a nightmare, not reality. A knock on the door brought him back to present time and place.

"Daddy, there is a phone call for you, it's the mayor," Barbara said through the partial opened bedroom door.

"Okay, honey, I'll be there in a minute." No. It hadn't been a dream. Joe was probably checking up on him. He picked up the receiver.

"This is Buster."

"Hi, Buster, this is Joe. You feel okay this morning?"

"As much as can be expected, considering…"

"I know, but I thought I needed to let you know."

"Know what?"

"Last night, after you dropped me off, I went by Marshall's place to tell him that Donnigan had appeared to you."

"And?"

"He died."

"Donnigan?"

"No, Marshall," Joe answered.

"What… How?" Buster stammered, somehow feeling there was a connection between last night and Marshall's death.

"Come to my office as soon as you can, and I'll give you all the details."

———◆———

"It wasn't a surprise to him," Joe said as he slumped into the overstuffed wingback chair across from Buster. He ducked his head as he caught a choking sob in his throat. Buster remained silent even though large schools of questions swam in his head.

"When I got home last night, Marshall called. I could tell he was in a bad way, so I went right over. He lives in the next mile section from you, you know, so I could get there fast," Joe explained the obvious as if he was buying some time before he told the details of the tragedy.

"Was he still alive when you got there?" Buster asked, hoping to prod Joe to the crux of the event.

"Yeah, but he knew...he knew the monster was in the room. He said the monster told him that he would die soon." Joe shook his head.

Buster saw it was not grief that Joe was experiencing, it was fear.

"Buster, what happened last night? How did you get him to go?" Joe pleaded with red eyes. "What did you promise him?"

"What? I don't understand."

"You know; he always wants something. What did he ask you to give him?"

"Nothing."

"Nothing?" Joe said in a mocking, incredulous voice. "He always wants something, and it is at somebody's expense. I think you gave him Marshall."

"Joe, I don't understand. He didn't ask me for anything. He mocked me for trying to be a hero, then he turned himself into the image of Mrs. Paul...you know the secretary who worked at the school that was murdered a little while ago."

"Then what happened?" Joe prodded.

"I'm not sure, let me think." Buster ducked his head trying to recover the memory of the awful event.

"Oh!"

"What?"

"I looked into his eyes—the coldest meanest evil eyes I ever saw—scared the living daylights out of me, so I started singing."

"You sang to the devil?" Joe smirked.

"No, not to the devil. I started singing about Jesus, and you know I can't sing, but I started singing a hymn."

Joe became serious once again. "Then what?"

"Then he put his hands over his ears, said 'Oh, crap,' and disappeared. The next thing was you banging on the window."

"You made him mad. That was it." Joe stood and paced around Buster's chair as if he were solving a math problem.

"Still in the dark here, Joe. What does this have to do with Marshall?"

"Every time the evil thing appears to someone in the form of Donnigan, somebody dies, and it is usually someone mentioned by the one who sees Donnigan."

"But you didn't mention anyone's name?" Joe queried as he stopped in front of Buster.

"Only my wife. But I didn't mention her, he took on her image and voice. I begged him to leave her alone."

"Hmmm, I don't understand. Is she okay?"

"She was when I left home this morning." Buster began to squirm; he wanted to get home to her.

"So why Marshall?" Joe asked.

"Did Marshall say anything else?" Buster asked.

"He said, he had seen the monster when he was a young man of good reputation. Marshall got into some trouble with embezzlement. It would have been a humiliating experience for Marshall's dad if the news got out. Donnigan promised to make it go away…and he did. The missing funds were replaced and no one ever questioned Marshall's integrity, but Marshall always knew Donnigan had done something mysterious. When Donnigan appeared to him last night, he said to Marshall that payday had come. Marshall was scared, really scared."

"How did he know the monster had come to get him?" Buster prodded.

"Merilee, your wife."

"What? She barely knows Marshall."

"It was the list of those who owned the mask."

"Merilee was the last to own it, but she took it back to the store."

"Yes, she took it back, but she didn't leave it."

Buster pondered the statement for a few minutes trying to make the connection. Finally, he gave up. "I still don't understand."

"The mask is supposed to stay in play, and when it's not, then…" Joe let the sentence fade.

Buster grabbed Joe by the coat lapels and shook him. "What man? What? Speak up." Buster was on the verge of letting his anger out. He clenched his jaws to keep it under control. Few people have ever seen Buster lose his temper, and fewer still know the destruction he can cause; and has caused. It had been almost seventeen years since he'd lost his temper on that day when Merilee was in danger. Only Merilee knew about it, but somehow the monster knew and at this very moment was prompting Buster with villainous thoughts of assault.

Joe grabbed Buster's wrists and held them tight. Buster calmed a bit and let go of Joe.

"I'm sorry, Buster, really I am, but Merilee took on more than she knows about. She still has the mask."

"How did Marshall know?" Buster asked.

Joe pulled the list from his pocket and handed it to Buster.

On the last line, new letters appear next to Merilee's name. He gasped in horror as he watched the letters m-u-r-d-e-r h-e-r appear on the paper one by one. Buster's knees buckled and he fell into a chair.

"Marshall was supposed to murder Merilee?" Buster said as he gazed in shock at Joe.

"Yes, that was the price that Marshall was to pay and he refused to do it." Joe sat down beside Buster, burying his head in his hands.

"You know Marshall's death won't stop the monster."

Buster nodded. "Can you tell me what happened to Marshall?"

"I can tell you what I saw, but even that won't be the whole story," Joe said. "When I got here, I saw Marshall alone. With a red puffy face, he was standing beside his desk for balance. I rushed toward him but ran into something unseen."

"Marshall kept screaming that the monster was squeezing him, and laughing as he squeezed harder. I tried to help him and I called the ambulance. But it didn't help. They couldn't get here in time because the monster wasn't going to let them. Marshall calmed and said one thing you need to know."

"What was that?" Buster asked, looking Joe in the eye.

"He said, 'Protect Merilee at all cost and help Buster. They are our only hope.'"

Buster stared at Joe. Then Joe completed the story of Marshall's death. "He said good-bye to me, and then he turned blue, gasped for air, and died. The monster squeezed the life out of him."

Joe sat down with his head in his hands and wept openly.

"Joe, the monster couldn't stay around when I started singing about Jesus. I was singing, 'I know that my Redeemer liveth.' That was why he had to leave. He can't be in the same space with praise to Jesus." Buster thought for a few minutes and then exclaimed, "That is our weapon, praise to Jesus. It says in Hebrews 13:15, 'Let us continually offer up a sacrifice of praise to God, that is, the fruit of our lips that give thanks to His name.'"

He laid his hand on Joe's shoulder. "Joe, if he comes to you, remember to sing or at least start saying these words, do you know the words to that song?"

"No," Joe answered.

Buster sang the song and wrote the words down as he sang. He gave Joe the paper with the words and said, "Sing it when you see him or sing Jesus loves me, I really don't think the song matters. It could be anything about Jesus."

Joe looked relieved as he took the paper.

"So you are saying that when you started singing this, Donnigan went away?"

"Yes, and it was reluctant, it was as if he had to leave," Buster added.

"Hmm." Joe rose from his chair and walked toward the door. He stopped right before he got to the door and turned to Buster, "Do you think this can really work?"

"If you read the story of the Ark of the Covenant being placed in a tent with the foreign god Dagon, you see that the god Dagon bowed to the Ark and lost his hands and head. I would say the one true God is stronger than an imitation god." Joe nodded and the two men left the room.

⬥

Jim Lawson put down his shovel for a short break. He truly thought he could do this job, but he had forgotten that it was fifteen years ago when he last worked at hard labor. On his way to the soda machine, he overheard a couple of the supervisors talking. He acted as though he didn't hear them, but he noted their conversation. It was an important piece of information to Jim. To everyone else it was just daily business information.

He entered the break room and took a drink of his coke. As it trickled down his throat, he wondered if Barry had burned alive or if he had been overcome by smoke. The thought made his eyes water.

"Hi, Jim." Sally the clerk entered into the break room. She was a cheery young woman.

"Hi," Jim muttered, hoping she wouldn't start a conversation.

"You okay?" she asked as she sat at the table across from him.

"Yeah, just thinking about Barry." He fought back the tears that threatened to spill down his cheeks and took a drink to give him time to think of an excuse to leave. Trouble was he needed his whole fifteen minutes to recharge himself for the heavy labor to which he would return for another two hours before lunch. Why had he asked for this demotion?

Dennis Goldman, his boss, wondered too, but Jim told him he was in a state of grief and couldn't keep his mind on the figures of his job as an accountant at the plant. Goldman seemed to understand and asked Jim what job he wanted. He knew exactly which job he wanted. The one he started with, the entry level job in the plan, moving product from truck to storage building. He knew the work was hard, but hard work was good for depression, plus it would help him with his recovery.

Goldman agreed to the demotion but told Jim his old job would be there for him as soon as he was ready. Goldman apologized for the drastic cut in pay. Jim didn't mind, besides his car and house were paid for, and now with only Jim in the house, the upkeep was minimal. He didn't need money, he needed the old job.

After Sally left the break room and went back to her desk, she put the form in her IBM electric typewriter and in a few minutes filled out a request for a quote, checked for errors, and mailed the request. Sally was good at her job and discerning people.

Mrs. Waithe felt good on this bright day. She took her coffee outside and sat on her back patio as she watched the sun come up. She loved being able to face the sun in the morning and have the shade at night. Probably one of the main reasons she bought this house was the patio, it was the perfect place to meet casually with her Lord. This morning was no different.

As Clara Waithe sipped her coffee, she began her conversation, which she called it. Her warrior prayer time came in the still of the night and she slept a lot in the afternoon. Her late-night prayer sessions always washed away the worries of the day. But they would soon start building as the day progressed. She didn't expect anything to change today, except that she did expect each day to be her last.

She looked up at the early morning glowing sky and could see a bit of a reverse mirage. "Is that for me, Lord?" she asked with a smile on her face. No one saw it but Clara because in reality it wasn't a reverse mirage, it was an angel approaching to escort her into her real home—heaven.

When Buster returned home, he told Merilee about the events of last night and this morning. She was visibly shaken. He put his arm around her and pulled her tight. "It'll be all right. There is one who can and has defeated him."

Merilee smiled as she laid her head on Buster's shoulder. "But…I have something to tell you." Her voice cracked. Buster could tell something else had happened. As he felt the rising tension in Merilee's arms, fear overcame him. Donnigan had threatened him with Merilee. But he felt comfort by her presence, so he asked her quietly and with deep concern.

"What now?"

"Clara Waithe went home to the Lord this morning. I just got a call from Montgomery's funeral home. Apparently I was listed as her nearest contact. Right now, I guess we are the only ones who know. She didn't have family around, except us and the many she prayed for every day. Buster felt her shudder and he held her a little tighter.

"You know what this means, don't you?" she asked.

"Like in the days of Methuselah...," Buster commented in a casual manner.

She rose up and looked at him. "What?" she said with a furrowed brow.

"I'm sorry, I guess I was thinking out loud," Buster replied.

"Yes, you were, and I need an explanation." Merilee leaned back into the crook of Buster's arm.

"Methuselah lived to be 969 years. The Bible tells us that his father Enoch 'walked with God' and Methuselah's son Lamech died shortly after his son Noah was born. Enoch must have had a prophetic message because the name Methuselah means '"when he dies, judgment."' Right after Methuselah died, the great flood of Noah's day came. Mrs. Waithe told us she would not see the battle but she was to strengthen and guide us in preparation."

Merilee clung a little tighter to Buster, "Sooo …?"

"Our trial is upon us. Let's pray we're ready for it." Buster said, and the couple bowed their heads simultaneously and prayed. At the same time a grating noise came from the incinerator.

Merilee whispered out loud, "Can we do this without Mrs. Waithe's prayers?"

Buster smiled and answered, "Oh, she hasn't stopped praying. She's just doing it in person now."

20

And So It Begins

> I will give them into the hand of their
> enemies and into the hand of those who
> seek their life. And their dead bodies will
> be food for the birds of the sky and the
> beasts of the earth.
>
> —Jeremiah 34:20 (NASB)

"I DON'T UNDERSTAND," Dennis Goldman said to Sally.

"I think something is going on, but I don't know enough to tell you." Sally hung her head in shame she had come to the Goldman's office with a hunch rather than with facts.

"Tell me what you think is going on," Goldman said.

"I saw Jim Lawson in the break room and he was crying."

"That's understandable. He just buried his wife after getting news of his son's death. He has lost his whole family."

"That's not it, I understand his sadness, and by the way, he came back to work way too early."

"I agree with you there, but he begged me to let him come back. Said he needed to be out of the house and he needed to work. He asked for his entry level job back and even took a big pay cut to do so."

"He isn't capable of doing the work anymore you know." Sally said in a low voice, ashamed of accusing the man. "He's a good man, but he is getting older, and the barn is really hard work, especially loading and unloading product. I know; I did it when I started."

Goldman laughed at Sally, "I remember you were quite a sight—this petite little girl trying to lift a shovel full of manure. But that's what I admired about you. You didn't give up." Sally gave a chuckle at the complement.

"Jim's a good accountant, and I miss him in that position," Goldman said. "He's a good manager too. He can manage people, put a plan together, and carry it out. It's hard to find a man with only a high school education who is as talented as he is."

"I guess it is all that mucking that teaches us." Sally smiled at her own joke. Goldman smiled too.

"Back to Jim. What do you think is wrong?" Goldman asked Sally.

"He's lost all hope," Sally said. "I think he may be suicidal."

"I've noticed that too but felt he would get better with time. Seems he's getting worse."

"He's brooding too much, and mucking gives one a lot of time to think or brood over unjust events."

"I'll talk to him." Goldman said.

"Thank you." Sally left his office and returned to her desk.

Jim Lawson leaned on his shovel to catch a breath when he saw Sally come out of Goldman's office.

He took a deep breath and pushed himself to the work. "Soon." He said in a low voice to no one but himself. "Soon.."

Merilee felt a bit apprehensive about going to the beauty shop, but it was a Tuesday and the shop wouldn't be as busy. She rescheduled her appointment since she remained in a state of constantly waiting for something to happen. Her stomach tied in knots. She didn't want to be around people any more than necessary. But she couldn't give up her hair appointment. The fact that Buster hardly let her out of his sight made it worse. His constant hovering served as a catalyst to move her hair appointment to the time when there were fewer patrons in the shop. She needed a break from the worry and fretting, it was giving her diarrhea.

"Good morning, Karen." Merilee said in her best happy voice, a smile on her face.

"Hi," Karen responded and then looked back at the newspaper she'd been reading.

"Have you seen this?" she asked Merilee. Karen handed her the paper and she looked at the headlines. "Arrest made in Dallas for Paul Murder."

She didn't read it; she didn't want to hear any negative news today. "So they found her murderer. That should be good news." She put the paper down and sat down in Karen's beauty chair.

"It would be if it wasn't for the name of the one they arrested." Karen said as she fastened a cape around Merilee's neck. "It's only going to fuel the gossip around this town." She sighed. "And most of it will originate right here and at the Enchanted Village Shop." She shook her head as she brushed the teasing out of Merilee's hair.

Merilee ducked her head for Karen to get to the lower hair. As she did, her eyes caught the name of Mrs. Paul's accused murderer on the newspaper she had laid on the counter, Mr. Jase Hamlin from Church Creek Falls.

Merilee took a deep breath. She didn't know the man, but she knew his character, first-hand. Just a few months after Merilee and Buster had moved to Church Creek Falls, he appeared at her doorstep with his big smile and his flattery. She had a new baby; Barbara was only a few months old the day Hamlin pushed his way into their home, and she knew exactly what he planned to do.

As he began to unbuckle his belt with a chuckle, Merilee reached behind her and picked up the bottle of coke she'd been drinking. Barbara squealed and Merilee broke the bottle on the sink. As Hamlin came nearer, she pulled the broken bottle out from behind her and slashed his face with a deep scarring cut.

He yelled and started toward Merilee as she headed toward the back door. She had to get him away from Barbara. She ran to the barn where Buster kept his rifle, always loaded and ready for rattlesnakes or coyotes, grabbed the gun, and pulled the trigger immediately. She knew Buster would hear it.

It didn't take Hamlin long to pull the gun away from her and snarl a most bitter hatred at her. "No woman ever tells me no."

"This one does."

About that time, Hamlin fell at her feet and Buster stood behind him with a shovel. They didn't know anyone in the town yet, and they didn't want this to be how they would be remembered. Buster tied up Hamlin and took him to a country bar. He dumped him there in the parking lot next to a broken beer bottle. He put some of Hamlin's blood on the bottle and left. That was the end.

Merilee did not ever see Hamlin again. He had always been a big topic of conversation in the beauty shop, and Merilee often wished she'd been able to put him in jail for all the damage he caused to families.

Karen was right; this would cause the gossip to go wild. He was a most handsome man with a reputation as a playboy, married to a homely woman. Sadly, Merilee was not surprised about the recent news and knew Hamlin was perfectly capable of murder. She'd heard horrific stories of his sadistic practices. She'd heard all sorts of stories behind the scar on his face—none were true, — but Hamlin used it to add to his mystery and appeal. He wasn't going to tell anyone the truth, not the whole truth anyway. A few of the stories came close, but Hamlin's story made him the victim.

As Merilee put the news behind her, she let her head rest in the bowl to get her hair washed. "Would you care for a massage today?" Karen asked her, "I'm not real busy today."

"Oh, Karen, that would be wonderful; I need it more today than ever."

She relaxed as Karen washed the tension and memory away.

———◆———

While there seemed to be a cloud of dissension and trouble hanging over class, no one talked about it. So after talking to her dad, Barbara felt confident in bringing up the gloomy atmosphere with Mrs. Wallace and stayed after school in order to ask her teacher about it.

Mrs. Wallace felt it too and had some theories about the cause but no real facts. They discussed each of their theories. It surprised Barbara that Mrs. Wallace talked so freely to her about the problem, especially her theory about Superintendent McCoy.

McCoy and Jim Lawson had been football buddies during their high school years at Church Creek Falls. Barbara never thought about her teachers being students even though their pictures were on the carousel of pictures in the school lobby and both McCoy and Lawson had their pictures in the trophy case. They must have been the star players on the football team. Mrs. Wallace told how they had been friends since grade school and remained friends their whole lives.

"How come we never see them together?" Barbara asked.

"They probably socialize in their homes more than in public," Mrs. Wallace answered rather casually. That made sense. The connection between Lawson and McCoy could be the source of the gloom, the grieving process over Barry and Joan Lawson, could affect a good friend, which, in turn, would affect his co-workers and workplace, in this case, the high school. Mrs. Wallace said the death of Mrs. Paul added to the strain and the atmosphere.

It made sense to Barbara, so the rest of the conversation was chit-chat, until Barbara realized the time and rushed over to pick up the boys. Her brothers would be standing on the school steps, cursing her for leaving them alone. But they didn't understand the situation at the high school.

After Barbara left, Mrs. Wallace went to Superintendent McCoy's office. She knocked on the door.

"Enter," McCoy called.

Mrs. Wallace went in and slumped in the chair across from his desk. "The Troye family is trouble," she said.

McCoy looked up, put his pencil down, and looked her in the eye. "What are we going to do about it?"

"Nothing. They only know it's going to happen, they don't when or how or who."

"Besides the Troye family farm is fifteen miles out of town," Mrs. Wallace said.

"He'll take care of that. He's already focused on them you know," McCoy said.

"Yes, I know, Buster keeps coming to the museum asking questions," Mrs. Wallace said.

"Have you told him?"

"You mean about his own ancestry? No, I didn't want to give him any fuel to fight the plan any more than he already has."

McCoy shook his head and said, "Do you think he's really seen the dragon?"

"Sure, the real question is whether it's his imagination or is it real?" Mrs. Wallace smiled a crooked smile. "I've certainly been feeding his imagination the last few weeks. When he first came in I thought this was the perfect opportunity to cover our tracks. You can imagine my shock and pleasure when I realized his heritage."

McCoy looked at Mrs. Wallace in a serious tone and said, "Why are we doing this?" Her answer was simple, but they both understood it. "Justice."

During lunch Jim Lawson went to his old desk and checked out some numbers, and then he took a stack full of journals and ledgers and placed them in a box. He looked around at the empty office, removed the boxes, and loaded them in his car. He then went to the back of the factory and checked out his handiwork.

Jim carefully set Barry's football jacket on top of his own. They were the same size and, aside from minor improvements, were almost alike with the same numbers and patches. Jim let his hand glide over Barry's jacket as he reminisced about the many yards his Barry had gained during his football years. There would be no future Lawsons to play the game and make touchdowns, but, there would be retribution. He then headed up to the school with Barry's football jacket.

Mrs. Wallace was coming out of McCoy's office when Jim approached. He nodded and smiled. She returned the nod but not the smile.

He knocked lightly and let himself in. "Here's the jacket for you to put into the display case with his memorandum. So if anyone asks, I have a legitimate reason for being here," he said to McCoy as he threw the jacket on his desk.

"How's it going?" McCoy asked as he twisted his pencil through his fingers.

"Everything's in place, this is the eleventh hour if we want to call it off."

"Do you?" McCoy asked.

"Hell no, I've been waiting for this ever since Joan's funeral. What about you and Mrs. Wallace?"

"We have out-of-town conferences, which last a week. By the time we return, the damage will be done," McCoy said with a smirk of satisfaction.

Jim stood and shook his hand, "Well, brother, this is it, probably won't see you again."

"What are you going to do?" McCoy asked.

"Stayin' right here. I'm goin' to watch the fireworks." Jim smiled.

"But---you might not...," McCoy Stammered.

"If I am lucky, I'll see the blast but not survive it. That's my prayer."

"Humph." McCoy replied.

"What was that for?" Jim asked.

"Prayer? For what we are doing. Look at who our mentor is in this whole thing, a dragon, a giant serpent. I hardly think prayer has any place here," McCoy said.

Jim laughed. "You know you're right, I'll change that. I'm asking that sneaky snake to give me a vision and peace." They both laughed as Jim started to walk away. "Oh, what time you making the call?"

"Six okay?" McCoy asked.

"Sure. Where you making it from?"

"The bus station."

"Good call, then you flying out?" Jim asked.

"Yep. What about Troye?"

"What about him?"

"You including him?"

"I don't think so, he hasn't done anything to any of us and he is a safe distance from town. He has enough worry with that old devil dragon hanging around his farm."

McCoy nodded. "I guess you're right."

21

Terror on Every Side

"For I have set My face against this
city for harm and not for good," declares
the LORD.

—Jeremiah 21:10

MERILEE PARKED THE car in the narrow garage. She generally didn't do that, but she needed the shelter today. Buster greeted her at the door of the garage. "How'd it go?

"You have to ask? You should be able to tell how pretty I am," she teased with a smile and a quick kiss to his lips.

"You're always beautiful to me." He took her packages and started toward the house with them. "How was it at the beauty shop today?" Buster asked with caution.

"It was good. Karen gave me a wonderful head massage. Just melts the tension away." She smiled. "But understand, I was the only one there, and it was such a blessing for the massage and the freedom from gossip. I must remember to pray for Karen more often. She hates that her shop turns into a local gossip place. But there's nothing she can do."

"Glad you had a quiet time. I had some quiet time too and spent it in Bible study."

"What are you studying?"

"Jeremiah, I never realized how current that book is and how it's actually the climax of the Bible. It's where the action takes place. Moses is the story of the beginning, but Jeremiah tells how man destroyed what God gave them…simply with their disobedience." Buster continued to talk about his study.

Merilee could tell it had been intense. She listened and followed as much as she could, but much of it was the reasoning of Buster's head. She didn't interrupt him. Instead she pulled out her Bible and began to read the things he mentioned.

They both knew that something was going to happen; Merilee prayed it would not be as significant as the Babylonian Captivity was for Judah. She even expressed the thought out loud.

"I know we're about to have a trial," Buster said, "but it's not part of the history of God and His people Israel. However, it is part of the same thing. When people disobey continually and violence replaces good will and peace and greed and cheating and all sorts of sexual misconduct, then God has to judge."

"Why?" Merilee asked, enjoying this precious Bible study with her husband.

"Because there has to be justice." Buster answered.

"I don't understand. Merilee said.

"He loves us so much He will not let us continue to run away from Him or to live in such a way that it separates us from Him. His desire is for reconciliation with us. Look at Jeremiah three verses 11–16. If we admit our sins and repent, then He will once again become our master. Merilee, do you realize that means if the town repents this monster will leave us because God will return."

Merilee sighed. "It sounds so simple."

Buster started again with enthusiasm he often expressed when he had gained understanding from the Scripture. "Look at verse 16, Merilee, it says the ark of the covenant of the Lord will be forgotten and not be missed."

Merilee smiled but felt a bit confused. She didn't understand the connection or what the verse meant. "It sounds great," she responded without any emotion.

"You don't understand, do you?"

"No, I don't," Merilee admitted.

Buster leaned over toward her and kissed her on the forehead. "Oh, my sweet Merilee, I love your innocence. You see, it means there is no need for a physical representation of God, because He will be with us always. We will not need the ark of the covenant of the Lord to meet with God. We can meet with Him through Jesus, Think of our children. When they disobey us, we can't give them good things. We can't enjoy a relationship with them; and we lose the good things of life when they are disobedient. In order for our children to see a parent's heart, they have to see a semblance of parental authority, like a time-out or loss of privileges. But as they grow they began to see our hearts and they understand us without any symbols. It's the same with us and God." Buster stopped and pondered his own words for a moment.

"Merilee, I think what is about to happen to us is a good-old fashioned spanking."

Merilee gave a slight laugh at the analogy. "We certainly deserve it. I can't think of a single couple we know that hasn't had some kind of marital affair that blemished their relationship."

"I see greed and cheating by the business people." Buster added.

"I see selfishness and gossip and bullying." Barbara said.

"Where did you come from?" Buster asked.

"My room, it is next door to the den you know. I could hear everything you said. We may have that ugly dragon in our field but we will not bow to him by disobedience to God's Word," Barbara said as she sat down between her parents. Merilee and Buster scooted over to give her room.

Merilee didn't like the interruption but knew she needed their comfort too.

The back door slammed and Zay came running into the house carrying a basketball. Rance was not far behind. Two dozen flies followed the boys into the house, and Buster shouted at them to stop running. They stopped and looked at their parents and sister sitting on the couch. "What's going on?" Rance asked as he pulled a pitcher of tea from the refrigerator and poured a glass for himself.

Zay came up behind him, "Yeah, why the long faces?"

"We were discussing the book of Jeremiah and how it relates to our situation today."

The boys grabbed their tea and some chunk of cheese and settled themselves in comfy chairs. The discussion continued, then Buster would relate a truth from the book. Each person contributed their opinion.

The phone rang and the entire family jumped. Buster answered. After a few minutes of listening, not talking, his demeanor changed from peaceful to concerned and he gave an answer over the receiver. "Of course I will Jim. I can be there in about thirty minutes." Then Buster turned to his family and said, "It's Jim; he wants me to come see him."

Buster had almost forgotten about Jim, a man who had lost his son in Vietnam in an incident called friendly fire. But when Jim called, Buster knew that the pain in his life had grown, not diminished. He was basically alone in the world except for his only grandchild. A child being raised by another family.

"Do I need to go with you?" Merilee asked.

Buster pondered the question, thinking where Merilee and the kids would be safest. It was difficult to leave them alone with that giant dragon lurking around in the fields, but something in Buster's gut said it wasn't the dragon that was the danger. The dragon was the intimidation.

"No, Merilee, I think he's losing it. His speech was totally incoherent and garbled. It sounded as though he may have been drinking. But I did catch one phrase."

"What was that?"

"I'm goanna kill all them sums-of-gums. Somebody has to pay."

"Oh, Buster, it's not safe for you to go." Merilee clung to him.

"I'll be all right if you stay here and pray for me."

He let go of Merilee and walked over to the other side of the room, as if attempting to remember something in a hurry.

"Do you know to whom Jim was referring?" Barbara asked.

"No, he was just ranting."

As Merilee spoke, Buster pulled on his jacket and grabbed his car keys. He knew what Jim had told him after the funeral, and now he wondered if Jim was going to take action. The drive into town seemed to take longer than usual, but Buster was relieved when he saw Jim's car still in the driveway and a light in the house. He ran up to the porch and banged on the front door. He hoped Merilee had been able to call the sheriff's office and ask him to check on Jim. Buster's concern was answered as the sheriff pulled up behind his pickup. Jim opened the door with the obvious signs of drinking. His face red and swollen, his clothes covered in spilled alcohol gave off the odor of strong whiskey.

"Oh, and what brings you here?" Jim asked Buster as he turned away from him and headed back inside. He motioned for Buster to follow him and left the door open.

"I came to see about you, remember? You called me."

"Yeah, I've come up with my plan. I'm just try'n to get the nerve to carry it out, but when you weren't there…" Jim laughed, took a drink, and then began to cry.

"Buster, I did it."

"Did what?"

"Made a bomb."

Buster felt his heart melt into his legs.

"Where?" he said almost in a whisper. At the same time, the sheriff stepped into the house.

"So, you already called him," Jim said with a scowl on his face.

"No---well, yes. I called him to come by and check on you."

"Now what?" Jim said as he eyed Buster.

"We have to stop the bomb."

"No, we don't, and I ain't goanna tell you where it is." He plopped into a chair and crossed one leg over his knee.

"When will it go off?" Buster asked calmly, hoping to catch Jim off guard.

"When I will it to go off," Jim answered.

Buster saw Jim was unstable. It could be grief and wishful thinking. Buster looked at the sheriff and silent communication went between them. Even if it was the ranting of a drunken stupor, they could not take the threat of a bomb lightly. Buster sensed Jim would reveal more if he kept talking. The sheriff was already out of the house calling the bomb squad to get prepared. Before he got out of range, Buster said to Jim.

"Did you put it at the school?"

Jim stopped his drink in mid-gulp and looked up at Buster. "What makes you think I would do that?" Jim sounded incredulous but at the same time sarcastic, and the hint of a smile confirmed to Buster of the great possibility the school would be the location.

Buster looked at the sheriff and pulled him out of earshot of Jim. "Start with the high school and the administration, especially Dr. McCoy's office."

—◆—

When the sheriff left Jim's house, he headed to the school and called the bomb squad, if it could be called that—two men who had taken a couple of courses and purchased a barrel to set off bombs. Nobody used a bomb; it was a waste of taxpayers' money to put so much money into something that would probably never happen. Sheriff Glenn knew his two young experienced officers calling themselves a bomb squad would be more frightened than anyone, so he sent a message to the next big city, eighty miles away. Probably wouldn't be any help, but at least he sounded an alert.

—◆—

Meanwhile, Buster kept talking to Jim, hoping to get more information. As he listened to Jim mumble about his boy Barry, he realized Jim's bomb would be similar. If Barry was killed by airplane fuel lighting up after an accidental spark, then the bomb didn't have a detonator. It was probably some kind of flammable fuel placed where a spark could ignite it at any random time. He could tell by Jim's countenance that the man fully intended to die in the blast when it occurred.

Buster walked outside and called Sheriff Glenn and related his theory. Glenn agreed, and this made it all the more dangerous. With farming all around them, there could be diesel fuel and fertilizer all over the place. There was even a fertilizer plant on the north side of town. Buster and Glenn had the same thought at the same time. It wasn't near the school; it was the plant.

—●—

Glenn called Dennis Goldman, the CEO of the plant. He explained the theory and Goldman conceded it was possible and that Jim had the ability and knowledge to do such a thing. "But…" Mr. Goldman hesitated.

"What." Glenn almost screamed at his hesitation in the moment of high anxiety.

"If Mr. Lawson did what you're suggesting, you need to evacuate the town. It won't leave anything untouched," Goldman said in a soft apologetic voice.

Sheriff Glenn moaned internally. "How far out?"

"At least five miles from town in any direction, but I would suggest more if one goes north of town."

"I will get my employees looking for a set-up now. Jim was working the product barn; we will start there."

"How much time to clear it if you find it?" asked Sheriff Glenn of Goldman.

"I have my men looking for such a bomb right now, but truthfully, without some idea of where, it's like looking for a watermelon seed in manure. I am evacuating my people as soon as we hang up. Prepare for the worst, pray for a failure," Goldman said then hung up.

Sheriff Glenn headed back to Lawson's house after sending a dispatch to start evacuation orders. Maybe, just maybe, the location of the bomb could be discerned through Lawson's drunken conversation.

Glenn told the dispatcher to start deputizing any volunteers to help with the evacuation and, if necessary, rescue operations. He prayed the latter wouldn't be needed, but in his gut, he knew Jim Lawson was an exacting man. After all, he was an accountant. A bomb created by Lawson would not be easily stopped.

Buster remained with Jim, giving him coffee and trying to console him.

"Buster, I think you're the only honest man in this town," Jim blurted in a drunken stupor.

Buster simply agreed with all he said because there was no reasoning with a drunk. He knew that first-hand, for he'd dealt with a drunken brother, and for a short time, joined his brother in drunken sprees. But, Buster discovered real fast, the high of the drink wasn't worth the pain of the hangover. His brother had died young and emaciated from alcohol abuse. Buster knew the best thing was to let Jim get a little more sober. In the meantime, he would ask questions to hopefully gain any helpful information.

Glenn pulled into the driveway just as Jim passed out again.

"We are evacuating the town," Glenn told Buster. "You better get going and get as many people as possible to go with you." Buster dragged Jim toward the door.

"I would leave him if I were you, put him out of his misery if it goes off," Glenn said.

Buster looked at him in earnest. "You know I can't do that."

———◆———

Jim stirred a little and declared in a loud voice, "What you doing with me? Let go of me!"

Buster helped him to his feet.

He looked around and grinned. Only he knew he was stone-cold sober; the drunken act served him well. He wanted to see as much as he could. He didn't know when McCoy would make the call that would wipe this gossipy, greedy, immoral little town off the face of the earth.

"Buster, come downstairs with me," he said. "I want you to see Barry's room."

Buster shrugged, looked at Glenn, and said, "Go, do what you have to do, I'll stay here and let you know if I learn anything worthwhile."

Glenn walked out the door to his waiting car.

Jim led the way down the stairs, forgetting his drunken act. It was no longer important; it was okay for Buster to know. It didn't look like Buster noticed the change.

"This was my boy's room. It's the same as the day he left for that damn war or police action as the great emperor Kennedy called it. Humph, it's still war and people still got killed and for what?"

"Jim, what's going on?" Buster said, wrinkling his brow. Maybe he noticed Jim's slurred speech was gone.

"I want you to see this." He walked over to Barry's dresser and pulled out a small box. He opened the box, pulled out a Bible and handed it to Buster. "Look at this."

Buster opened the well-worn book and stared at the hand-written notes throughout; most of them were quotes. Things Buster had said in Sunday school when Barry was in his class as a fourteen, fifteen, and sixteen-year-old.

"He talked about you and your class all the time. He wanted me to go to church with him. He wanted me to get to know you. He said, " "You'll like him, Dad, he's genuine.""

Buster stared at him

"Go ahead' read em."

Buster read through some of Barry's notes, Barry had written Buster's name beside a date. He remembered talking to Barry after Sunday school class but never realized the young man's spiritual hunger.

"This is humbling, Jim," Buster said without looking up.

"He always had something good to say about you. He noticed you and your family lived humbly and he said he never heard you talk about another person in gossip." Jim wiped a tear from his eye. "I wanted you to see that and to thank you for what you did for my boy. Because of that, stay down here and maybe be protected against the blast." Jim started back upstairs. Buster grabbed him by the arm.

"Jim, think this through. This is not what Barry would want."

"You're probably right, Buster, but it is out of my hands now. I did my part," he said as he started up the stairs.

Buster processed what he'd heard. Jim Lawson was not in this alone. "Jim, who helped you?" Jim stopped near the top of the stairs and looked at him.

"Aw, it don't matter if you know now. But you'll be surprised. Mrs. Wallace and Dr. McCoy."

Buster was not surprised, but mostly hurt, "Why Mrs. Wallace," he asked Jim.

"She hated this town, but it was her husband's home, so she moved here and made the best of it and made a pretty decent life. But it still sucked the life out of her."

"I don't understand."

"She had a daughter." Jim said.

Buster tried to hide his surprise.

"She had a daughter, just as sweet as she could be. The apple of her eye."

"What happened?"

"She killed herself when she was fourteen—hung herself in her closet. Mrs. Wallace found her."

"But why?"

"Not sure of all the details, but I think she was the object of a certain man's lust and she got pregnant." Jim said.

"You said man, not a boy?" Buster questioned, a sick feeling rising up in his stomach.

"Now you're getting the picture and today that Mr. Kearney is going to get justice."

Buster stood there in silence for a few moments, then he asked the question to which he needed an answer. "Did he rape her?"

"In a way, her daddy put her up in a poker game, Kearney won."

"He did what?" Buster shouted. "How, what kind of man…"

"A desperate one," Jim said matter-of-factly. He'd run up a sizable debt and was about to lose everything. He thought he had a winning hand, but old Kearney had one card better. Wasn't too long after that, Mr. Wallace went fishing alone and his body was found tangled up in a fishing line at the bottom of the lake. Accident? Who knows?"

"I wonder why Mrs. Wallace stayed here."

"Because old Kearney owned her, he held all the notes on her property. He told her she could live here as long as she needed, but if she left, he would demand full payment on the notes. She worked hard Buster, to pay them off and dagnabb it, she paid it off last year."

"What about McCoy?" Buster asked.

"He was just a sorry son-of-a-gun who got tangled up with other men's wives. I think he's filled with guilt and blames the enticement of loose women of the town for his predicament."

"Me, you know about, and you are naive, honest but naive." Jim said.

Buster opened his mouth to refute Jim's assertion of his naivety.

Boom!

Seconds later, windows shattered and wood splintered around Buster and Jim. Deafness and blackness swallowed Buster, and the words were lost forever.

Tragedy struck Church Creek Falls.

When Buster awoke, he could smell the diesel fuel and immediately knew what had happened. He looked around and saw nothing but debris and sky. Jim Lawson was on top of him trying to get up.

"Buster, I think there's something on top of me," Jim said, "I can't get off you."

Buster crawled his way out from under Jim and helped Jim up. He took the few stair steps to the ground level. The dirt and debris falling from the sky made it almost impossible to tell what he was looking at, but then there was nothing to look at. He saw no houses or buildings standing, only debris. Afraid to move too far, he called out. He listened but his ears picked up nothing—only eerie silence.

After a few cautious steps, he found three people lying on the ground, one of them the sheriff with a large piece of broken glass protruding from the back of his head. He was dead and so were two other officers.

He picked up a walkie-talkie and asked if anyone was listening, but he only heard static. Buster stood and gazed at the once-beautiful and pristine town now a scene filled with debris and terror. But no chaos, because there were no other people.

"Don't much matter where I hid it now, does it." Jim said as he sauntered beside the bodies of the policeman. Buster gazed out over Jim's front porch into the town of five thousand people, or rather what was once a town. How many could have survived such a blast?

Jim smiled in an awkward way, as if he wanted to smile but was too much in shock, the reality of the tragedy sinking in to his wounded heart.

"Jim, I- I don't understand," Buster stammered as he gazed over the field of debris.

"It was friendly fire that killed my boy and took my wife and left me all alone, so it's friendly fire that killed this town. Now if you'll excuse me, I have one more task." He walked over to the sheriff's body, pulled his gun from his holster, and opened it to make sure it was loaded. Slowly he raised the gun to his head.

"What are you doing Jim?"

"I wasn't supposed to survive," Jim said.

"Think about what you're doing," Buster pleaded with him.

"I'm thinking about it. I'll be with my boy and my wife," Jim replied, a blank look on his face.

"Only if you have Jesus as your personal Lord and Savior," Buster said.

"What do you mean?"

"I mean that if you pull that trigger and you don't know Jesus on a personal basis not only will you be without your family, you'll be alone forever and always. But if you know Jesus, then you know He will carry you through."

"Hogwash," Jim shouted.

"Look at Barry's Bible." Buster pulled it from under his coat. He opened up the back pages where Barry had made notes. He'd written his testimony and ended it with, 'I pray someday my dad will find this truth so we can share eternity together.'"

Jim read the testimony, dropped the gun and fell on his knees atop the debris.

"But look at what I have done…" Jim moaned.

"Jesus is not surprised, and He still loves you," Buster assured him.

"But… how?" Jim began to weep as he stared at the loaded gun pointing toward his face.

"I don't know exactly how, I only know He does, He suffered extreme torture and rejection and a most awful death to show us that He loved us enough to take the punishment for our sins. The penalty for this tragedy has already been paid." Buster sunk on the debris beside Jim and held him as he wept. He gently took the gun from his hand.

"I need to understand like my boy did." Jim sobbed.

"The best thing you can do for me is to help me find people who are still alive and let's get them out."

Jim nodded and both he and Buster stood. No other people had come from the debris yet. Could it be that he had truly wiped out an entire town? He thanked God his family was fifteen miles out of town, but the sudden thought occurred to him that Jim could have set more than one bomb to reach the environs of the town.

"Jim, can you tell me why?"

"I done told you, because this town killed my family."

"No, they didn't. His death was an accident."

"That ain't what I mean, the gossip killed my boy and my wife."

"The gossip?" Buster said.

"Yes, isn't it delicious," the serpent's voice coming from behind. "I had the best time when his boy got the beauty queen from the best family in town pregnant." The laugh came from a deep guttural sound of pure evil.

Buster fought the anger rising up in him. He knew what he'd see, but he turned anyway and saw Donnigan standing behind him.

"Hello Jim." Donnigan said as he walked toward Jim Lawson and stood beside him.

Jim picked up the gun again, "You better say good-bye because this gentleman is going to blow you to hell, and, of course I'll meet you there but you'll no longer be off limits."

Buster didn't say anything; he was too busy praying for wisdom. At that moment he began to assess his life as he prepared to meet Jesus face-to-face. But how did one prepare for that? He thought of all the things he'd wanted to do. He thought of leaving his family and never seeing grandchildren. He tried to sing but it wouldn't come.

Donnigan laughed. "You can't do that again, I tied your vocal chords."

Buster realized he couldn't speak anything but garbled sounds. But he kept trying until he was able to say, "Jim, do you see the other man?"

Jim looked around for someone else, shook his head, and dropped the gun to his side still holding his finger over the trigger.

"You stupid turd, he shouted. "There ain't no one here but us and we gonna be gone soon."

He swung his arm around to aim at Buster.

But Buster fought Jim to either get him to drop the gun or at least get his hand over Jim's to prevent any shooting, which wasn't that hard to fight a weak and hopeless man.

Donnigan was talking first to Buster in a taunt and then to Jim as a cheerleader and encourager. Buster noticed when Donnigan was taunting him instead of Jim, then Jim relaxed and almost gave up.

"Hey, Donnigan, why don't you pick on someone your own size?" Buster yelled out not knowing what to say. His concentration was now split between Jim and Donnigan.

"You mean someone like you?" Donnigan tossed his head back and laughed.

At that moment Buster wrestled the gun from Jim and Jim fell against him in a state of resignation.

"I need Jesus," Jim yelled out, "will He take me?"

"Yes," Buster said as Donnigan turned into a serpent writhing in pain.

He pushed Jim behind him and headed toward the dragon who now was shrinking in size. "I did like you said and researched my ancestors too." Buster said to him with authority.

The serpent returned to the form of Donnigan and stood up but didn't say a word. Buster could tell that Donnigan had lost some of his spitfire.

"Seems you couldn't get to my grand pappy either."

"Oh, but I did." Donnigan replied. "You didn't get all the history?

Donnigan was right; Buster hadn't searched to the end of his grandfather's life. "You still don't know why or how he disappeared. Aren't you the least bit curious?" Donnigan said with a smirking laugh.

"I don't have time for you right now." Buster replied as he took Jim by the arm and walked away from the remains of the Lawson house. Buster had a job to do; he needed to be looking for survivors, not arguing with the devil.

Buster's mind was exploding with two details at the same time; the state of his family and the devastation before him. He walked through town step by step, looking for people and a way to get home. When he reached the place where his truck had been sitting, there was only a mass of crumpled metal, barely recognizable as his vehicle. His heart felt heavy as he attempted to find a way to get home. He would walk the fifteen miles if he had to. Still his ears kept listening for sounds of life.

The piercing sound of a baby crying gave him both hope and dread. "Jim, do you hear that?"

Jim stopped and listened with Buster, and they both headed toward the sound. In that moment Buster focused on nothing but the sound of a crying infant.

At last he could tell the infant had to be in arm's reach; he looked for debris but there was none. The sound was magnified at that spot. He became frustrated as he rummaged around the area, being careful where he put his feet and still could hear the cries of the helpless infant. Where are you little one?

"Frustrated?" The evil voice of Donnigan said.

Buster looked up and saw the murderous eyes.

"What do you want?" Buster screamed at him.

"Just watching you is entertainment enough."

Buster took a swing at the man hitting him squarely on the jaw.

Donnigan fell to the ground, rubbed his chin and smiled a twisted smile. "Good jab; didn't know you had any fight left in you."

He realized his anger was feeding Donnigan and making him more powerful. He turned away from him and focused on the child. "Lord, you know where that baby is, please point me in the right direction, and if you could block that evil behind me or better yet, banish it to the abyss."

Donnigan groaned and fell, writhing on the ground pleading. "No, not the abyss." Buster couldn't be sure if it was real or if Donnigan was play-acting. He was a deceiver. He tuned his ear for sounds of human life. He heard the faint whimper of the baby running out of energy, but still fearful.

He bent down to the ground and found a piece of rolled-up carpet lying on what appeared to be a porch. Who lived in this area that had a baby? He could only think of the Alexanders'. Were they getting some new red carpet? Threads hung down from it, and then he heard the baby make one more cry from beneath that roll of carpet.

Oh, thank goodness. Surely that floor covering had protected the baby. He pushed the carpet off the baby and noticed it was sticky wet.

Then he saw the bright-crimson liquid surrounding a person's bright blue eyes, fixed and frozen staring. He gasped as he realized he was looking at a young woman clutching her tiny infant even in death. Her body had been ripped in two He almost lost his lunch when he realized the roll of carpet was actually the woman's torso, and the strings were her long hair soaked in blood.

He turned away and took several deep breaths to ward off the shock of seeing the scene. With no other choice, he turned back to check on the baby. It appeared to be uninjured. Even though the baby's skin was covered with the shed blood of his mother, she had protected him; and nearby lay another child—a toddler, too terrified to scream, speak, or cry.

Buster pried the infant from the dead woman's arms and wrapped him in his T-shirt. He reached out to the toddler who gratefully accepted the welcoming arm. As he drew the child toward him, he put his arms around Buster's neck and clung to him. The infant leaned into him. Buster felt his throat getting clogged up with emotion.

Jim watched. "I-I didn't think…," Jim stuttered, as if barely able to get out the words, "children from parents… I never thought…"

Buster nodded but didn't speak, Jim needed to be alone in his own head with the consequences of his actions.

He had to get the children to some assistance and he had to get home. Right now it seemed the two things were actually one. The only place there would be help for these children was his home. But the big question was how to get there. Jim gained some of his senses and reached over and took the toddler.

"We need to get out of here, Jim," Buster said as he thought out loud.

"What about other survivors?"

"Listen, be careful, but we need to get these babies out of here."

Jim nodded in agreement, and the reality of the children's plight pulled him out of his stupor.

With no cars that were travel-worthy in sight, Buster began walking toward the west side of town toward his home. The whole town as far as he could tell was leveled. They traveled toward the setting sun. The night would grow long and weary if he did not find some mode of transportation. He kept looking for survivors and listening for sounds of people or animals, but he was engulfed in an eerily quiet and deserted town.

Buster kept plodding on, putting one exhausted foot in front of the other. Occasionally he would see a few people rising from the debris. They were all in the same state of shock as Buster had been at first. He called out but no one acknowledged him. Suddenly, his foot touched a level piece of ground. He looked down and saw that the debris was not as great. A tinge of hope filled him as he again focused on finding suitable transportation. Then he saw a figure of a horse against the fading light in the west sky. At first he looked around for something to entice the horse toward him, then he simply whistled and the horse came toward him. It was his own horse! He realized Rance was driving the wagon.

"Dad!" Rance called out. He stopped the horse, put on the brake, and ran to him. He stopped when he saw Buster holding the infant covered in blood. "Are you all right?"

"I'm fine, son." He put his hand on Rance's shoulder. "Thank you for coming to look for me"

Some quilts sat in the back of the wagon. Merilee must already be on the rescue. He attempted to put the children in the buggy but they whimpered and cling to him and Jim even tighter. Even the infant steeled himself against Buster's chest. Awkwardly the four of them climbed into the back of the buggy and Rance picked up the reigns. Rance clicked his tongue at the horse and they headed off into the western sun. This little band of troopers had a destination in mind.

22

Church Creek Falls Burns

"For I have set My face against this city for harm and not for good," declares the LORD. "It will be given into the hand of the king of Babylon and he will burn it with fire."

—Jeremiah 21:10

THE TROOP TRAVELED about five miles from town when they saw a strange sight: cars, trucks, and people coming toward them. Garrett Bosley was among them. He walked over to the wagon and said, "I can't believe you're alive. It looked as though Church Creek Falls expanded and then fell to the ground. It was as if it was plucked up and uprooted."

Buster shuddered as he thought of what had happened. The people got out of their cars and questioned him.

Buster told them the town was devastated and needed help, but cars wouldn't be able to travel in town. He made a plea to all who owned horses and wagons to get them. Keep the vehicles close, for if any survivors would be found they'd need to be taken to hospitals in nearby towns.

In the midst of the chaos and questioning, a sense of dread enveloped Buster. He saw a sea of worried and scared faces and realized all the community knew as a governing body no longer existed. They were on their own; the country people were the first responders. He handed the clinging infant to Barbara. The baby whimpered and he wanted to take him back, but he knew there was work to be done and someone had to organize it.

Barbara took the children to her car and drove back home to her mother. She cried when she recognized the children as nephews of her best friend, she knew this must mean their mother was gone.

Garrett opened the door of his pickup, stood up on the step, and stared. He couldn't comprehend what he was looking at, and there was no way to drive any further. He headed into town, but with all the destruction, it was difficult to tell his location.

Buster was grateful for the horse and wagon ride, but it was much too slow. The horse trotted at a good clip, but Buster longed to get back into town faster; there might be more survivors. The center of the blast was located near a residential area north of town where the new houses and pristine lawns sprung up in the last few years. Beside the new addition lay a nice older neighborhood.

His jaw dropped, there couldn't be any survivors left due to the massive destruction. Jim truly had brought a major disaster of biblical proportion upon Church Creek Falls. Most of the city leaders and first responders lived in that part of the community. The culture, the government, all which made a community operate no longer existed.

Near the south edge of town, the Daniel residence stood intact. Buster stopped and knocked on the door. When Harry came to the door, Buster could tell he was visibly shaken. "Did you hear it?" he asked Harry.

"Yes, what was it?"

"A bomb. Looks like it was from or near the fertilizer plant, most likely an accident," Buster said with Jim in earshot. "We need to get a message to some of our neighbors. We need help and lots of it. We need the Red Cross, anything."

"I will gather all the medical supplies I have and then organize the neighbors. We'll meet you in town to start looking for the wounded."

23

Search and Rescue

> For I have heard the whispering of
> many, "Terror on every side! Denounce
> him; yes, let us denounce him!" All my
> trusted friends, watching for my fall, say:
> "Perhaps he will be deceived, so that we
> may prevail against him and take our
> revenge on him."
>
> —Jeremiah 20:10 (NASB)

BUSTER LOST TRACK of time during the search and
rescue, He'd taken naps on a cot in a tent set up by Red
Cross for at least a week or more. Meals were brought from
out-of-town churches. He marveled at the response from
nearby communities and yet they barely made a dent in the
work. While everyone still hoped to find a survivor or two,
most had lost hope. The only survivors found were the two
Alexander children.

The official statement read the explosion was an unfortunate accident caused by a series of small mistakes. Dr. McCoy and his wife returned from their conference within a few days after the blast. Mrs. Wallace was never found. Her house was completely demolished and small bits of flesh were found among the rubbish leading the search and rescue to assume she had been killed in the blast.

No one ever questioned Jim or seemed to consider he had a part in the explosion. People's anger focused on Dennis Goldman, the CEO of the plant. The people couldn't understand how he could have let such a thing happen. Of course no answer would be coming since he perished with all the other employees on the grounds. Occasionally, a worker would speculate whether the town would be rebuilt or not; there were so few people left of the five thousand that once occupied this little spec of dirt. The survivors were the farmers and their help who lived on the environs of town.

Jim now lived with Buster's family and spent his time helping with the recovery. Merilee and Barbara cared for the Alexander babies. And Buster kept hoping they would find their father. Those people closest to the plant were disintegrated when the blast hit. No workers at the plant escaped, the same with the north and west side of town. It just didn't seem worth the hassle to turn Jim in to the authorities, and everyone was satisfied with the accidental explosion theory. However, Buster really questioned whether Jim could have done such damage. There were powers at work much greater than Jim, Mrs. Wallace, or Dr. McCoy.

Buster returned to his farm to be with his family and rest. He needed the normalcy of home rather than the constant destruction in town. When he drove toward his house, he saw the monster in the field and slammed on his brakes. This time he used no disguise of a dirt devil or sinkhole or Donnigan. He was a big, ugly, large horned dragon sitting in the middle of Buster's cotton field watching the events before his eyes. Buster no longer cared about the hideous monster, other than getting rid of him. At least there was nothing for him to destroy anymore; he had done the most evil in those five seconds that had ever been done to Church Creek Falls.

"I thought you were sent to the abyss." He snarled at the monster.

The laughter of the monster reverberated through the field. A sadistic laugh. "You can't get rid of me that easy. You are not that strong, buddy," the serpent said to Buster telepathically. "Besides, the best is still to come. Have you discovered whatever happened to that grand pappy of yours?"

"Buster ignored the serpent. His history just didn't seem important, especially if this thing thought his family history was something to laugh about.

"So Donnigan had to go?" he said, changing the subject.

"Donnigan is my most loyal servant." Buster looked at the monster.

"What do you mean?"

"I've had Donnigan since he was a young boy, got him when his mother died of starvation. You should have heard that little boy bawl. I gave him training that hardened him like stone. But the best part was the day I was able to take possession of his body."

"What was different about that?" Buster asked.

"It was the day your great grand pappy thought he could stand up against me too."

Buster didn't want to waste time with the monster. All he wanted was to be rid of it. Attempting to act cool and unafraid, he still avoided any visible acknowledgment. The statement about his grandfather made him wonder but didn't make him want to engage in conversation, even though it sounded as though it would give him answers about his heritage. He knew the dragon was a liar and the father of lies, and when he speaks from his heart he is lying.

The Alexander toddler squealed with delight when he saw Buster. "Momma! Dada!" He tussled the toddler's hair and shook his head. "Sorry, buddy, I didn't find them."

He saw his family sitting at the table, praying.

"Hi, Dad," Rance said as he took the toddler from Buster. "It's my turn to get him ready for his bath. Glad you're back, Dad." He headed to the bathroom.

"Glad to see you Dad," Zay said as he hugged Buster.

"We have been so worried about you." Merilee said as she stood and greeted him at the kitchen door. "Didn't know what to do besides pray."

"I guess it worked." Even though his whole body ached. He gave his wife a big kiss and a genuine smile. How he loved them all!

"Any survivors?" Merilee asked.

"No. The town's almost all gone. The survivors came out the first hour after the blast, none since then. Only the buildings on the outskirts of town are left standing with minor damage. I am surprised these two made it. I don't think they would have if their mother's body had not protected them. As far as I know, the sheriff's entire department, along with every municipal officer, has been killed."

Merilee cradled the clean-smelling baby girl in a towel. Jim took the clean little boy from Rance and rocked him to sleep. He had really bonded with this little one, it was if God had given him a second chance to have his son.

"Did you see the thing out there?" Buster asked his family.

"Yeah," Barbara answered. He's been there ever since the blast. Occasionally he laughs and heckles. Mom still can't see him, but she can hear him."

"Dad, he doesn't scare me anymore. Zay said.

"And why not?' Buster asked his son.

"Because he can't do anything."

"I don't think that's right, he just blew up a town," Buster replied with half-interest.

"No, all he can do is put fear in our hearts and tell lies. Then his lies get spread by us and we do his dirty work.

"But that thing out there is the one who plotted this whole thing." Rance said.

Buster shook his head, deep in thought. "I don't think so," he finally said.

"What do you mean?" Merilee asked as she pulled a baby bottle out of the warmer and handed it to Jim.

"I'm not sure that thing is the architect of this," Buster said, still in the reasoning process.

"Okay, explain." Barbara said as she sat down next to her daddy.

"Look at what we've learned about our little town, it was filled with immorality and corruption from its beginning." Buster started a soliloquy to bring reasoning to his thinking. "If the serpent of old—the dragon in our field—knows all that is happening, he knew this was going to happen, and he just showed up for the fireworks."

"Dad, are you trying to say that evil thing had nothing to do with this?"

"No, he definitely had something to do with it, but his work started back with Donnigan, not with the fertilizer plant."

Jim smiled at the sleepy toddler in his lap and shook his head.

"Still not with you, Dad," Zay inserted.

"The deception began some years ago and continued to grow, but there's one thing that bothers me."

"What's that, Dad?" Barbara asked.

"My history—it keeps coming up," Buster said thoughtfully.

"You think your grandpa who disappeared had something to do with all this?" Rance said.

"Yeah, I do, but I can't figure it out, and now with the town gone I don't know where to start looking."

Rance walked up to Buster and placed a large black book in front of him. "What's this?" Buster asked.

"It's your mother's family Bible," Rance said.

"I know that but why are you giving it to me?"

"Open it up." Rance sat down across from Buster.

"There is a family history in it, see. If there is anything in there to help, you know where to turn."

"Good idea, son." Buster said. He began to thumb through the large Bible until he came to the center pages. The names of his ancestors were listed. His missing grandfather was listed as Robert Troye.

There was an asterisk beside Robert's name. Buster looked at the pages in the back of the Bible to find an explanation. An envelope full of newspaper clippings about the disappearance of Robert Troye. The first articles expressed sympathy and concern for the missing man and his family. The tone of the articles changed from helpful to scornful as time progressed.

The last letter was written by Donnigan, a soliloquy about the possibilities of Robert Troye's disappearance. They were skillfully written in an accusatory manner of wrong-doing.

But the final sentence stood out to the family.

"Since Robert Troye or his body will never be found, this incident should be placed behind us."

"He knew." Buster said.

24

Nothing but Lies

> I have forsaken My house, I have
> abandoned My inheritance; I have given
> the beloved of My soul Into the hand of
> her enemies. My inheritance has become
> to Me Like a lion in the forest; She has
> roared against Me; Therefore I have
> come to hate her.
>
> —Jeremiah 12:7–8 (NASB)

JIM LAWSON KNEW the blast would be devastating, but he had no idea how devastating. He often found himself thinking back to the days he was misplacing the diesel fuel, knowing the location was volatile and a small spark could set off an explosion, even the small spark from a ringing phone. A few years back when a tank had exploded on the Nigel farm, two children nearby were burned. They both died a few months later, much to the relief and sorrow of the family. Their sorrow paralleled his own; Barry had burned in a sea of jet fuel. Whether anhydrous ammonia or jet fuel didn't matter; both burned hot and long. Tears trickled down Jim's cheeks as he thought of the precious lives lost. Jim looked around at the cleanup crew and found Buster.

"I need to talk to you," Jim said.

"Okay."

"Why haven't you turned me in?" Jim asked.

"For what?" Buster replied, not in ignorance but in an attempt to give Jim an opportunity for confession.

"For…what I've done," Jim answered.

"And what is that?"

He looked up at Buster almost in anger. He flung his arms around him. "Look!"

"Are you sure you did this?" Buster asked him.

Jim didn't answer. He looked around and thought about what had happened. "Do you think this was an accident?" he finally asked.

"I think only you can answer that question," Buster said.

"Buster, I think…I did it." Jim said in a quiet voice.

Buster sat down on a flat surface, most likely a refrigerator. "Want to talk about it?"

"Yeah, I do." Jim sat down beside him. "How can God forgive me for this?"

"I don't know how, but I know He does. The Bible tells us that while we were yet sinners Christ came and took the blame for our sin."

"What?" Jim said.

"Christ came to earth in the form of a man to fulfill the law of God. Then by doing so, he was the perfect sacrifice for the sins of everyone once and for all."

"Still not gettin' it."

"That's okay, I've been a Christian for fifteen years and I'm still working on 'gettin' it," Buster replied. "All you have to know is that forgiveness is found in the person of Jesus Christ when you recognize his taking your sins upon himself."

"That sounds too simple."

"Yes, he did all the work himself. All we have to do is recognize the work, accept it, and then give ourselves to Him as our Lord."

"What do I have to give up?"

"Nothing, or maybe your selfish pride that says you can save yourself."

Jim chuckled at the thought. "What do I do to accept His sacrifice?"

"Tell Him."

"How?"

"Just talk, He can hear you." Buster said as he got up and left Jim alone. He looked back and saw Jim looking up and talking.

Buster took a break at the Red Cross tent. He picked up a cola and a newspaper. He asked the volunteer if he could have the newspaper.

Buster went back to Jim. Jim looked up at him and said, "I don't think He hears one as bad as me."

"Have you ever heard of John McCain?"

"No." Jim shook his head.

"He was on the Forrestal with Barry." Buster said as he picked up a few stones and tossed them into a broken receptacle that couldn't be identified.

"Oh, did he die too?" He joined Buster in the stone-tossing action.

"No. But there are some rumors that if he hadn't been transported off the ship quickly, the others may have killed him."

"Why?"

"Because there are many who think he started the fire."

Jim stopped tossing stones and looked up at Buster. "How did you find this out?"

"I've been reading about it lately in this newspaper." Buster showed him the paper he'd been reading. There are some minor details here that turn out to be pretty important." Buster said. "Do you want to know about this kid?"

"Yes." Jim said through gritted teeth.

"He was a young Navy pilot, following in the footsteps of his father and grandfather. They were both admirals."

"So do you think he was…you know, 'full of himself?'"

"Yeah, probably."

"How did he start the fire?" Jim calmed down as he wanted to know more.

He handed the paper to Jim as he returned to his perch on a chunk of debris. Jim took the paper and opened to the story about the Forrestal fire. It was all pretty much the same he'd heard, and besides he'd read this version before.

"Look at the last column." Buster said.

At about 10:50 (local time) on 29 July, while preparations for the second strike of the day were being made, an unguided 5.0 in (127.0 mm) Mk-32 "Zuni" rocket, one of four contained in an LAU-10 underwing rocket pod mounted on an F-4B Phantom II (believed to be aircraft No. 110 from VF-11), accidentally fired due to an electrical power surge during the switch from external to internal power. The surge, and a missing rocket safety pin, which would have prevented the fail surge, as well as a decision to plug in the "pigtail" system early to increase the number of takeoffs from the carrier, allowed the rocket to launch.

Likely source of the Zuni was F-4 No. 110. White's and McCain's aircraft.

The rocket flew across the flight deck, striking a wing-mounted external fuel tank on an A-4E Skyhawk awaiting launch aircraft No. 405 from VA-46, piloted by Lieutenant Commander Fred D. White. The Zuni rocket's warhead safety mechanism prevented it from detonating, but the impact tore the tank off the wing and ignited the resulting spray of escaping JP-5 fuel, causing an instantaneous conflagration. Within seconds, other external fuel tanks on White's aircraft overheated and ruptured, releasing more jet fuel to feed the flames, which began spreading along the flight deck.

The impact of the rocket had also dislodged two of the 1000-lb AN-M65 bombs, which fell to the deck, and lay in the pool of burning fuel between White's aircraft and that of Lieutenant Commander John McCain. Damage Control Team No. 8 swung into action immediately, and Chief Gerald Farrier, recognizing the risk, and without the benefit of protective clothing, immediately smothered the bombs with a PKP fire extinguisher in an effort to knock down the fuel fire long enough to allow the pilots to escape. The pilots, still strapped into their aircraft, were immediately aware that a disaster was unfolding, but only some were able to escape in time. McCain, pilot of A-4 Skyhawk side No. 416, next to White's, was among the first to notice the flames and escaped by scrambling down the nose of his A-4 and jumping off the refueling probe shortly before the explosions began.

"Notice the source of the bomb that caused the fire was White and McCain's planes." Buster pointed to the single sentence paragraph.

"So what are you saying?" Jim asked.

"I'm saying McCain started the fire." Buster said. "His plane sat in front of White's, and when he started his engine a plum of fuel shot out of his tailpipe hitting White's plane and setting off the rocket."

"It was an accident?" Jim said in resignation.

"It was said by some of the survivors that McCain wet-started his plane." Buster replied solemnly. "Even knowing the bombs were unstable."

"Wet-start?" Jim looked at Buster.

"He let fuel pool in the engine before he hit the start button. By doing that a plume of fire would've come out of his tailpipe."

"Can't prove it, and sure can't prove he did it on purpose, but, one thing is sure, John McCain started that fire, however, it went down."

"What is your point?" Jim asked between clinched teeth.

"A helicopter came and took McCain off the ship. He was the only man air-lifted off that ship."

"So, I don't understand."

"His father and grandfather had some influence, they most likely sent that helicopter to rescue him."

"That stinks, why didn't they get the other boys?"

"Good question, but the point is, in the midst of calamity, McCain's father and grandfather had the ability to rescue him and they did."

"Still don't get your point." Jim said.

"God has the ability to rescue through His Son Jesus Christ. All you have to do is grab on to the rescue rope and be air-lifted out of the fire."

Buster sat silent as Jim bowed his head and moaned deep and guttural. Buster didn't understand what Jim was saying, but he knew it was a conversation that did not include him. Thirty minutes later, Jim came to Buster with a smile across his whole face.

"I did it. I grabbed the rope. He just saved me." Jim said with a new spark in his voice. Buster gave him a firm hug and pat on the back.

"Now, you may be ready for the rest of the story," Buster said.

"Sure, tell me, I can take anything now.

"So you know where McCain is now?" Buster said.

"No, and don't care." Jim announced.

"Maybe you better." Buster said as he handed Jim a list of MIAs.

Jim looked it over and then gasped, "You think…"

"He's now a prisoner of war," Buster said.

"You think God is punishing him for starting the fire?"

"Can't say, but I do know what the Bible says." Buster then quoted two passages.

"'The LORD is slow to anger and great in power, And, the LORD will by no means leave the guilty unpunished." That's from the book of Nahum. And it says in Isaiah, "therefore, a curse devours the earth, and those who live in it are held guilty.'"

"God is sovereign," Buster sighed. "And whatever He wills will be for our well-being."

Jim ducked his head in shame. "What do I do, Buster?"

"Pray for McCain and obey the sovereign God," Buster answered.

"But I am guilty of---"

Buster stopped him. "If you are guilty, you will not escape His punishment, but you will be held forever in His keeping," Buster said as he turned, leaving Jim to ponder.

Jim bent over and picked up a piece of debris that looked like a woman's jewelry. "You know Buster, I felt punished when I lost my beloved wife. Could I be punished before I commit the deed?"

Buster chuckled. "Don't try to read the mind of God; you'll only get lost. Trust in His heart."

Jim nodded, "I want to help right now. I'll tell the state police after some order has been reestablished."

"Know that whatever you do, the Lord will carry you through it." Buster said as he went back to work.

For the first time, Jim looked closely at the man he'd planned to rescue, but who ended up inadvertently saving his life. Dark circles had grown underneath his drooping eyes, and his shoulders slumped.

"Buster, go home, get some rest. You're no good to anyone if you collapse."

"Okay." Buster did not argue and headed for his horse.

"Buster?" Jim called to him.

Buster turned, "Yeah?"

"Thanks for the talk."

"Anytime." Buster turned and headed for home.

Jim watched him go, why on earth had he ever tried to kill such an honest, hard-working man?

—◆—

When Buster walked into the farm-house, he collapsed onto the couch. Merilee brought him a glass of iced tea and a piece of German chocolate cake. "Oh, thank you, I barely have the energy to eat it, but I'll most definitely eat it and enjoy it." Buster smiled at Merilee, giving a little pat on her bottom as she sat down beside him.

"How bad is it?" she asked. Buster nodded but didn't say anything. He ate his cake in silence. He handed his empty plate and glass to Merilee, "I need to sleep." Buster went to their bedroom and slept for the next three hours.

━━●━━

As the family finished their evening meal, Merilee noticed Buster gazing into space.

"What's wrong?"

"Just thinking about my grandfather. The monster keeps telling me to search out my history, but how can I do that when there's no history about him after he disappeared?"

Merilee sat her tea glass on the coffee table and motioned to Buster to follow her. She rose from her seat. "I may have something to help you."

"This came in the mail today," she said as she pulled a large envelope off the top of the refrigerator. "It's from a genealogy society, so you're getting an answer to that question."

Buster opened the envelope and read the introductory letter at the front of the packet.

"Mrs. Wallace survived."

The rest of the family watched him, waiting for word of its contents. Buster handed the letter to Merilee to read as he began to examine the contents of the thick package.

She took it and read in a clear voice.

"Dear Buster and family; I apologize for deceiving you when you came to the museum seeking information. I wanted to give this to you, because I knew it belonged to you. There's more in a safety deposit box in a bank in Toulouse. Here's the key. Happy discovery. Sincerely, Mrs. Wallace.

"P.S. Yes, I'm well but will not return to Church Creek Falls. I decided it was time I started over and let go of my anger. I'm working on forgiveness, because I need the peace and relief from bitterness. I'm so glad I got to know you because you were the one who taught me the power of forgiveness.

Merilee looked up at Buster, "What does she mean you taught her the power of forgiveness?"

"Not sure, but you never know when the Lord's going to use your life as a testimony." Buster smiled and put his arm around her. He knew why she said it, but there would be no good in revealing to Merilee that most of the town either knew or thought they knew about her encounter with Jase Hamlin. They also knew Buster never spoke ill of Jase but only spoke of forgiveness when Jase came up in their conversations. When Jase was indicted for Mrs. Paul's murder, Buster didn't gloat but prayed for the man. Mrs. Wallace had said to him, "When wicked people see righteous people, it scares them, but it has a deep impact upon them in that fear."

"So, what is in the package?" Zay asked.

"It's the story of my grandfather and his disappearance. It contains some of the evidence collected at that time." Buster held up the key. "Apparently, there's more evidence in Toulouse. Do you feel like a drive?" The whole family stood up and said, "Yes."

On the thirty-mile drive to Toulouse, Zay broke the quiet when he said, "This is more fun than a mystery movie or a book."

"Yeah, 'cause it is real."

"Real and personal," Barbara added.

The safety-deposit box presented more thick packets, each packet labeled. The family sorted through some of the contents but it made no sense to them.

"We need to take this home and study it," Barbara said. The family agreed. They packed up the contents of the box, returned the key, and all went to a local Mexican food restaurant for some much-needed rest and recreation. For just a few moments, the family forgot about the tragedy in their hometown and the mystery packets setting in the car.

25

The Mystery of Ancestors

"But this is the covenant which I will make with the house of Israel after those days," declared the Lord, "I will put My law within them and on their heart I will write it; and I will be their God, and they shall be my people."

—Jeremiah 31:33

BUSTER AND MERILEE sat down at the kitchen table after all the dishes were done. Merilee rocked the baby and the toddler played with toys in his high chair next to Barbara. Buster brought a packet to the table. Zay and Rance poured everybody a glass of ice tea and brought a plate of cookies to the table.

"Here we go again," Buster said in a weary sigh. The first packet had been full of pictures both before and after the dust bowl days. Many of the group pictures contained the likeness of Phillip Donnigan at the same age. The only significant finds in the box was that Donnigan looked a lot like Jase Hamlin, and there were many pictures of Buster's boyhood home. One picture revealed the house tipping to one side. It appeared as a strange apparition. As if someone had chopped a portion of the house away. Buster knew a sinkhole might cause that, but then this picture was taken when he was an infant so he wouldn't have seen it tipped. No one in their right mind would rebuild a house over a sinkhole. There were no inscriptions or explanations on the pictures, only a date of April 1918. It remained a mystery.

The next packet contained a few pictures and many newspaper clippings. One clipping showed a toddler on a trike in his underwear. The child was identified as Buster Troye. The family all laughed at the picture.

"I really don't want to do this tonight." Buster said after a while.

"I understand, Buster, but we're almost through, let's get through it," Merilee urged.

"I just can't. It's painful to look at all this stuff. Still, I don't understand why these were in a safe-deposit box; they all look like trash to me." Buster whined as he sat back down.

"Daddy that's a good observation." Zay added.

"What?"

"Why were these old things in a bank deposit box? Only reason I would put these away would be because they have vital information, or someone wants them destroyed." Rance said in his best detective voice.

Buster pondered the silliness of the kids for a moment. Then he made a moaning sound. The family turned and looked at him. "What's on your mind?" Merilee asked as she noticed a new spark of energy in Buster's demeanor.

"Let's think about this," Buster said, "I think Rance is right. There is a vital piece of information in these packets, maybe something that will banish that ugly thing in our field."

"We need to keep looking, but let's go through these things with our inspector's glasses on," Zay said.

The family laughed.

"I agree." Merilee said as she pulled a pile of newspaper clipping toward her.

The others followed her lead. Each family member examined the paper more closely.

Buster noticed Barbara staring at the same newspaper article for nearly five minutes as she rubbed her head and frowned. "What's going on over there, Barbara? he asked. "Are you okay?"

"I've got a headache."

"I'll get you some aspirin," Merilee said as she scooted away from the table and went to the bathroom. She returned with pills and a glass of water.

"Thanks, Mama."

"Daddy, what do you think this means, it's really strange."

Buster read it and then looked at the top of the page to notice the date- April 25, 1918.

"I think this is my birth announcement." Buster replied with a weak voice.

"What-How can that be a birth announcement?" Barbara stuttered. "It's tragic."

"Thanks." Buster said with a smile. "The article is not about my birth but rather a gruesome death; and I think that was my birth announcement to the spiritual world. I think I was set aside for this role the day I was born." Buster said as he examined the paper with some renewed enthusiasm. "Keep looking for anything around the date in 1918. We need a bigger picture, but I think we just found the path to the answer. We need to be looking into this city-wide fire that occurred the day I was born." Buster pulled up a pant leg and revealed an ugly scar on his calf to Barbara.

"Where did that come from?" Barbara winced as she looked at the ribbed and twisted skin on her daddy's leg.

"I never knew, but that's pretty much what I look like on both legs."

"Daddy, how did the fire start?" Barbara asked as she perused the pictures.

"I don't know. I never heard anything about the fire until now."

"I wonder if your house had something to do with it, and maybe that is why there are so many pictures of it sitting at an angle." Barbara stared at another picture.

Buster took the picture from her, along with a few others of the house. He took a magnifying glass and examined them. "Barbara, I think you're on to something. Look."

Buster pushed the picture and magnifying glass toward Barbara.

"What is that?" she asked.

"It's black, like it's been burned. The house wasn't leaning into the ground; It was leaning on the ground after having been burned on one side."

"But---" Zay started to speak, but Buster continued.

"A house doesn't burn like that, unless…it is a controlled fire." Buster closed his eyes as if trying to remember.

Buster pulled the piece of burned leather from his pocket that Mrs. Wallace said would have meaning to him. It must be from that day. Buster wanted to capture the stories from his childhood, starting with the origination of this piece of memorabilia.

"Dad, look," Rance said. "Here's an envelope addressed to the children of Robert Troye." He pulled a well-stuffed number ten envelope from another packet. Buster took the envelope and stared at the signature on the yellowed package for a few minutes.

"Do you recognize the handwriting?" Merilee asked.

"Strange as it sounds, it looks like mine."

Merilee leaned over and gasped, "It does."

"It's not unusual for family members to have similar handwriting, they have similar structures that may cause a certain look." Zay interjected. "We learned about this in school. They have similar bone structures that may cause a certain look."

"Open the envelope and read it."

To whom ever may find this letter:

My name is Robert Troye. If anyone is reading this, I pray that you will accept the following as truth as it happened and disregard the menagerie of rumors and speculations, which have been formulated over my disappearance.

I did not disappear; I am currently in Church Creek Falls and never left; but because I am still alive, there will never be a body found unless someone finds this letter and acts upon it. I pray the letter falls into friendly hands. I am a victim of Phillip Donnigan, who is a man most mad of mind and cruel of soul. It was his clever machinations that have put me into this dungeon unknown by anyone other than himself. He is the only face I see, and the only voice I hear, except for the torturous voices that he allows me to hear outside my underground home. But on those occasions he deftly mutes my own voice with a devious muzzle that is designed to inflict extreme injury upon my face and throat if I speak. The injury would most surely be fatal. Therefore, I must listen to my friends and family speak ill of me while I languish in sorrow.

My most valuable possession was always my good name, but that was sullied by Donnigan when I crossed him. Yet, if I had it to do over, I would still stand up to the wicked man. I do not believe him to be a man but merely an evil fiend in the garments of a man. It seems that I occasionally see him as a man-size serpent flicking a split tongue at me as if to antagonize me.

He has not left me without the comforts of home, my dungeon is well-furnished, comfortable temperature year round, and my nourishment comes directly from the kitchen of Donnigan's private gourmet chef. Yet, I am always alone and defenseless against his cruel dissection of my character. It hurts me most to see him flatter my beautiful wife. She is a sensible woman and will not give in to him, but I do worry that he will force himself upon her just to hurt me. He is a man who is cruel to women and has no respect for them. He plays with them the way a cat plays with a mouse. He has often brought a young woman to my dungeon. It makes me ill as I am forced to watch him peel away her dignity and clothing. The look of horror on their young faces brings me to tears as they realize the evil that has enslaved them in his perverted desires only to leave them physically dead or worse yet mentally disturbed so that they can tell no one of their ordeal. I attempt to comfort those who survive his treacheries, but only for a while before Donnigan removes them, to where, I do not know. I never hear from them or about them again. I pray my own daughter will not succumb to his deceptions, for I do not think my heart could bear his atrocities on my precious Margaret.

I wander in my story. I fear it will never be told, for one of Donnigan's favorite games is to provide a little hope and then to snatch it away. I think that once I have completed writing this he will merely burn it in front of me. Since the night he took me away from my wife and newborn son. I've watched my Reuben grow and have even observed my grandson, Buster. My arms ache to hold them as infants and to teach them as boys and to honor them as men. But all of this has been denied me because of the jealousy of one cruel man.

You are probably wondering how I came to be here. So let me renew my story of deception and capture.

I lived my life as hardworking honest man. I stood alone against Donnigan at first. Other men had found themselves attached to Donnigan by monetary traps and torturous chains of ancestry.

I did not buy land from Donnigan. It was a freakish mistake that allowed our family plot of land to still be held in the hands of the Indian Territory and the Great Plains Indians. Thus when I wanted to homestead the land, I purchased it from the tribe. Donnigan did not hold any notes on our land. I stood up to Donnigan, and called him a bully. When I built a church near the town square with our own money and labor, Donnigan could not stop the building. It soon became the favorite place of the community and provided peace to the people and financial aid to the weary. Donnigan hated it and the community loved that he hated it. He started brooding, and it was evident that Phillip Donnigan had begun to plot the ruin of this town. The bad part was that it was also evident that he was getting some spiritual help and not from the good spirit. Black was the heart of Donnigan, a selfish man, but he changed to the void of an evil dragon, both physically and spiritually.

I'm not sure who it was that saw the vile thing first, but it wasn't long that the scaly reptile began to conceal himself from view until he wanted to be seen. He was pretty small at first but with each little wicked victory he grew. We tried to get rid of him by using the spiritual weapon of prayer and the armor of Bible study. The church grew and was used every night for some form of warfare. As the spiritual life of the community developed, the blessings began to pour on us and the vile serpent and his alter ego Donnigan, faded into the background.

One day, as I was transporting my cotton to the gin, I saw Donnigan sitting beside the road. I felt a chill come over me. I knew the man was up to some horrible scheme. I should have prayed but I didn't, I started trying to figure out how I would defeat this man. That was a stupid thing because I could not imagine the evil that lurked in his soul. As I returned from the cotton gin with the family paycheck in my pocket, Donnigan swept down upon me and knocked me from my wagon. I fought him but he took out his pistol and shot me. It was only a grazing shot to my head but it was enough to knock me out.

When I awoke I found myself in this dungeon with no way out and have been here ever since. But because I am in the middle of town, I hear the activity and the talk from those who sit under the gazebo and pass the time sharing their tales.

The community soon forgot the evil Donnigan. I can't prove it but I believe that it was Donnigan that started the fire on the community on April 25, 1918. I think his plan was to burn my son, Reuben's home. He had sworn to me that he would wipe out my family name so that no one would ever remember us. Ironically, the only building that was not completely burned was Reuben's home. One side burned, the side upon which my newborn grandson lay in his crib next to his mother. If I had been able to be there, I might have been able to stop it, but by that time Donnigan had already imprisoned me and started the poisonous rumors which caused my family to be despised and rejected.

When my baby grandson was born, the town was collectively angry at me and questioned my wife. It was only she and the midwife in that little hut that day. Donnigan made sure I saw the damage. After he applied my muzzle, he took me up on a hill, safe from the fire but in the sight of my own little home where I could hear the cries of my grandson as the fire enveloped the house. I wept as the flames licked up the south side of the house consuming the base, I begged God to take me home with my family. Instead a small rain shower came up and poured itself upon the fire, before it burned the house. I know not what damage the fire did to my wife and baby, but I know they both lived. My wife called the boy Buster, it was a nickname she always liked and would often call me, but the baby's real name was Robert Troye II.

Merilee stopped reading as she looked up at Buster. "That was you," she said.

"It appears so, but it still doesn't answer the question about this piece of leather, but it certainly answers another question I had," Buster said.

"What?" Zay asked.

"When I met with the mayor and some of the other men of the town, they took me to a room underneath the courthouse. It was a nice room and was quite comfortable. When I asked them about it, they said they found it accidentally and that no one else knew about it. They told me what they found: rich furnishing, a four-poster bed with large wingback chairs, and a library. The fireplace was huge and beautifully appointed. They didn't know what it was for, nor did they ever identify the skeleton found in the bed."

"Dad, did you say skeleton?"

"Yeah, it was the weirdest thing I ever saw."

"Did it scare you?"

"No, in fact it seemed to send out signals of peace. The weirdest thing was that it was completely intact and kneeling beside the bed as if praying."

"The men assumed it was Donnigan." Buster let his gaze wander for a few minutes. "But they were wrong. It was my grandfather, Robert Troy."

The family sat in silence as the realization of the creature in their field grew. It was the serpent that had been seen three generations before. It had just revealed itself, and they would never be rid of it. It could lay dormant for years, maybe even centuries.

"Look guys." Barbara pulled a small package from one of the boxes. It was the mask, the dreaded mask. She dropped it--"Yeow! The thing is moving!" she screamed as she pulled her hand back. The thing grew to the size of a large man.

"Phillip Donnigan, I presume?" Zay said, almost in a trance and with a silly little grin on his face.

"Correct, Master Zay, I always knew that you would be my next target." The look on his face was the same disgusting smirk that had been on the mask.

Merilee ran and stood in front of Zay. "You keep your slimy hands off of my son!" she said with fierce determination.

"You have no place in our home, and your pet dragon has no place on our farm. Today is the end, do you hear me? The end." Merilee was screaming and red-faced by the time she said the last the end.

Donnigan stepped back from her anger and the smirk left his face. Buster noticed the fear in Donnigan's face. He stood beside Merilee, "You cannot intimidate innocence," Buster said. "Because we have the truth in our heart you cannot deceive us and because we wear the righteousness of the only true righteous one, Jesus Christ; you cannot condemn us. And because Christ is our peace, you cannot disturb us. Therefore, according to the pure water of the Word of God, you are condemned and enslaved by that righteousness. In that name above all names and with the Sword of the Spirit, the Word of God, we banish you from our home, our community, and our church."

The family clung to each other tightly and prayed with all fervency as the mask grew to fill the house and display its filthy agenda. They all said it together loudly, "Go!"

And he did. Even with the breath of vile wind he left behind, Buster had no doubt it was gone.

The family collapsed in nearby chairs, spent and exhausted.

"It's gone," Barbara said with a huge sigh.

Rance rose up, "You're right, I can't feel its presence anymore."

Zay looked at his siblings, his face pale, "Thank you guys, I could feel him in my head and his grip tightening on my heart."

Merilee watched her children relax for the first time in years. She had not known the fear they had experienced but now she understood.

"Why do you think he left?" Merilee pondered.

"Because once I realized my heritage and that my inheritance was the heart of a praying man, the dragon could no longer intimidate me or my family. He had to leave us, just like he failed with my grandfather. He may have imprisoned his physical body but he never imprisoned his spirit. It belonged to Jesus Christ. Our heritage is we belong to God both past and present."

"But Daddy, what is that piece of leather?" Zay inquired.

"I don't guess we will ever know. But I am sure it was something in the fire, possibly something that saved my newborn life," Buster replied. "It does have the initials RT on it so it must have been in our family." Buster felt a connection to that little strap of leather. He slipped it into his pocket as a beloved friend. After all, both Buster and the leather strap carried mysterious burn marks.

Claire Waithe stood tall in her young and sparkling body on the ridge of heaven looking into the living room of the Troye family. Beside her was the light of a messenger angel explaining an event to her.

"It was a rough day back in 1918. The evil had spread so far into the hearts of the people, but one man never gave up. He fervently prayed for his son and grandson. He even mentioned the new saddle he had bought for his son Reuben. It was to be a surprise for him on the day he was captured and taken prisoner. He had taken on extra jobs and saved to buy that saddle. He couldn't wait to give it to Reuben. He always asked what happened to it. One day Robert asked in his prayers if we could make sure Reuben got the saddle.

"It was on that day in 1918 that Reuben found the saddle. He brought it in to show his wife who had just given birth to a baby boy. He didn't know where it came from, but he knew it was his. He put the saddle in the baby's room. It would make a fine decoration and maybe someday the boy would want to be a horseman too.

"When the fire started, the prayers of Robert Troye became urgent and God sent me to cover Robert's family with grace."

The angel stopped the story for a moment as he recalled that day in April, 1918.

"I placed a never-used saddle over a crying infant only seconds before fire engulfed the baby. The flash fire quickly burned the saddle, but a quick and localized sheet of rain doused it before the baby and house were consumed. But I could not have done it without the constant prayer of a missing grandfather. He caused miracles to happen that day."

"As well as this day." Added a glowing Clare Waithe.

Epilogue

THE DISASTER AT Church Creek Falls inflicted a wound so deep there were no words for description or communication. Among the dead lay Kearney, a man who had cheated most everyone in town, laid down a bad bet and bedded a beloved daughter or wife. He was a scoundrel that would not be missed. His house was in the direct path of the blast. His wife survived because she had been away from home at the time. The most difficult one to understand was the death of Mrs. Alexander. She was the mother of two babies who needed her. Why would she be taken? Her husband was never found.

On day 100 of the cleanup, the townspeople watched the last of their volunteer help leave. They had been told this would happen, now the clean-up duty fell upon the shoulders of the residents.

Sorrow found its way into the hearts of the survivors as they realized the great amount of work still to be done. With so many deaths, there were only a few people to complete the work. On the other hand, with so few survivors, there seemed little need of rebuilding.

Some municipal funds had been brought to the town with the rescue teams taking municipal responsibility. They used the funds to hire a cleanup company to remove the rest of the debris. The large tractors and trucks made short work of the mess. With the small amounts of funds leftover, the few remaining citizens erected a memorial on the site of the court-house. With that last action, the remaining people returned to their farms or left the area and Church Creek Falls fell into the annuls of time as a ghost town. A few stout-hearted town folks put up awkward buildings to help supply goods to the farmers. On the site of Robert Troye's land, a small one-room school was built on the site, which had become the town square. Ironically, it also served as the community church. Other than the sparse rebuilds, and the memorial, the land appeared almost the same as it did the day Phillip Donnigan arrived.

The children of Mrs. Paul came and looked at the devastation of her house, made a quick walk-through and then signed everything over to the city. They walked away as quickly as they could. They knew people wondered about their mother, but they didn't want to relate the details of her murder. It was enough for them to know she had been found in a compromising sexual position and had probably been tortured for hours before she finally fell into a permanent sleep. Her pain must have been brutal. The man Jase Hamlin, was captured a few months later and convicted by the testimony of one of his other victims who escaped his murderous hand. He was charged with Mrs.

Paul's murder along with twenty-three other counts of murder, the bodies left in hotel rooms across the country.

Wylene had rented a small house in the blast area; she was critically wounded and died a few days later in a hospital in a nearby city. She told the nurse she needed to make peace with her baby. The nurse informed her she didn't have a baby. Wylene broke down in tears and told the nurse about the abortion she had in years past, because Mr. Troye didn't want children. She was afraid he would leave her. She never even told him she was pregnant. Still, that was the point when their marriage began to deteriorate.

Garrett Boseley didn't live in the blast area, but his mother did. As he cleaned up her house after her death, he stepped on a nail and developed a bad case of tetanus. He died several weeks later. Before he died he wrote a letter to Buster and included a cashier's check for the stud fee that Buster had paid him. The explanation in the letter stated that the bull had been sterile and he'd discovered it a few days before Buster paid Garret for stud service to his cows. Buster's first thought was he also owed him for twenty-six calves that were never conceived and thus lost income. But Garrett covered that too. He left his impregnated cattle to Buster.

The mask's owner list contained the names of most all the dead, including generations past all the way back to Donnigan. A few names had the inscription, redeemed by their names. Beside Mrs. Wallace's name the words were justice served. McCoy was not on the list. He moved to a small town and found a teaching position at a state school. He decided to change his name from Dr. Matthew Phillip

McCoy to Mr. Phillip Donnigan McCord. The dragon had a new body with an old name. But the significance of the list was the changed inscription at the bottom of the list, "The planting of seed is singular but the reaping of the harvest comes in multiples." <><

Notes

The aircraft carrier USS Forrestal experienced a fire on July 29, 1967. This caused a series of chain-reaction explosions that killed 134 sailors and injured 161, after an electrical anomaly discharged a Zuni rocket.

The Forrestal was engaged in combat operations in the Gulf of Tonkin during the Vietnam War. The damage exceeded $72 million (equivalent to $511 million in 2017), not including the damage to aircraft. Future United States Senator John McCain was among the survivors. The Forrestal was repaired and remained in operation for several years before she was moored in Philadelphia, Penn. She was dismantled in 2014 and sold for scrap metal.

To learn more about the historic fire on the U.S.S. Forrestal and the role John McCain (R-Arizona) played in the sequence of events which that caused the fire, an Internet search is suggested, since there is more information than one link can provide. YouTube® provides film of the actual fire taken from the ship's camera.

All the characters of The Dragon and the Mask are fictional, including Barry Lawson, the sailor on the

Forrestal. The events are real, including the rumors of McCain being the cause of the fire, there is also evidence refuting these rumors.

The plot of The Dragon and the Mask is loosely based upon the plot line of the biblical book of Jeremiah. The accompanying Bible study of Jeremiah will provide new insights and truth into the biblical book of Jeremiah.

The Author

The author lives in Oklahoma City with her husband,
She earned a doctorate in biblical counseling from Trinity
Theological Seminary in Newburgh, Indiana.. Dr. Cooner
has served as a biblical counselor since 2006.

Book Two in the Dragon Series to be released Winter 2017:

A GATHERING OF DRAGONS

AT THE SOUND of rustling paper coming from down the hall, Barbara Troye froze in mid-stroke while putting on mascara. *Who is there?* She pulled the drawer of her vanity open and picked up the 22 caliber revolver her dad gave her when she left home. *Please Lord, don't make me shoot anyone . . . or get shot.* She stepped into the hallway hidden in shadow. She took a deep breath in an attempt to calm her rapid beating heart and steady her breathing. *Maybe it's just a rat.*

The shadow of the intruder moved toward her. Her free hand flew to her mouth and her breathing stopped. Beads of sweat tickled her spine. Her addled mind searched for an escape. She felt body heat and a drift of air when a shadow passed. Standing still she didn't perceive the second shadow until it towered over her. She flattened herself against the wall. The entity pressed closer, standing from floor to ceiling.

The man moved toward her desk. The dragon followed. Her lungs were about to burst holding in her breath, she exhaled knowing it would reveal her position. It appeared neither of them heard her gasp for air. The man walked around the living and kitchen area as though he lived there. He made no effort at stealth. The dragon followed close behind the man, tracing each of his steps. Barbara wondered if the man knew a large dragon followed him. She shuddered at the sight.

A cold crept up over her body like a glove covering a hand. She held her gun close but she could feel her whole arm shivering. Surprised to see a dragon again, she groaned inside at the unexpected sight.

She watched the man rifle through the papers on her desk. The make shift desk of a poor college student made of a plywood board with screw-in legs couldn't stand under the rough search. A moment after the intruder pushed everything to the floor with a swoop of his muscled arm, the desk toppled onto the floor. Paper, pencils, pictures, and a melee of various brick-a-brack sprawled broken around the room.

Barbara raised her left hand in front of her face. Again, she held her breath. Neither figure looked at her. She eased back into a dark corner. The second form stood next to the first, but they didn't acknowledge each other. The dragon raised his serpent-like head over the intruder.

A strange noise reached her ears. *A growl?* Barbara yelped. The man turned away from her, toward the window. A strange, orange glow emitted from the dragon and surrounded the man like a cloud.

Barbara gasped. This time the intruder heard. With quivering hands, she slipped her finger over the trigger. Her legs felt like they were made of wax. How could---

At that moment the man looked directly into her eyes. One side of his mouth turned up in a smirk. Barbara gripped her gun and braced herself to shoot. He walked toward her, snickering.

Barbara wanted to run for the front door but the dragon blocked her path. She had nowhere to go except deeper into the hallway.

"Hello there; it's been a while," he growled.

"Who . . . who are you?"

"You don't recognize me?"

Barbara shook her head. He did look familiar. Still she didn't recognize him.

"I'm not surprised," he said. When she reached the end of the hallway, he kept coming.

Barbara fired.

He kept coming. The dragon no longer followed the man, but settled on his haunches in the dining room. He flicked his forked tongue over the man's head.

She fired again; he jerked a little. She hit him, still he kept coming. The dragon lowered his head over the man.

"Take whatever you want!" Barbara screamed.

"I found what I wanted," he said as he placed a sheet of paper in his shirt pocket.

"Then leave," Barbara demanded.

"Oh . . . you don't frighten easily."

"Why should I be afraid of a clown in orange?"

He hesitated. His facial expression changed. "Orange?" He looked down at himself and brushed his chest.

"You think I'm a clown?" he mocked. With the statement he raised his arm and pointed directly at Barbara's head.

Something knocked her to the floor. Her hands trembled and she heard gunfire as she fell.

Orange man groaned. She both felt and heard him fall beside her. Staring into his blood-stained face he exhaled. His breath stank of sulfur.

With great effort she pushed herself up only to fall into something wet and sticky. Blood.

She heard a voice say, "The planting of seed is singular, but the harvest comes in multiples."

A wispy orange cloud floated in front of her just before blackness engulfed her.

Barbara Troye goes to college, where she falls victim to the destructive plot of a demon led by a gathering of dragons.

In Barbara Troye's disappointment, the dragon uses the lies of the second wave of feminism to entrap her. She follows the dragon's path of destruction thinking she is doing good. Does she belong to the dragon and will his deception take her to the depths of moral depravity?

Dragon Series

Buster Troye comes face to face with a horrid Dragon. Will he overcome the dreadful beast?

Barbara Troye is lured by her selfish needs into revolt? Can she be rescued from the Dragon's demon?

Dr. Zay Troye sees a Dragon carrying the secret of hell. Can science find the truth?

Rance Troye's wedding is cut short when the Dragon steals the bride. Will Rance's search save her or destroy him?

The pain of Buster Troye's Dragon bite grows from a family division. His final battle is fought by the Dragon warrior.

During World War II, military "Operation High Jump" explores Antarctica and finds the Dragon's lair.

www.StonesInClay.com

Stones in Clay
PUBLISHING

www.AlongSideYou.org

Available wherever books are sold.